unthinkable
NANCY WERLIN

Dial Books
an imprint of Penguin Group (USA) Inc.

DIAL BOOKS
An imprint of Penguin Group (USA) Inc.
Published by the Penguin Group
Penguin Group (USA) Inc., 375 Hudson Street, New York, New York 10014, USA

USA/Canada/UK/Ireland/Australia/New Zealand/India/South Africa/China
Penguin Books Ltd, Registered Offices: 80 Strand, London WC2R 0RL, England

For more information about the Penguin Group visit penguin.com

Library of Congress Cataloging-in-Publication Data
Werlin, Nancy.
Unthinkable / by Nancy Werlin.
pages   cm
Sequel to: Impossible.
Summary: "Fenella, the first of cursed Scarborough girls, is challenged to accomplish
three tasks of destruction against her family in order to finally leave her miserable life of
purgatory in the faerie realm and return to the human world"—Provided by publisher.
ISBN 978-0-8037-3373-2 (hardcover)
[1. Magic—Fiction. 2. Fairies—Fiction. 3. Blessing and cursing—Fiction.] I. Title.
PZ7.W4713Unt 2013 [Fic]—dc23   2012050174

Printed in the United States of America
1 3 5 7 9 10 8 6 4 2

Designed by Nancy R. Leo-Kelly
Text set in Minion Pro

For Jim

Chapter 1

"I demand to speak to the queen!"

Panting, shouting, a redheaded human girl named Fenella Scarborough raced toward the center of the forest clearing, barely in front of the willow-tree fey chasing her. She felt the flick of a long thin branch start to twist around her waist, but she wrenched it aside before it could yank her backward. The full-moon court of the fey was assembled, with countless faeries crowding the ground and trees and air, but Fenella ignored them all. She kept her eyes fixed firmly on the tall figure of the queen as she zigged and zagged and fought toward her.

The girl's desperation was real, but the chase was staged. The queen's tree fey guards were helping Fenella Scarborough. They might not approve of her quest, but she had convinced them of her need to try.

Bless them, Fenella thought as she evaded another feint at capture.

She reached the queen and staggered to a stop. The queen had risen to her feet, and Fenella looked a long way up into her face, for the queen was taller than tall. But the queen's half-mask of reptilian skin, which nestled over her forehead and around her left eye, made it hard to read her expression.

"You must hear me." Fenella put an unconscious hand to her side, where she had a stitch from running.

The assembled court stared and pointed and chattered. The tree fey whipped restraining vines around Fenella's waist. In a moment, they would have to drag her away.

But then it happened, just as Fenella had hoped and planned. The queen's wings rose with interest and she held up a clawed hand. "I will hear this human girl."

The tree fey guards loosened their bindings, though they did not remove them.

Fenella knew to wait now, until she was bidden to speak. She stood still beneath Queen Kethalia's examining gaze. She did not let her eyes slip even once to the thick, curved knife that the queen wore in a sheath on one forearm.

Her involuntary shuddering made her glad for the support of the tree fey's vines. Would the queen think she was afraid? Fenella jutted her chin out. She was not. Not of the new young Queen of Faerie, not of anyone, not of anything. Fear had burned out of Fenella Scarborough years ago.

"You look like a young girl," mused Queen Kethalia at last. "But you are older."

A discreet tug at Fenella's waist cautioned her not to reply.

It was true that Fenella Scarborough looked young, eighteen at most. But an acute observer with knowledge of magic—and the queen was nothing if not that—would stop and look again, questioning the surface. And it would not take knowledge of magic for an observer to notice the firm tilt of Fenella's chin, the thrust of her strong nose, and the character hinted at by her wide, mobile mouth. There was none of the uncertainty of youth.

"Also," continued the queen thoughtfully, "someone, sometime, has put a foot on your neck, and kept it there."

"Never again!" Fenella snapped. The willow fey warned her with another tug, and immediately, she compressed her mouth.

Now there was not a muscle of her body that she wasn't holding tautly. But it was even more disconcerting than she had expected, to be under the gaze of the young queen. She knew exactly what she was doing here, but she had not anticipated feeling so naked. She had not known, really, what to expect from this new young queen. Her friends the tree fey had not been willing to share their thoughts beyond agreeing to help her gain an audience.

Unlike Fenella, Queen Kethalia really *was* only eighteen. There was a whiff of the human about Queen Kethalia too. It was not in her blood; it was culture and upbringing. The queen had recently spent several years in the human realm, in disguise as an ordinary human girl. The queen had had a human foster mother, and had attended human school, and—worst of all, according to some of the fey—had had a human best friend whom she actually loved.

Whispers said that Queen Kethalia missed those days and she missed that friend, and it had affected her judgment.

There was no telling any of this, however, from the impassive face meeting Fenella's gaze now. "Speak now, girl," the queen said. Her voice, if not gentle, was calm. "What do you want?"

Fenella unclenched her hands. Her voice rang out firmly. "I want to die."

The entire watching court leaned forward.

"What?" said the queen.

"I want to die."

Three of the insect fey winged to the human girl and examined her with their multi-faceted eyes nearly in her face.

A human seeking death was incomprehensible to the long-lived fey. In the old days, many humans came to Faerie seeking the opposite. Plus, the entire faerie race had only just managed to claw itself away from extinction; the threat of which had been why the queen was sent to the human realm to begin with.

"Please," Fenella added huskily.

The spotted lizard that rode the queen's shoulder poked his head out from the glorious mass of her hair. He flicked his tongue toward Fenella, as if to taste her sincerity.

Then the queen's partial brother, Ryland, padded up beside the throne.

Ryland was a manticore. To human eyes, he seemed a monster, with his enormous, muscled lion's body, dragon's tail, wings, and human head. But to faerie eyes, he looked like what he also was: royal.

Seeing him, Fenella wondered about other rumors she had heard. Would Ryland have been a better ruler than Queen Kethalia? It was said his ideas were different from his sister's and unmarked by any fondness for humans. And yet their mother, the old queen, had at the end chosen Kethalia—firmly.

"Sister," Ryland said formally. "I know about this girl. May I comment?"

Ryland had not been in Fenella's plan. Panic pushed at

her throat. "*I* don't know *him*! It is my life. I will speak for myself." The last word emerged only as a squawk, as the tree fey tightened their hold on her. A leaf even brushed her mouth in light reproof. Fenella subsided.

What was that fleeting expression on the queen's face as she glanced from her brother to Fenella and back again? Fenella squinted at her, suddenly uncertain she had seen anything at all.

The queen nodded to her brother. "Go ahead."

"It is an old tale. The girl was once the human slave of the Mud Creature." Ryland put an expression of polite inquiry on his face. "Sister, you may not know the Mud Creature. Long before you were born, he made a nuisance of himself at court, posturing as noble."

Fenella frowned. The Mud Creature?

"You are correct. I have not heard of him," said the queen.

"Who do you mean?" Fenella blurted, despite the reproving tug of the tree fey. "Why do you call him the Mud Creature? I know him as Padraig."

Ryland shrugged. "The Mud Creature no doubt told you his name is Padraig. It means 'noble,' but it is a name he chose for himself. His mother had nothing to do with it. He was never noble."

"Another old tale?" asked the queen.

"The ordinary tale of an unwanted bastard," said Ryland,

with a dismissive swish of his tail. "Unworthy of song or poetry. But the first tale, of the Mud Creature's kidnapping of a human girl—that has elements of interest."

"Tell it, then," said the queen.

Fenella clenched her fists again. It was her story to tell, not his.

Ryland lowered his lion's body comfortably to the ground. "Some four hundred years ago, the Mud Creature kidnapped this girl—who we see before us now—and kept her here in Faerie. He took her female descendants too, one by one in turn, over the generations. They were all under a curse."

Meeting the queen's eyes, Fenella was at least able to nod grim confirmation.

"Yes," said the queen. "The curse on the women of the Scarborough family is famous."

Ryland snorted. "That's as may be. But one does not care for the Mud Creature. He is . . . low. As evidenced by his bothering to torture a human for so long."

"Really?" drawled the queen. "What are you saying? You disapproved of a situation you did not consider important enough to fix?"

The manticore drawled back, "What should I have done, sister? A curse is a curse. Anyway, it was not my business what the Mud Creature did or did not do." He paused. "The queen your mother, and mine, did not intervene either."

Some of the fey murmured agreement.

Fenella bit her lip.

The manticore rested his chin on his paws. "Its maker aside, the curse was an interesting one. And clever. To break it required three tasks of creation; three symbols braided together to describe the behavior of true love. First the creation of a seamless shirt, representing warmth. Second, the location of dry land amidst water, representing home. Finally, the sowing of corn, representing nourishment. The Mud Creature set the curse with herbs—never mind that he stole them; even back in the days of our full power, he had little strength of his own. He secured the curse with haunting, powerful music. It should have been impossible to break."

"But it wasn't, was it, Fenella?" The queen looked at her.

At last Fenella could speak. Of this at least she was proud. "My many-times-great-granddaughter Lucinda Scarborough broke the curse. With her true love at her side," Fenella felt compelled to add.

"I know Lucy," said the queen unexpectedly. "I saw her— from a distance—when I was in the human realm."

Fenella caught her breath in surprise.

"There is little resemblance between you and Lucy."

"Lucy is dark-haired," said Fenella cautiously. "And athletic. And taller." Fenella was herself deceptively fragile of build.

"I was not thinking of surface differences." The queen paused. "Lucy carries herself with a certain confidence. It is the confidence of one who has always been loved."

Hearing the queen's comment should not have hurt. Fenella kept her face blank. She had once known love too. But that had been a very long time ago.

"The Mud Creature was predictably incompetent," Ryland remarked. "Letting a snip of a human girl break his curse."

Fenella had previously had no particular opinion about the queen's brother. Now dislike flamed. "He was competent enough to destroy twenty girls of my family before my Lucy got the better of him."

"Not difficult," said Ryland equably.

Fenella's fingers bent as if they would gouge his eyes out. She turned back to the queen.

The queen said, "The Mud Creature must have valued you a great deal, Fenella, to set such a spell on you and your family."

"Valued?!" Fenella took an involuntary step forward, and was stopped only by the tree fey's vines. "He wanted me the way a spoiled child wants a toy. He was obsessed. He entangled twenty innocent young girls. It was evil and senseless and wrong." She took in a hard breath, regaining control. She made a movement with her hands to to push it all away.

"But all that is over. It is not why I came here."

"You want death," said the queen.

"Yes." Fenella's entire body leaned tensely toward the queen. "When Lucy broke the curse, I was so glad. For her, for her mother, Miranda, and for her baby. But I thought my suffering would also end. I thought she had saved me too." Suddenly she needed the support of the tree fey. "I don't understand. Why didn't I die?"

The queen considered Fenella once again. Finally she nodded. "I see why. There is a net of vitality around you. It seems the Mud Creature cast another spell, separate from the curse on your family. This gave you inhumanly long life and health.

"Yet you are not immortal, Fenella. Eventually, you will die of old age, like all creatures."

"When?" Fenella demanded.

"In a few hundred more years."

Dismay rocked Fenella back on her heels.

At the queen's side, Ryland's teeth gleamed canine. "Unless of course the humans destroy the entire world before that. That would take you down early, Fenella Scarborough, along with everyone and everything else. Including us. Feel free to desire that."

Fenella recovered enough to throw him a look. "Believe me, I do."

The watching fey had been fairly quiet to this moment, murmuring only occasionally as they listened. But now one of the rabbit fey screamed, and a disturbing rattle arose from several other quarters as well.

Queen Kethalia's brow quirked. Or possibly it was a frown. Again she looked from Fenella to her brother and then back again. "Fenella, you are rash. You know little of the fey and our place in the world, or of the intertwining of the human and the fey and the earth."

Fenella's jaw hardened. "What I know is that I want death. I want peace. It is the proper end for all living creatures and I have earned it."

"Oh, look. She feels *entitled*," jibed Ryland.

Fenella managed to snap her mouth shut on more words, and cast an *I'm-in-control* glance toward her friends the tree fey.

The queen straightened to full height. Her hawk wings flared behind her and her hair rippled down in its thousand shades and textures, green and brown and orange, moss and fur and leaf and feather. Her cobweb skirts swirled around her as if they were alive. The spotted lizard who rode her shoulder again sent out his tongue. A tiny insect fairy swerved just in time, and landed on the bough of a nearby tree fey.

"Fenella, most humans would do anything for more time

on this earth," said the queen. "You can build a life for yourself here in Faerie. Or if you wish, you could even visit the human realm. In recompense for your suffering, which I do acknowledge, I would allow you this." Her voice gentled. "You could visit Lucy. She has a family, yes? They are your family too."

Fenella's head moved in a gesture that was neither a nod nor a shake.

"Also," said the queen encouragingly, "there is a new small daughter belonging to Lucy, isn't there? A sweet child who will never be cursed. A little girl you could hold and love."

Fenella clutched her arms tightly around herself. "No!"

"Consider—"

"I *have* considered! I have spent the last four hundred years helpless while every girl in my family suffered. They blamed me for their fate, along with blaming Padraig. I caused the curse, and then I failed to break it, and then I failed to protect any of them. I failed!"

Fenella sank to her knees and raised her head on a rigid neck. "I have already tried to die in every way I know. Poisoning and drowning. Fire and blade. Hanging and leaping. Nothing worked. Show me mercy. Undo this life-spell that Padraig cast. Let me die. It is long, long past my time."

One of the elk fey whispered to a rabbit, and the mossy

rock face of a stone fey glowed phosphorescent in the moonlight.

"I beg you," said Fenella.

The night wind moved through the leaves of the tree fey.

The queen wore an inward expression.

Ryland pointed his tail in Fenella's direction. "She is determined. If I were you, sister, I would help her. Why not?"

The queen retorted, "Because it is my job to husband the earth's powers, not to squander them recklessly. Her death will occur in its own time, as I have said. It might well be that she still has purpose here on this earth, though she knows it not."

"Or could it be"—the queen's brother paused suggestively—"that you have not the power to help her?"

Fenella glanced up as Queen Kethalia met Ryland's mocking eyes. Only when the queen had stared her brother down did she look away, out at her people.

The bird fey cocked their heads. The insect faeries angled their antennae. One of the rock fey rumbled low, and a spider replied with the almost inaudible flex of her eight legs against the rock. Far away, among the large mammals at the edge of the clearing, the huge pronged antlers of the huntsman could be glimpsed.

The queen said, to all of them, "Undoing a spell cast four

hundred years ago is no easy task. We fey are not now what we once were."

"Consider it a test, sister," drawled Ryland. "Your test."

Feathers and skin and feet were still. Thousands of eyes and antennae and ears and receptors awaited the queen's answer.

The queen did not seem intimidated. She took her time looking at her brother.

"Come here," Queen Kethalia said finally to Fenella. "Let me touch you. I will discover what is required to undo the spell." She paused and then added dryly, "I advise you not to have much hope. The spell seems . . . tangled."

"Hope is all I do have," said Fenella. Her pulse was pounding, pounding in her throat. She had not told the tree fey of this part of her plan. She rose from her knees. She took one firm, quick step forward, and then a second.

The queen was an inch away.

Desperately Fenella lunged. She fell against the queen and grabbed the hilt of the queen's ceremonial knife. For a split second, the knife's jagged blade gleamed in a shaft of moonlight.

In the next second Fenella plunged the blade viciously into her own body.

Chapter 2

Immediately she threw herself to the ground, curling into a ball to protect the knife. She felt the blade slice through flesh and muscle as she twisted it up under her ribs, aiming for her heart.

Warm blood gushed onto her hands and the ground.

There was, however, no pain. Fenella twisted the knife with all her strength. She was succeeding, she must be. Please, please, please. It was the queen's sacred ceremonial knife. It had been used to kill the old queen. If anything would have the power of death, it would. Please—

Firm hands on her shoulders. Gentle despite their claws, the hands rolled her over. Fenella's body uncurled. She looked up into the face of Queen Kethalia.

She knew then that it was useless.

The queen pulled the knife smoothly out of Fenella's body.

Now there was pain, but Fenella made not a single sound as her body healed and her flesh knit back together inexorably, even her dress fabric renewing. By the end, the bloodstains on her dress and hands and on the knife had also vanished.

So, Fenella thought. She swallowed hard, exactly once. Then she got to her feet and wiped her palms on her mossy skirt.

"I'm sorry, Fenella," said the queen. "No knife can help you. Not even mine."

"What if you were the one to wield it?" Fenella challenged. "Or the huntsman?"

"No," said the queen. "Your body is enchanted and protected. You cannot die before your time."

Fenella nodded. She said belatedly, "I am sorry for grabbing your knife."

"I understand," said the queen.

It was generous of her, Fenella thought. She kept her gaze steady on the queen's face. For a moment Fenella felt almost as if it was only the two of them there; as if she was understood. She said dully, "Is there a way to undo the spell, as you were first trying to determine? I will do anything to die."

There was silence in the clearing. Silence among the fey. And that emotion again that Fenella could not read in the queen's face, as she glanced once at the impassive tree fey guards, once at her brother, and then back to Fenella.

The queen slid her knife back into its sheath and regarded her hands. "Now that I have touched you, yes. I see a way to break the spell. But *you* must do it, not I. It will be difficult. I shall not tell you how to do it unless I am assured that you are—are fully sane."

Fenella felt a grim smile curl her lips as new hope flickered dimly in her.

"I am sane. I was enslaved to Padraig—he whom you call the Mud Creature—for four hundred years, and I did not lose my mind. I never will. I never can."

Someone else had, though. But Fenella would not think of Bronagh. One after another Scarborough girl had come to Faerie, remained eighteen years, and then died and was replaced. But none of them had been more damaged than Bronagh. Fenella's very own daughter, Bronagh.

A slender, flexible willow bough sneaked out from one of the tree guards, slipping round Fenella's waist. She heard the whisper of leaves as the other tree guard murmured something to her in leaf language. She sensed that the murmur was meant to be comforting. However, despite some practice, Fenella could not translate what was said. Leaf and flower language was so nuanced, so subtle, so complex.

The queen was speaking to her tree fey guards, also using

leaf language. Of this, Fenella caught the gist. "Bring the Mud Creature here."

The queen was summoning Padraig? Why? Why did he need to be present in order for the queen to explain to Fenella how to break the life-spell? Was it because Padraig had cast it? Abruptly, Fenella's stomach roiled.

Fenella had not seen Padraig since Lucy broke the curse on her family. She did not know how he had managed during the recent crisis that had nearly decimated the fey. She had not cared. She had only hoped that if all of the fey died, she would too.

And Padraig. She had not been above hoping Padraig would die first, so she could see it. So she could spit on his corpse—no, no. Fantasies were too dangerous.

She knotted her fingers together. She allowed the tree fey to stand with her, in their way.

Once upon a time, in her long-ago human life, Fenella would have walked by the tree fey without thinking them anything other than slender saplings. Even now, her human vision wasn't sharp enough to distinguish tree fey from ordinary trees unless the trees wanted her to.

Which they sometimes didn't. At the beginning of her life in Faerie, the tree fey had played pranks on Fenella. They'd lay snares of flexible green fronds to trip her, or grow a thorny branch across her path, or shift around in the forest so that she became hopelessly lost. Fenella eventually—it took decades—understood that the tree fey were interested in her, even liked her, and she learned to distinguish them from normal trees by smell. The tree fey had a subtle scent that, if you closed your eyes and stilled your mind, made the world around you feel softly, indescribably green, and wrapped in calm.

You could have a good talk with a tree fey, if you were patient. She was still learning.

The sapling on Fenella's left wrapped a second vine around her waist. It supported her as Padraig was marched into the clearing between four tree guards. But the support was not necessary. After an initial instinctive flinch, Fenella stood firm. I am not afraid of him, she thought. I hate him, but—no matter what my body thinks—he has no power over me or Bronagh or anyone anymore, and I know it. I do not fear him. I fear nobody.

She folded her empty arms around herself.

Still, the tree fey kept its vines in place around her, and as Padraig came closer, the vines tugged Fenella gently away so that there was room for him to stand with her before Queen Kethalia.

All the fey of the court, in their varied ways, focused on Padraig. Fenella too looked at him straight on. She stared boldly, scornfully, and—

She inhaled and borrowed some calm from the tree fey.

Padraig's beauty almost assaulted the senses. He knew it too. For the last four hundred years, Fenella had watched him tend his body and face; had seen him strut around like his beauty entitled him to anyone and anything he wanted. She had even seen many of the Scarborough girls dazzled and enticed and seduced by his looks—at first.

Padraig was the rare fey who needed little magical guise to appear human. Fenella had been surprised to learn that he was not considered attractive by those of the fey with more flexible, more mixed blood. Or, at least, that had been Fenella's understanding until today. What did it mean, she wondered, that the queen and her brother called him the Mud Creature? Ryland had said Padraig was not noble, and that he was a bastard. But what did the word *bastard* even mean, when there was neither marriage nor simple two-person parentage among the fey?

Padraig had lied to her about himself; at least that was clear. Interesting. No, wait, it wasn't interesting. It was the past. She did not care. She wanted only death. Soon the queen would tell her how to achieve it.

"Your Majesty," Padraig said, inclining his head to Queen Kethalia.

Fenella saw then that he had changed after all. Yes, his black hair grew as thickly as ever from his scalp, and his eyes gleamed more brightly than sapphires, and he stood straight, tall, his shoulders square, his body taut and youthful looking. And yet.

Fenella's descendant Joanne Scarborough had described to her a mechanical contrivance called a copying machine. Padraig seemed like a replica of himself. He actually looked *blurred*. Fenella thought about rubbing her eyes and looking again. But she didn't, because she didn't care about him and she wasn't afraid of him anymore and she wouldn't voluntarily waste another moment on him.

The queen spoke to Padraig courteously enough. "Fenella Scarborough, who was once your slave, has come to us with a request."

Padraig swept Fenella a low bow. "My love."

Fenella did not reply.

The queen said, "Fenella seeks to reverse the life-spell upon her."

"She can't do that," said Padraig instantly.

"Oh, but she can," said the queen. The small leopard-patterned gecko that rode on the queen's shoulder stuck his head and neck entirely out from her wondrous mass of hair. "There is a way."

Fenella leaned forward. "How? What must I do?"

The queen said, "You must complete three tasks of deliberate destruction in the mortal realm."

Three tasks of deliberate destruction.

It took a moment to penetrate. "You mean like before?" A leaf brushed Fenella's cheek and she pushed it away. "Three tasks? As with the first curse?"

Padraig was looking at her. Fenella saw his sneer.

They both knew she had failed at the previous three tasks. Everyone knew.

"Yes and no," said the queen. "These are tasks not of creation, but of destruction."

Fenella opened her mouth to ask a question, but the queen's brother Ryland spoke first.

"How poetic. I feel the beginnings of a new ballad. What shall we call this one? Scarborough Fair, part two? Summon the minstrels."

Fenella whirled on him. Ryland thought her life—her death—was a joke. "You want minstrels? I'll rip you apart and use your forepaw for a lute!"

"Ooo la la," said Ryland. "I am terrified."

"Stop it," said the queen. "Both of you. I said that this is not like before. Ryland, that means there will be no riddles, no tricks, and no song. And, Fenella, not a single one of these three tasks is impossible. It is only . . ." She paused. "It is only that your choices will be . . . difficult. Terrible. Also, as they must be done in the human realm, they will be terrible in human ways."

Hope had touched Fenella with the lightest of fingers, however. "No riddles? No tricks?"

"That is correct," said the queen.

"How dull," Ryland said.

Fenella knew better than to react, and yet—

"Oh, sorry," she said. "I'll make my death quest entertaining in other ways, shall I?"

"Please do." Ryland bared his teeth at her. She scowled back—and then, abruptly, realized that she was focusing her attention on the queen's brother in order to ignore Padraig. But she felt Padraig's gaze. Hot, as always. Possessive. Vindictive. And angry; always angry.

Well, she was angry too.

The queen's brother was laughing now. He beat at the ground with one large paw. Then the other fey joined in, everyone save the queen, the tree fey, Fenella, and also Padraig. It was laughter at the irony of it all. It was laughter at Fenella's expense, and also at the expense of the despised Mud Creature.

But it was also simply the laughter of those who have lived too long without it. "Three more tasks for the Scarborough girl!" they chorused. "Better luck to her this time!"

Chapter 3

When the laughter stopped, the queen's gaze was intent on Fenella. "You can do these tasks. I have no doubt. You see, destruction, unlike creation, is easy. There will be many possible solutions to these tasks. But I warn you, the ease will be only on the surface."

She paused, and then added, "My advice to you, Fenella, is to live out your life instead, long though it may be. I advise you to reject this challenge. To give up your quest for death."

"Continue with your long life," murmured Padraig. "Your lonely life, filled with memories. Like when Bronagh came to me. Fenella, you remember your gawky daughter? That big overlapping front tooth she had . . ."

Fenella looked only at the queen. She listened only to the queen.

The queen said, "Don't allow yourself to be provoked."

"I'm not listening to him," Fenella said. And she wasn't, though he was still murmuring provocative poison in his low, resonant voice.

The queen had said the tasks would mean difficult choices, terrible choices. But at least, finally, Fenella would *have* choices. She met the queen's globed eyes and thought that they were beautiful.

"Your Majesty," she said. "Thank you for this chance. What are the tasks of destruction?"

Padraig was silent at last.

The queen leaned forward. "You will destroy three things, but you will get to pick each one, to fit a prescribed condition."

Fenella listened carefully. "I will be in control? I will choose all three of the destructive tasks? I will not need to destroy anything—or anyone—that I do not decide to destroy?"

"Yes. There will be one guideline per task."

"I see. Yes. I agree to it."

"You are not committed, Fenella, until you have said yes three times. Consider one last time that these are tasks of *destruction*. This means—"

Fenella lifted an impatient hand. "I am not a child. I know what it means. So I am responsible for destroying this thing or that thing. What does it matter? Life destroys everything too. Nothing lasts for long. Especially in the human realm."

Feeling many critical eyes on her, she whirled and out-stared a unicorn, only a foot away. She met the gaze of a speckled faun with wings. She glared at a large, mossy stone that had shuffled closer.

"Life destroys all of us anyway. At the end we are broken. At the end, we are dust." She discovered she was looking at her friends the tree fey, and that her voice was quiet, steady, and certain. "At the end, it is all meaningless. Life *is* death. Life *is* destruction."

"Ah," Ryland drawled. "A philosopher."

Even he could not irritate her now, however. Not now that she saw her path before her, shining strong like the sun on water. Fenella merely looked at Ryland. "Yes. I am a realist."

She did not wait for his reaction. She did not care whether he realized she was no longer the uneducated peasant girl she once had been. "I absolutely agree to do this," Fenella said to the queen. "I agree thrice. Yes. Yes. Yes."

As the sound of her final yes faded, Fenella realized that her waist was free and bare. It felt strange, to be without the touch of the tree fey. Then excitement welled up in her. She was on her way at last. She held her own fate in her hands.

The queen's brother stretched, front paws extended on the ground, muscles rippling.

"Very well, Fenella," said the queen. Her gaze moved. "Padraig, Fenella has accepted the three tasks of destruction. Now comes your part."

Padraig had a part? Before she could control herself, Fenella found she had swiveled to face Padraig.

He looked straight back at her. "Why did you think she summoned me?"

Fenella turned to the queen. "You said there would be no tricks!"

"There are none. Padraig cast the original spell. Breaking it will affect him."

Of course. Fenella gritted her teeth. Why had she not realized this?

The queen said, "Padraig, your fate will depend on Fenella's actions, just as hers for so long depended on yours. If Fenella Scarborough succeeds in breaking the life-spell you cast on her, you will die."

There was a stirring of deepened interest from the surrounding fey. The only change in Padraig's expression was a slight flaring of his nostrils.

But Fenella caught her breath. Padraig, dead? Dead as a result of her actions? Before she had a chance to soak it in, Padraig said, "May I ask a question?"

The queen inclined her head.

"What if Fenella fails? What is the consequence to her? Surely there is one."

"You are correct," the queen said. "Everything must balance."

There was a pause, a long one. Fenella waited for the blow that she should also have expected. She had been a fool to trust this unknown queen. A fool not to realize that nothing was ever straightforward with the fey.

The queen said, "If Fenella fails, Padraig, then her life will again belong to you."

"My slave again?" said Padraig, slowly. "In my power again?"

"Yes."

No, Fenella thought. And then: *What have I done?*

Padraig threw back his handsome head and laughed. It was a raucous laugh, like a crow.

Despite all her resolve, despite all her best intentions, Fenella flung words at him.

"Laugh all you like, Mud Creature!" She took pleasure in using his new name. "We shall see."

"We shall indeed." His gaze swept Fenella up and down in the old way.

And her control snapped.

When the red haze lifted from Fenella's eyes, she discovered that the tree fey had her in their grip. All she had was a vague memory of having lunged, again, for the queen's knife. Padraig was still leering, but he had stepped prudently back.

It was the smallest of victories, his stepping away from her, but it would have to do. For now. When she won freedom, when she won her death, she would see him lifeless first.

"I was wrong. This is far from dull," murmured Ryland.

All the fey were talking excitedly, laying bets, exchanging thoughts, like in the old days. The murmurs rose and strengthened—

"Silence!" The queen got to her feet.

She looked measuringly at her brother. "I have allowed you too much leash of late, brother."

"Allowed?" Ryland yawned. "You have little power over me, sister. We both know it."

The queen did not answer with words. She drew her knife and shaved its blade sharply along her inner arm. A viscous line of deep green-blue blood welled up.

"Consider this a test, brother." The queen smiled, but it was a smile that did not change her expression. "*Your* test."

"Wait," said Ryland, half rising. "What are you—"

"Or perhaps it is a punishment." The queen spoke over him easily. "You will go with Fenella to the human realm.

You will be her adviser. And you will do it well, or you shall not come back here. Do not doubt I have sufficient power for that."

Queen Kethalia stretched out her bloody arm and laid it on her brother, blood to his skin.

A spasm passed through Ryland's body. His shape went smoky. It writhed and shrank.

When Ryland came back to solid form, he was a medium-sized, fluffy-haired tomcat. His fur was mostly white, but he had one black forepaw and, on his chest, a second black spot. This spot was in the exact shape of a heart.

Indignantly and unmusically, the cat yowled.

The queen yowled back. Their voices rose—warred— and then died out. Ryland turned his furry head slowly. He looked at Fenella.

He meowed contemptuously.

The queen said calmly, "Ryland has agreed. Or, rather, understood that he must obey me." She nodded at Fenella. "Your choices and your actions—yours alone—will guide the destructive tasks. Ryland can only give you advice. But that he will do."

The leaves of the tree fey rustled.

The queen appeared to listen for a moment before she swept on. "In the human realm, Fenella, if you are careful, you can get away with talking aloud to your cat. As for my brother, he will send thoughts to your mind." She turned to the cat. "We can't have you talking aloud, can we? You'd end in a science lab with electrodes attached to your poor wittle head."

The cat's hair was standing on end. He presented his rear to his sister.

The queen only shrugged. "Fenella, Ryland also has the power to return to Faerie when necessary and—if you are in physical contact with him—to take you with him. Finally, when you give him a direct order, he must obey."

The cat screamed.

"Oh, it's true, brother," purred the queen. "And you know it."

She turned again to Fenella. "My brother is a cruel and callous individual. He thinks this is a strength. However, I have found him reliably strong in only one thing: He always knows how best to undermine and destroy. This, you may find useful. I certainly do not."

The cat was now silent.

Fenella found her voice. "But I don't want him!"

At the same moment, beside Fenella, Padraig protested. "How is this balanced? How is this fair, that she has help? At the very least, she must have a time limit!"

"There is a time limit," said the queen.

"Nine months?" asked Fenella sarcastically. It had been the amount of time allotted to try to break the previous curse.

"Three," said the queen. "The span of a single season."

The cat meowed. Fenella discovered that she could indeed hear him in her head. *She's right that you'll do better with me to help. Unless you don't really want death? Do you secretly want to belong once more to the Mud Creature?*

The cat's mental voice was surprisingly calm. Perhaps too calm, as if he were forcing himself to be rational. Meanwhile, Padraig was standing straight, looking—was Fenella suddenly imagining this?—confident. She contained a shudder.

She looked back at the cat, and then at the queen.

"Decide, Fenella," said the queen. "Do you go alone, or with Ryland?"

Fenella hesitated. The tree fey murmured their opinion.

Fenella said reluctantly, "I will take Ryland with me."

"Good. He knows the human realm, and so will also assist you in navigating and understanding it. It is a long time since you have lived in that world, and you will find much has changed."

Fenella said, "I know more than you realize."

It was true. She had learned about the modern world from her descendants, starting with Minnie Scarborough. Minnie had been educated before Padraig's curse took her. She had been Fenella's friend. Because of Minnie, Fenella had at last allowed herself to become close to every Scarborough girl that followed. Jennie. Mary. Ruth, and Joanne, Deirdre, and finally, Miranda, Lucy's mother.

Fenella had helped each of them in turn endure Padraig. She had learned to adjust the way she spoke English, and even the way she thought, to better communicate with them. Of course, each relationship had ended in pain and, yes, destruction. But still, she had learned. She was no longer the inexperienced girl who had failed herself and her family.

She could do this. She could free herself, and see Padraig dead in the bargain—and she would.

"I talked with each of my—my daughters, when they were imprisoned here with me. They told me about their lives, and about their world."

The queen nodded. "I am glad you mention your daughters. You will go to the two that survive, Lucy and her mother, Miranda. Tell them you have been freed and are coming to them for help to restart your life."

"No." Fenella was firm. "I will do this destruction my own way. I will keep Lucy and her family entirely out of it."

The queen continued as if Fenella had not spoken. "They will want to love you and take care of you. They will not be suspicious."

"I don't wish to go to them," Fenella repeated. "I would

rather simply begin on the first task of destruction. Tell me. What must I destroy first?"

The cat butted his soft head against Fenella's ankles. He did not make a sound, but Fenella heard his mocking voice in her head.

"No," she said sharply. "No, you're wrong." She looked at the queen. "Isn't he wrong?"

"He directed his thoughts to you, not to me. What did he say?"

"He told me—" Fenella broke off. "He said that my *family* must be the target of each act of destruction. He said it would not be human destruction if there was no pain for me. For people I care about." Her eyes were hot flame. "Tell me it's not true," she demanded.

The queen said, "Your first task is the destruction of your family's safety."

"No," said Fenella.

"Yes," said the queen, steadily. "You have agreed. You must go forward toward the death you desire, sowing destruction about you, or you will belong again to the Mud Creature."

Chapter 4

With the white-and-black cat in a plastic carrier in one hand, Fenella stood on a sidewalk before a big, shabby house. She had been standing there for several minutes. Her throat was dry and her palms were sweating. Here she was, back in the human realm after all these years. She had dreamed of this in her early years of captivity. That was a long time ago, though. Now she was in a world she did not recognize.

How had she ended up tasked with destruction instead of in her grave? This was not what she had intended. But here she was and she would do it. She would destroy her family's safety. She had her choice of how. She would find something to do that wasn't too bad. After all, it wasn't like she had to murder anybody. She didn't even have to listen to Ryland's ideas; his own sister had called him cruel and callous. The queen had only wanted to get rid of him, Fenella thought. She had not really believed he would be of valuable assistance to Fenella.

She thrust her chin out determinedly, dismissing the subject of Queen Kethalia's motivations. She needed to focus on her tasks.

Now. This was the house where her family lived. Lucy. Lucy's mother, Miranda. Lucy's foster parents. Lucy's young husband. And—and—

And it was a beautiful morning in late September. The front garden of the house displayed a scattering of dandelions amid grass, a few bushes, and patches of bare earth. An odd little vehicle, pink with three wheels and with the word *Playskool* on its side, lay overturned on the front porch of the house. There was a large oak tree to Fenella's right, and many other trees around the neighborhood as well, maple and willow and more oak, none of the trees very old. The leaves of the nearby maple were beginning to turn.

Fenella wondered whether the trees would be friendly. She put a hand out to touch the oak. Nothing—oh, of course. These trees were not fey.

Are you going to stand there all day long? This is a small cage I'm trapped in, and I would like to be out of it. Go up those stairs. Move into your new home already.

"Shut up, Ryland," she said to the cat. "I don't trust you, and I don't have to listen to you."

I plan to help you, said the cat, with exaggerated patience. *In fact, I'm being forced to help you. You'd be stupid not to take advantage. I want this to end successfully every bit as much as you do.*

Fenella snorted. "Only because it's in your own interest."

Whose interest should it be in? And here you claim to be a realist.

She didn't answer.

He was right about her next move, she thought. She did need to walk up those stairs to the door of that house. Instead, she looked down at her unfamiliar clothes. Queen Kethalia had given her a soft white cotton shirt and a white hooded sweatshirt, and a skirt that was frankly wondrous. It was deep green as a summer leaf, and long to her calves. It swung pleasurably at the hem, and had a comfortable stretchiness woven into the fabric. *One percent spandex,* Ryland had told her, in her head, authoritatively.

"What's spandex?"

He hadn't answered. Instead: *Tell my sister you need ballet flats. Pale pink. Not those sneaker things.*

Fenella had ignored the fashion advice. But now she looked around and understood at least why shoes were a necessity. Much of the ground in the human realm was covered with a smooth, hard surface that would hurt the soles of bare feet. The ground in this place was also covered with houses, and everywhere you looked, there were vehicles that operated artificially, without horses or donkeys, which was—rather fascinating. All she had really known of machinery, in the old days, was the watermill that Robert's parents ran, and it had been a long time since she had allowed herself to think of those days.

Go up the stairs, Ryland said with irritation. *One foot at a time. Then do something called "ringing the bell." It's not a real bell. You push a button. It makes a noise that summons the people within.*

Fenella would have, she absolutely would have, because there was no sense in running away. But suddenly from within the house came the muffled but unmistakable sound of a child's demanding screech.

The baby. Who would not be such a baby. Eighteen months? Nineteen?

Fenella dropped the cat carrier. It landed with a thud on the ground.

The cat said something nasty as the house's front door opened and a young woman with short, dark hair catapulted onto the front porch

"I have to go right now or I'll miss my bus," she called back over her shoulder. "Listen, Zach, ask Mrs. Spencer about taking care of Dawn next Wednesday, okay?" The young woman hefted a backpack onto her shoulders and sprinted down the house steps and onto the walk. She went past Fenella, mumbling, "Sorry, excuse me."

Lucy Scarborough, I suppose, commented the cat.

Fenella knew who it was. Her heart had taken on a rapid rhythm. "Her name is Lucy Scarborough Greenfield now," she murmured.

She watched Lucy's back until the girl turned the corner. Then Fenella remained quite still, looking at the empty street and feeling her heart thud with—something.

Ten seconds later, Lucy reappeared. She stared in Fenella's direction. It was too far away to see her expression.

Involuntarily, Fenella stepped away from the cat carrier. She felt she couldn't breathe. She raised one hand in an uncertain gesture, reaching out, pulling back. She took another step forward. Confusion filled her. Then numbness.

Then terror. Terror, even though she had honestly believed she could never fear anything again.

Lucy began walking back rapidly.

"Shut up, Ryland," Fenella whispered to the cat, even though he hadn't said anything.

Then Lucy was in front of her, close enough to touch. Her gaze straight into Fenella's eyes was intelligent, and clear— and amazed. She was several inches taller than Fenella.

"I went right by you," Lucy said. "But I could feel you watching me, and . . . I had to turn. Then—I knew you. Even from the end of the street, I knew you." She paused. "Fenella? Fenella Scarborough? It is you?"

Fenella clutched the back of her own neck beneath her red hair. She managed a nod.

"Are you real?" Lucy touched Fenella gently, tentatively, on the upper arm.

Fenella didn't think about what to do. Her body knew. She put her hand on top of Lucy's. "I'm real." Her voice came out choked.

"How?" Lucy's gaze was intense. "How can you be here?"

"The fey." Fenella remembered some of the things the queen had advised her to say, and she got one of them out past the obstruction in her throat. "They let me go."

"Like Miranda was let go?" Lucy asked. "Free to live out the remainder of her life?"

Fenella nodded. "I—yes."

"But what about all the others? If you're here, then maybe, could they all be alive again somehow, or . . .?"

"No," said Fenella steadily. It was a relief to find her way to saying true things. "They died each in turn, in their time, according to the curse, every eighteen years. They are at peace. It's just me who—who kept on living forever." She paused and added, "Until now."

"It's a miracle. Oh, my God. They gave you your life back!"

The cat meowed plaintively.

Lucy looked down. Ryland pushed his soft little face against the wire mesh of the door and blinked at her with gorgeous eyes.

"So, this cat," Fenella said colorlessly. "Someone gave him to me while I was on my way here. I—I want to keep him."

If Lucy found it strange that Fenella had been ejected from Faerie and made it her first order of business to adopt a cat, she didn't say so. She squatted. "I don't know if I've ever seen a cat with markings like that before. Adorable." She extended a finger inside the wire mesh and stroked the cat's head.

The cat purred.

They will all love me, he said arrogantly to Fenella. *Watch. I'm going to be ever so sweet.* He pushed his head against the mesh toward Lucy's hand.

"Boy or girl?" asked Lucy. "Name?"

"Boy. Ryland," said Fenella, full of hate for the cat. And then for herself. She pressed her hands together. She wet her lips. "Lucy?"

"Yes?" Lucy looked up.

Fenella reached for her rehearsed words. "I have come to visit you. I hope—that is, I hope it is all right that I've come."

She added in a rush: "I didn't know where else to go." She discovered she could no longer look in Lucy's face.

Lucy said, "Oh, Fenella. Of course this is where you should be. There's no question."

Fenella forced out more words. "My cat . . . ?"

"We'll make room for him too."

Lucy jumped up. She fell upon Fenella, hugging her, enveloping her. "I don't believe you're here, but you are. Just wait until Zach sees you—and Miranda! I've been worried about Miranda, but maybe it will help her to see you. And you haven't ever met my parents. My foster parents, I mean. You'll love them."

It was too easy. Fenella felt sick. She wanted to pull away, but Lucy had her cheek on Fenella's hair, and her arms were tight.

"And my baby, Dawn—you were there when Dawn was born. You appeared to us when the curse was broken. I will never forget it, or you. Of course you're welcome!"

The child. How could she live in a house with the little girl, how? She pulled away from Lucy.

"I'm sorry." Lucy put one hand up to cover her mouth. "I wasn't thinking. Maybe you don't like to be touched?"

"It's all right." Fenella looked down. "I was only—this is all strange for me."

"I understand. Fenella? Listen. We don't know each other,

but I'm your family. We all are, here. We know more about you than you probably realize. Miranda talks about you. She says you kept her steady for those eighteen years she was trapped in Faerie with you . . . and with *him*." Lucy's pause was almost imperceptible. "She says you told her never to give up hope, never to stop trying to help me figure out the curse. And never to stop loving me, even when she was here in the human realm trying to communicate with me and I—well, you know. I was horrible to Miranda sometimes."

"It's all right," said Fenella. "Miranda understood what you were feeling. So did I. Anyway, that's over. It's over because of you, Lucy." The memory swept through Fenella of how it had felt when Lucy and Zach defeated Padraig. The rush of gratitude, the huge relief. The love and joy.

It had not lasted, not for Fenella, not when she discovered her personal ordeal would continue in a different form. But that moment had still been real. Lucy had broken the Scarborough Curse. She had saved herself, and her baby, and her mother, Miranda.

Lucy was moving her shoulders awkwardly. "I was lucky. I had help. Zach, and my parents."

"I know," said Fenella. "But all the same, you were glorious, Lucy. Glorious."

They were quiet for a moment. "Well," Lucy said at last. "Obviously I'm not going to my class this morning. Let's go inside. You have to meet everyone." She held out her hand for a second, before letting her arm fall back to her side when Fenella did not take it.

Fenella discovered that even with Lucy beside her, she needed to stand on the sidewalk in front of the house for another minute, just breathing.

She had figured out that the pink toy on the front porch must belong to the child.

Lucy was patient. Miraculously, so was the cat. At last Fenella reached for the cat carrier.

"Wait," Lucy said. "Can we leave your cat outside? On the porch? The thing is, we have a dog. We'll have to go slow."

No, said Ryland instantly. *You need me with you.*

"Yes, fine," said Fenella to Lucy. "Let's leave him outside."

Chapter 5

Fenella had never realized before that five people (plus a dog) could constitute an enormous crowd. The family crammed around her in the kitchen. They stared and talked and marveled and fussed. Several of them mentioned places they were supposed to be: jobs, school. But then they pulled out little communication devices and gave notice that they would be late, or were not going today. After that they looked at Fenella as if they thought their staying with her would make her happy.

They were happy. A little alarmed, a little anxious, but genuinely glad to see Fenella. The Scarborough-Markowitz-Greenfield family was accustomed to fantastical events. They could take it in stride when a woman showed up, claiming to be their relative released from captivity in Faerie after hundreds of years.

"Like Rip Van Winkle," said Leo, Lucy's foster father. "Only you didn't get older."

Fenella didn't know who Rip Van Winkle was. She smiled tentatively anyway. She took a seat at their kitchen table, well away from where the child sat in her high chair. She did not look at the child, or at the child's dimpled hands, or at the child's softly curling dark hair, or at the child's gently rounded arms, or at the tiny bubble of clear spit at the corner of the child's pink lips. She closed her ears to the happy babbling that came from the child's mouth.

The kitchen was full of unfamiliar things and she was able to pay attention to them. One was a fascinating box that heated food. The box whined and gave out a demanding beep as it finished.

Lucy's foster mother, Soledad, put something called tea in a mug and placed it before Fenella. Her husband, Leo, gave Fenella a bowl of strawberries and blueberries.

The berries looked delicious, but Fenella couldn't control a shocked face after she bit into one. Leo said, "Are those strawberries terrible? Yeah, look at that. Completely white inside. What else can I get you? Toast? We have granola somewhere."

Fenella didn't know what granola was. She managed another smile as she shook her head. "I'm not hungry."

The liquid in her mug was hot, which Fenella appreciated. Under Soledad's supervision, Fenella put in five lumps of sugar. "It helps with shock," the woman said, putting several lumps in her own.

Under cover of drinking the tea, Fenella stole another glance at Lucy's daughter. The child was much occupied with catching little circular food items with a fingertip and putting them in her mouth. She raised her head to peer shyly over at Fenella. Fenella looked away then, quickly.

Not quickly enough. Lucy's husband, Zach, asked, "Fenella, would you like to hold Dawn after she finishes her Cheerios? If she's in the mood to be held, that is. These days, she's into everything."

Fenella shook her head. She muttered a question about Dawn's age, even though she already knew. Eighteen months, nearly nineteen. She lowered her gaze to her mug and sipped frantically at the liquid in it.

Others kept talking. Was Fenella tired, scared, or confused? She should not worry, they said. They were her family, they said. They would take care of her, they said. Oh, and her cat too.

"Thank you," she managed.

The talk around her began to seem like a roar of unindividuated sound.

She got their names sorted out, though. Soledad and Leo Markowitz were the married couple who had raised Lucy as their own. The dog, Pierre, wore an eye patch, and had a black, curly coat that was growing back from a short summer cut. Of course there was Lucy herself and her young husband, Zach Greenfield.

The child was called Dawn. She had been named to celebrate a new day.

Soledad Markowitz was saying something about arrangements; that there was a second bed in Miranda's room. Belatedly, Fenella was appalled; how could she have forgotten about Miranda, even for a short time?

"Where is Miranda?"

"She's on a meditation retreat. It's a kind of vacation. We don't have a lot of quiet here for her."

Fenella nodded uncertainly. She remembered that Lucy had said she was worried about Miranda. "What is a vacation?"

"A break from routine," Lucy said. "You go away from home, for pleasure, or to have time to rest or think. Miranda will be back tomorrow. We could call her to tell her you're here, but they don't allow communication except for emergencies. Mom? Is this an emergency?"

"No. It's a lovely surprise."

Soledad was a tall, splendidly curvy woman in her late forties. She had a short cloud of black hair with gray beginning to lace through it. Her brown face was marked with laugh lines. She reached out and patted Fenella's hand.

Fenella looked at the hand patting hers. It was square and

strongly shaped, though feminine. What is safety, she wondered. Was it a mother holding you, in hands like these?

Uncontrollably, she looked across the kitchen to where Lucy had taken up the child in her arms. She was rubbing her cheek gently on the child's head, and at the same time, was saying something to Zach. The child was peeping right at Fenella, her hazel eyes wide and mischievous—

Fenella snatched her hand away from Soledad. She leaped to her feet. "Please," she said frantically. "Can I bring my cat in from the porch?"

There was silence in the kitchen, but only for a moment.

"Sure," said Leo Markowitz easily. "No problem. It's good that Lucy was careful, but Pierre has met cats before. He likes cats better than nasty, eye-scratching thorn bushes. Right, Pierre?" Pierre raised his head briefly from where he was lying on the floor outside the kitchen. Then he lowered it back down onto his paws.

"Good old boy," said Leo. "It'll be fine."

It was not fine, though.

Pierre growled and then barked as the cat carrier came in. He would not stop. He would not be soothed. In his turn, Ryland stood up in the carrier, hair on end, eyes manic, keening inside Fenella's head in a language she did not know.

In a quick discussion that Fenella could barely follow,

the family decided what to do. The cat would be placed in the bedroom that Fenella would share with Miranda. "Just until we figure out how to get them acquainted," Zach said over his shoulder as he mounted the stairs with the cat carrier.

Fenella went after him. "Could I stay in the bedroom with the cat for a while? I could nap. I know it's only morning, but I would like to rest." She felt as if she might collapse.

"Of course," said Zach.

"I can't believe I didn't think of that," said Lucy, beside Fenella.

Zach murmured quick agreement.

A few more negotiations were necessary: a small room used for personal bodily matters was pointed out; a box of dirt was put together for the cat; Lucy pressed clothing called pajamas upon Fenella. But finally the bedroom door closed and Fenella was alone with Ryland.

She stood still, listening to the footsteps of the family as they retreated back downstairs. Ignoring the pajamas, she sank down onto the bed that had been allocated to her.

She breathed.

The cat's voice in Fenella's head was not entirely calm, but at least he was speaking English again. *That dog can't get in here?*

Fenella found the strength to whisper wearily, "The door is closed."

Maybe there's a lock?

Fenella dragged herself up. Following the cat's instructions, she found a metal button on the doorknob. When she pressed it, something in the door snicked audibly into place.

Even in her exhausted state, Fenella was vaguely intrigued by this lock, which was nothing like the sort of lock she knew. She snapped it open and closed it again. Peering, she could see that part of the lock had slipped into the containing wall. Later on, she thought, she might figure out exactly how it worked. She had understood completely how the watermill worked; this interested her in the same way.

Only not now.

Back to the bed.

Aren't you going to let me out of this cage?

With one hand, Fenella reached out from her prone position. Ryland stepped out of the carrier one cautious paw at a time. Fenella closed her eyes as he began sniffing suspiciously at the floor.

That dog's been in here.

"He's not here now." Fenella kept her voice low.

We have to get rid of him. I won't be able to help you if he's around.

She didn't move. "Can't you make him love you? By being ever so sweet?"

No! A frantic note returned to the cat's voice. *He smells Faerie on me. I'm not safe with him around.*

"I don't care."

Fenella! You need my help!

Why wouldn't he let her sleep? "Couldn't you enchant him, so he thinks he's friends with you?"

These are not the old days. I can't just wave my paw. Anyway, my abilities are limited here. My sister told you. All I can do is give you good advice, and get us back and forth into Faerie. And, he added bitterly, *obey you.*

The cat leaped. He landed next to her on the bed with a thump. Fenella could feel his stare. She opened one eye and found he was nose to nose with her.

You're really going to nap?

"Apparently not," she snapped.

Good, he said tensely. *Because we need to get started. First, you get rid of the dog. Once he's out of the way and I have free rein over the house, I can observe everyone here. I'll figure out what makes each of them feel safe. Then we can discuss destroying that safety—*

"Stop," said Fenella.

The cat's eyes narrowed.

"Listen to me," said Fenella softly. "You're not in charge here. I am. I'll decide what we're doing and when. Now, let me nap. That's a direct order."

Chapter 6

Fenella had not believed she would sleep. No matter how exhausted her body, there were a million jumbled thoughts in her head. She had planned only to close her eyes and be silent.

When she awoke, the shadows of afternoon had moved across the carpet on the bedroom floor. She could smell something cooking downstairs, and she could feel the cat stretched out alongside her legs. He had one silky paw extended across her ankles. She pulled her feet away.

She rose and stretched. The cat opened his eyes. Before he could say a word, she grabbed him and stuffed him into the carrier. "For your own protection," she told him.

I hate that dog. He wrapped his tail around himself.

"I know."

She put the carrier on a high dresser. Then, with a deep

breath for courage, she unlocked and opened the door. She tilted her chin. She went down the stairs and into the kitchen.

"Hello." The word seemed to stick in her throat.

"Hello," said Soledad.

"Hello," said Lucy.

They were the only ones there. The direction of Soledad's gaze made Fenella raise a hand to her hair self-consciously. It had not occurred to her to groom. But both Soledad and Lucy were smiling.

"Did you have a good sleep?" asked Lucy.

"Yes." Fenella looked around cautiously. "Where's the dog?"

"Outside," said Soledad. "Pierre can live between the back-yard and the basement, so your cat can be here in the house."

"That's very kind." Fenella thought of what Ryland had said about wanting to observe everyone. It would do no harm to let the cat do that. "Can I go get him, then?"

Lucy looked startled. "Sure. All right. Of course you don't want him cooped up."

When Fenella returned to the kitchen, Ryland in her arms, it was clear that the two women had been talking in low voices, and equally clear that they had been talking about Fenella. It was only natural, Fenella knew. It felt odd anyway. She couldn't help wondering what they truly thought of her having shown up like this. It could not possibly be convenient. Were they really entirely unsuspicious? It seemed so.

Soledad said, "Dinner won't be ready for an hour yet, and the guys won't be back until then anyway. Can we give you a tour of the house? We'll have to be quiet—Dawn is sleeping."

"I'd like a tour," said Fenella. She was relieved to learn the child was out of the way.

Soledad smiled once more. So did Lucy.

This felt so awkward.

Their first stop was a half-bathroom located off the kitchen. Fenella had been shown the upstairs bath earlier, but now that she was not so tired, she found she had questions. It was good to have something impersonal to talk about.

"What happens to the waste water from the toilet?"

"Underground pipes collect everything from our house and the other houses into sewers under the streets," Lucy said.

"Then what happens to it?"

Lucy looked at Soledad. Soledad looked at Lucy. Soledad said, "It flows to a treatment plant."

"What's a treatment plant?"

"A place that cleans dirty water."

"Really? That's possible?" Fenella was intrigued.

"Uh. I believe so."

"How?"

"Well. I'm not certain. I'll look it up online."

"Online?"

Soledad looked at Lucy. Lucy looked at Soledad. Lucy said, "It's a way to find out information. I'll explain it to you later. Watch." She demonstrated the cold and hot water taps.

"This water too goes down the drain and into those sewers?" Fenella said.

"Yes. It's called a plumbing system." Lucy had Fenella put the cat down and practice mixing the water to a good temperature. "The shower works the same way. You'll want to test the water temperature before you get under the spray to wash."

"It's so interesting," said Fenella thoughtfully. "You know, in Faerie, you don't need to worry about personal grooming, or cleaning, or really, anything to do with taking care of your body."

"No toilets, even?" said Lucy incredulously.

Fenella shook her head. "Not needed."

"Miranda told me that too," Soledad said. "But I can't wrap my mind around how it would work. Your digestive system doesn't process what you eat? What about other organs? Does your heart still pump blood?"

"Oh, yes. Everything works the same, physically. It just doesn't have the same consequences." Fenella paused. "I never questioned how it worked before. But now I'd really like to think about it."

"There must be some scientific principle that explains it," Soledad said. "Even if it's a principle we haven't discovered yet. That would make sense."

"Not everything makes sense, Mom," said Lucy.

"I don't accept that. I will only accept that I don't understand *how* it makes sense."

"Oh, Mom."

Fenella picked up Ryland again. They moved into a large room beyond the kitchen that was called the family room. This was furnished with many large chairs, one of which was called a sofa and was wide enough to seat three or four people. On the floor was a worn carpet with faded blue and pink roses on a yellow background. There was a large knitting basket next to a rocking chair. A half-finished child's pink garment lay partway inside the basket, on needles, amid balls of yarn.

Lucy gestured toward a few rectangular objects. One was called a television. Another was a computer. Lucy explained and briefly demonstrated these devices. Fenella felt a slight impulse to open up the boxes and see what was inside, but the boxes were not quite as interesting to her as plumbing. Or even the lock on her bedroom door. The cat struggled in her arms. Absently, she released him to the floor. She turned to Soledad and said impulsively, "I'm remembering that Minnie had the same questions as you, about how the body worked in Faerie. It drove her crazy that it was just magic. She wanted reasons and logic. She was a nurse." Fenella pronounced the word proudly.

"Why, so am I," said Soledad. "I work mostly with pregnant women."

Fenella regarded her with interest. "Miranda told me that about you, but I forgot."

Lucy seated herself on the arm of the sofa. "Which one was Minnie?"

"Minnie Scarborough was your—" Fenella paused to count. "Minnie, then Jennie, then Mary, then Ruth, then Joanne, then Deirdre your grandmother, and then Miranda your mother."

"My great-great-great-great-great-grandmother," Lucy counted on her fingers. "Seven generations ago. Wow. She was a nurse?"

"Yes. She took her training at the New England Hospital for Women and Children, in Boston." Fenella had long since memorized the name. "She told me all about it."

"How amazing," Soledad said. "What year was that?"

Fenella knew this too. "She entered the program in 1879.

She was seventeen, so she only had a single year before, well, you know. That was one of the things she resented most about the curse, that she didn't get to finish her training. That was Minnie. She loved learning. She had wanted to become a doctor."

Lucy looked surprised. "Could women do that then?"

"Yes, and a determined few did," said Soledad. "It was a breakthrough time for women in medicine."

"It was so frustrating for Minnie in Faerie," Fenella said. "I couldn't understand her at first, but she said it was like being intellectually starved. She even asked Padraig for books. She couldn't help herself."

"I'm sure he didn't get her any books," said Lucy tightly.

"But he did," said Fenella. "Everything from poetry to scientific treatises to philosophy and literature. Something new every single week, for eighteen years."

"Really? I'm surprised he—"

"Just for the pleasure of keeping them where Minnie could see them. Where she could read their titles, but nothing more. Often, he would read a page or two aloud to her. He always knew what she'd find particularly involving or fascinating or moving. Then he'd stop at the best part, rip out that page, and burn it."

Lucy and Soledad stared at Fenella in horror.

"Oh, Minnie got revenge," Fenella said. "She taught *me*

to read. She scratched letters in the dirt with a stick, and I learned. She insisted, and I wanted to do something that would give her happiness. It was all I could do. Then, after Minnie was dead, Padraig threw out the books. He didn't have any idea they mattered to me. I hid them. They were like—like a gift from Minnie. They kept her with me every day."

She had read the books aloud, one by one, finger tracing the words, while she sat in the bough of one of the oldest and wisest tree fey. The tree fey had helped her keep the books hidden, and she had shared her gift with them. She and the tree fey had learned about the human world through books, together.

"Minnie sounds like an amazing person," said Lucy, after a long silence.

"Yes," said Fenella simply. "Minnie was the most *alive* person I've ever met. Even after Padraig got hold of her. Most girls of eighteen—and I've met my share, you have to admit—they tend to be passive. But even though she was so young, Minnie always had plans, even in Faerie, even when there was no apparent purpose in planning. That was who she was. She *planned* for me to have those books when she was gone. She gave me the education she wanted for herself, as best she could."

Lucy and Soledad were watching her with soft eyes.

"She was the first daughter I really loved," said Fenella. "Since, well. Since . . ." She shrugged. Bronagh, she thought. She was abruptly aware that, from the floor, Ryland was staring at her too.

Nobody said anything.

Fenella wanted to stop talking, and she knew she should, but her mouth kept moving. "Forgive me for going on and on. I've never talked about Minnie to anyone."

"Not even to Minnie's daughter?" Lucy's voice was high and thin. "What was Minnie's daughter's name again?"

"Jennie," said Fenella.

"You didn't talk to Jennie about her mother? Didn't tell her how amazing she was?"

"No. Not really."

There was silence.

"There was no point," Fenella said in a rush. "It's hard to explain, but Jennie didn't know her mother. She was too worried about her own daughter to think of her. That was the way it usually was, for all of us. Surviving Padraig, and trying to help your own daughter. Hope was always centered on the future. But Minnie was different. She had room for other things too. For other people. She had room for— for me. I don't know why, but she did."

Soledad reached out and put her arm around Lucy's waist. Lucy leaned into her mother.

Lucy said passionately, "I wish I had known Minnie too. I wish she were here. I wish she had the second chance you have. And Jennie, and—and all of them. We'd make room for all of them here, if we could."

Soledad gave a choked laugh. "Think of all the air mattresses we'd need. I think we could manage, though."

"We *would* manage."

Fenella said harshly, "There's no need for fantasy. Minnie's dead. Bronagh's dead. Everyone is dead."

"Not me," said Lucy quietly. "Not Miranda. Not Dawn. Not you." She paused. "Who's Bronagh?"

"Just another one," said Fenella. "It doesn't matter."

Soledad said, "What matters is that you're alive. And as soon as Zach and Leo get back, we'll have dinner and—" Her face changed. "Bad cat! Get away from there!"

Ryland was inside the knitting basket, clutching a ball of pink yarn. In four steps, Fenella crossed the room. "Let go, Ryland!"

It's soft! said the cat insanely. *It rolls! It unwinds!*

"You're a guest in this house!"

She had to wrestle him for the ball of yarn. Fenella put the yarn back into the basket and picked up the cat. What was *wrong* with him? He needed to act like an ordinary cat, not a bizarre one.

Pretty, pretty yarn, Ryland said longingly.

Fenella looked across the room at Lucy and Soledad. Their faces told her that they were still moved by what she had said about Minnie. But she knew it had been a mistake. She mustn't get too close to them. There was no point.

Also, they were wrong. She was not alive.

"Is there a cover for your knitting basket?" she asked Soledad.

Chapter 7

Leo was late getting home for dinner. This wouldn't have mattered if, upon coming in, he had remembered that Pierre was an outside dog now. But he didn't, and he let the dog in with him.

An instant later Pierre and Ryland were locked in combat, a rolling, screaming mass of legs and heads and fur. Fenella stood frozen. The last she'd known, Ryland had been under the table, listening to the conversation while lying on top of her feet.

Lucy yelled Pierre's name. Soledad snatched the crawling child up off the floor. Zach and Lucy and Leo threw themselves into the fray, and then so did Fenella.

Then a strange, deep, male voice broke into the mayhem.

"Pierre," the voice said sternly. "Down."

The dog lifted his head. In that second, Fenella was able

to snatch Ryland away. He came into her arms like a fury, nails raking deeply across her skin.

I'll claw out his other eye!

Lucy and Zach pulled Pierre into the corner of the kitchen by his collar. Leo threw himself down across the dog's belly.

"Walker," Lucy said, panting, to the stranger, who was standing behind Fenella. "Talk about being the right person at the right time."

"Nah, you were handling it," said the stranger called Walker, in a humorous, unrushed voice. There was something about that voice. It seemed to draw a lingering, easy line down along the bare skin above Fenella's spine. She suddenly wanted to see what the speaker looked like.

No. She did not. She bent over the trembling cat.

The dog was still growling, low in the throat. "Let's get Pierre out of here, Leo," said Zach. They dragged Pierre out of the room. The dog kept his single eye fixed on the cat the whole time.

The newcomer was close to Fenella now. He said, "Your arms are scratched and bleeding."

As large warm hands fastened on top of Fenella's, Ryland went limp, a bundle of fur and bones. The hands gently, competently, lifted Ryland away. The cat did not struggle.

The kitchen went quiet. Fenella looked around, but not at the stranger called Walker.

Soledad stood with Dawn in her arms, looking as if she might laugh hysterically. The child's gaze was on the cat. She leaned forward yearningly, her face alight. She babbled something.

"It's a kitty, Dawn," said Lucy. "Nice kitty." She reached for and took the child from Soledad.

Soledad said to Lucy, "Don't you laugh. If you start, I'll go off."

"*Nice* kitty." Lucy's shoulders were suddenly shaking.

"Stop it, Lucy."

Then the two of them were, inexplicably, roaring with laughter. Soledad wiped her eyes. "Walker? Would you like a square of lasagna?"

"I would, but first I'd like someplace safe to put this cat," said Walker.

"I'll get the cat carrier," said Fenella, and escaped from the kitchen. A minute later, she was back with the carrier. She held its gate open while the stranger bundled Ryland inside.

She still had not seen his face. All she had had was a quick impression of height and strong arms. Fenella's heart beat faster with what was surely anxiety about the cat.

"Now," said Walker. "Those scratched arms of yours. Can I see?"

Oh, no, wailed the cat. *Tell him he imagined it.*

Fenella tilted her chin and forced herself, finally, to look at the stranger. She looked slowly and thoroughly.

Walker was indeed tall. He wore pants that had been hacked short to reveal bare, knobby knees and long shanks. He'd paired the pants with a grubby shirt and its shoulders were slightly tight—or maybe it was that his shoulders were themselves a fraction too wide. Above the shoulders, he had a sturdy neck and dark brown hair the exact shade of a dead oak leaf that clings stubbornly to its branch. The hair needed cutting.

Walker's face was deep brown too. It featured a wide mouth and a misshapen nose that had plainly been broken some time ago. You wanted to smile at the nose, except that you forgot to do that once you looked into Walker's eyes. They were beautiful eyes; brown with amber lights, dark-lashed, crinkled at the corners.

Silently, Fenella held out her smooth, unmarked arms.

Walker's gaze moved from Fenella's arms, to her face, and then back down again.

"I guess I was seeing things. You're not hurt." His fingers brushed along the soft inside of her forearm, as if seeking tactile proof.

Fenella's pulse jumped in her wrists and at the base of her throat.

He smiled into her face. "I'm Walker Dobrez."

Fenella knew what to say. Fenella, she thought. My name is Fenella Scarborough. She moved her lips to say the words, to introduce herself as anybody would.

Nothing came out of her mouth.

Then Soledad was there beside her. "Walker, I forgot you were coming over. How lucky."

"Glad to help," said Walker. "But you didn't actually need me. You guys were coping."

"Opinions differ," said Soledad dryly. "Fenella, Walker is our vet."

"Vet in training," said Walker. "Not as good as a licensed vet, but a whole lot cheaper. I'll work for food, actually. When Soledad cooks."

"A vet is a doctor for animals," Lucy said.

Fenella was grateful for Lucy's translation. Then she realized that Walker might find it odd that she had needed it. Her mind was spinning. Again.

Walker hadn't even seemed to hear Lucy, though. He'd squatted down beside the cat carrier and was looking at Ryland. "Huh," he said thoughtfully.

The cat hissed again. *Fenella! An animal doctor? I am not an animal. I am fey. Don't forget it.*

Fenella tried to think of how she could answer Ryland in front of people. No ideas came to her.

"I only have a few more courses," Walker said to Fenella.

"And tests and things. But I'm going to make it. I'm nearly sure. So, this is *your* cat?"

He was evidently the kind of person who liked to chat, and who would tell you more than you had asked for or wanted to hear. At least he had ended on a question that was relevant. It could also be answered in a single word.

Fenella opened her mouth. "My name is Fenella Scarborough." Which had been the right thing to say. A minute ago.

A hot flush crept up her cheeks.

Walker said, "Nice to meet you, Fenella."

Lucy stepped in. "Fenella's a relative of mine. She's staying with us for a while." Dawn was squirming, uttering frustrated little noises, trying to get closer to the cat. Lucy hitched the child up in her arms.

Soledad added, "I guess we'll figure out how to deal with the animals, and get them to be friends. Somehow."

"Usually a cat and dog can learn to tolerate each other." Walker paused, opened his mouth again as if he was going to add something, but then closed it. A furrow worked its way across his forehead as he stared into the carrier at Ryland. Ryland, sitting, stared back. "Male cat, right?"

He was talking to Fenella, who was now able to answer. "Yes."

"Age?"

"I don't know."

"Shots?"

Fenella sent Lucy a quick, frantic look of appeal.

Lucy shrugged. "We have no idea."

Walker nodded. "Tell you what, I'll take the cat with me tonight and give him a checkup at the clinic."

Inside Fenella's head, Ryland's protest was instantaneous and shrill. *Fenella! Do not let this man take possession of me!*

"No," Fenella said reluctantly. "The cat has to stay with me."

"But it's important—" said Soledad.

At the same moment Lucy said, "Fenella, I should have thought of this before, we can't take any chances with Dawn—"

Walker spoke over them both. "You come too, Fenella. You can keep me company, and you'll also help keep your cat calm." His entire face was made mysteriously radiant by a smile.

He was young, Fenella realized. This Walker Dobrez was not many years older than Zach and Lucy. She had been deceived by the way he conducted himself before—by his authority, and perhaps also by his size. But now she saw that the owner of this smiling face had experienced little of the world. Certainly little of the darkness in it.

He was so—so sunny.

"Fenella can't go with you, Walker." Soledad gave Fenella a motherly, reassuring nod. "She's had a long day. But you can take the cat."

"Fenella doesn't want me to take the cat without her." Then he added, directly to Fenella, "Does the cat have a name?"

"Ryland," said Fenella. "What will you do to him?"

"Just a wellness exam. It won't take long. It won't hurt him. Then we'll come back here and I'll check out Pierre's scratched eye." Walker paused before finishing tactfully, "If it turns out that you folks need the cat to stay with me overnight, that's fine too."

No! said Ryland. *Fenella!*

"No," said Fenella.

"Probably not," said Lucy. To her daughter, who was squirming again, and babbling something in a demanding tone, she added, "Dawn, you can see the kitty later. I promise."

Soledad said, "Should we consider declawing the cat?"

No! cried Ryland.

"No," said Fenella cautiously.

"We can trim his nails," Walker said. "Come on, Fenella. The sooner, the better. Soledad, could you possibly save me that piece of lasagna? And, um, could it be big?"

"Sure, but—"

"Unless Fenella would prefer to stay here and rest—" Lucy and Soledad were practically in unison, but both stuttered to a stop mid-sentence, unable in front of Walker to make a logical objection. They looked at Fenella helplessly.

No vet! snarled Ryland again. *I don't want to be examined. Plus, we need to stay here. We have work to do. Remember?*

Work to do. Oh, yes. Fenella remembered, all right.

"Are you afraid of being examined, kitty?" she asked, choosing her words carefully and using a light tone, the kind that the family used when talking to the child. "Do you think there might be something wrong with you?"

No, of course not. I'm fine. We just don't need to do it.

Walker said, "Fenella? I've got my truck outside. We can zip there and back."

Fenella looked at him. Then she looked at Soledad and Lucy. Finally, she looked at the child in Lucy's arms. The bright-eyed little girl who was attending to everything as if she understood.

All at once she wanted only one thing: to get away from this house and the family inside it. To get away from that child.

To get away from how, this whole time in their company, while they were being so kind to her, she was thinking, compulsively, horribly, of what she must do to them. Destroy their safety . . .

"Yes, let's go," she said to Walker.

Chapter 8

Holding the cat carrier, Fenella followed Walker outside. The sun had begun to sink toward the western horizon, but there was still plenty of light.

Ryland was yowling in protest, both inside Fenella's head and audibly.

"I'll stow Ryland in the back of my truck," Walker said as he waved an arm at a vehicle that stood in the street before the house. "Unless you want the carrier on the floor of the cab with you? It'd be a tight squeeze, but we could do it. We could also take him out and put him on your lap."

"The cat can go in the back." Fenella glanced sidelong at Walker. She was only guessing what he meant by words like *truck* and *cab*. She would say as little as possible. Luckily, he was the kind of person who gestured while he talked.

He talked a lot. And he talked fast.

Fenella! was the desperate shrill cry from Ryland. *Keep me with you up front. You need too many things explained.*

It was true. But it wasn't as if Ryland had been much help so far. She was pretty sure he had started the fight with the dog, for example. Pierre certainly had not gone under the table looking for Ryland. Also, she didn't want to listen to his complaints.

"Sorry, kitty," Fenella said. She felt inexplicably cheerful. "You're going in the back."

Walker strapped the carrier into place on what he called the *flat bed*. The *cab* was the word for the enclosed portion at the front of the truck, which contained two wide, comfortable chairs. Walker helped Fenella climb up and sit on one of the chairs. She smoothed her skirt around her legs. It was interesting, sitting high up like this. There was a different view of the world.

Should she be nervous? She had heard about vehicles from the more recent Scarborough girls, but had never seen one before today. Vehicles traveled fast, she knew, faster than horses. Yet she did not feel even slightly anxious.

Walker sat at the controls on the other side of the cab. He pulled a wide strap down around himself. Fenella found a similar strap beside her own chair and pulled it into place with some fumbling. It was easy to guess that it was meant to function for safety.

Once you were strapped in, Fenella discovered, you felt ready. Ready to travel.

Walker did something and the truck seemed to come alive. It vibrated in place.

Fenella sat bolt upright.

Walker moved his hands and feet on the controls, and the truck responded. It moved! They moved! She moved!

Inside the truck, safe within its shell, she was moving. Moving with such speed.

Fenella caught her breath. Now she understood the smooth hard surface over the earth. It was to make travel easier. How clever was that? Of course, of course! You could not go at high speeds if you were forever encountering rocks and depressions and other irregularities in the ground!

And there was more! If you were a passenger, you could look around as you traveled, and, because you were going so fast, the things you saw and the things you thought kept changing. What was that gorgeous color in the little boy's shirt, over there? It was not found in nature! Why did the people put the buildings so close to each other? Why were the trees so few and so small? Now they were on a bridge, going over a river, and there were ducks! Oh, and look! There was a girl in control of that other vehicle over there. It was a small red vehicle, and the girl looked careless, confident, at the wheel.

Now that Fenella was looking for it, there were women in

control of vehicles *everywhere*. The educated, independent Minnie Scarborough would have loved seeing that. If she were here, Minnie would have been driving a vehicle of her own; Fenella knew it.

Also, there were so many vehicles, small and large. You'd think they would all crash into each other, but it was as if they were dancing together to the music that came from the vehicles themselves. It was not a perfect dance, nor even a pretty one, and the music of the vehicles was odd and discordant. But it was compelling, urgent, fascinating.

It was lovely!

Fenella clutched the seat on either side of her legs and leaned forward. She twisted around and looked again at the things they had passed. All she wanted was to keep moving and looking, moving and looking.

Walker had to say her name twice before she heard him. "Fenella? Hey, listen, you're making me seriously nervous. I can almost promise we won't have an accident."

"Accident?" Fenella craned her neck. "Where? Everything seems all right to me."

"No, no. I meant—could you please relax, Fenella? I'm a good driver. Well, pretty good."

"I'm not afraid. I'm only—I'm looking around."

"Oh. Okay. Fine. Sorry."

"I like traveling in this truck," Fenella said. Some of her

excitement ebbed as she realized she was surely behaving strangely. She forced herself to lean back. She looked at Walker and discovered that, at the same moment, he had glanced at her.

"Your cheeks are all pink." He smiled—a quick shy flash—before returning to managing the truck.

Fenella blinked, caught by surprise. Oh.

Oh!

Even in this new world—a world that had fast, glorious traveling trucks in it, a world where women drove vehicles— boys still gave girls glances. Quick glances. Quick, wondering glances.

Like that.

She was glad that she had allowed Ryland to be tucked away in back where he could not see that little glance she had just received.

Or the one she gave back.

Far too soon, Walker slowed the truck to a stop beside a small white building. The building bore a large placard that Fenella read silently to herself: *Veterinary Hospital. All Animals Welcome.* The word *hospital*—the mere reading of it—reminded her again of Minnie.

Minnie, who had fought Padraig every minute from her capture to her death. Fought stealthily, cleverly, idiosyncratically.

Fenella curled her hands into fists. The one she would destroy was Padraig. If she had had this truck in Faerie, she would have run Padraig down with it. She'd have had Minnie beside her, yelling encouragement. Smash him!

"Fenella?"

Walker was outside the truck. He had opened her door and had his hand out to help her. "You seemed sort of far away?"

She didn't answer. She released her strap with little difficulty and jumped lightly down, avoiding Walker's offered hand. She looked away from him, but could still feel his interest, centered on her. She took in a deep breath. Padraig had looked at her like that too, at the start of it all, and she had hated it. Hated it! But this didn't feel like that. This felt like—like Robert.

The thought hit her with a shock. It had been so many years since she had thought of Robert. Robert, her lover; Robert, Bronagh's father.

No. She would not think of Robert. He was no longer important. The past was not important. Also, this Walker was not important. Boys liking girls, and girls liking boys, just because of what they looked like, or felt like as you walked beside them, or—she inhaled—because of what they smelled like, that was not important.

Another moment and Walker had given her back the cat

carrier. Again Fenella was careful not to touch his hand.

Inside the carrier, Ryland was looking tense. She listened to him as she followed Walker into the building. *Let's get out of here quickly. We need to focus on the first task.*

Fenella said, "Now, Ryland. Be a good, obedient kitty for Walker and do what he says."

Walker laughed. "Hey, I don't know if he'll listen. I'm thinking your Ryland might be trouble. No offense."

"Oh, he'll be good," said Fenella. "Gentle as a lamb. And obedient. Right, kitty? That's an order."

Walker held open the animal hospital's front door for Fenella. "Fenella? You probably want him neutered, if he's not already. Right? I can't do it, I'm not qualified for that yet, but I could schedule it for you."

Ryland issued a screech so loud and so ugly that three people in the veterinary hospital's waiting area startled.

Fenella hesitated. Neutered? Could that possibly mean what she thought it meant?

Don't do it!

Fenella said to Walker, "Tell me what that would involve."

Chapter 9

Neutering was exactly what Fenella thought. She told Walker she would think about it. She didn't look at Ryland in his carrier as she said this, and while he refrained from screaming at her again inside her head, nonetheless she could feel his rage and fear. It felt a bit heady having this kind of power—and over the brother of the Queen of Faerie too.

She found herself wondering about his sister. Why had the queen transformed and banished her brother, delegating him to help Fenella? Was it a trap of some kind?

Walker had taken Fenella and the cat into a small room.

"I need to check in with my boss," he said. "Wait here for five or ten minutes?"

Fenella nodded and gave Walker a bright smile. Walker left, although at the last moment he gave Fenella another half-shy, half-bold backward glance that brought a flush to her cheeks.

When the door closed behind Walker, Fenella stooped to peer into the cat carrier. Walker had placed it on top of a counter that reminded Fenella of the uncannily smooth surfaces in the Markowitzes' kitchen. The cat's white fur was on end and his tail was low.

"Don't worry," she said. "If you were Padraig, I'd do it, but you're not. I'm curious, though. Would this neutering affect you in your real form?"

No, said the cat, with dignity. *But I am not interested in having the experience.*

"I understand."

Fenella caught herself wondering about Ryland's sex life. All talk—at least among the tree fey—about the queen's brother was centered on his purported resentment of his sister, his desire for power, and his cleverness. She tried to think whether there were any other manticores at present in Faerie. She didn't know. She knew the form was exceedingly rare. Perhaps he thought himself above others because of it? Or perhaps, like the tree fey, his form of sexuality was impersonal? But no, he was a mammal. Also, there he was, shuddering at the thought of being neutered.

Attend, Fenella! Ryland's tone was aggressive. *You seem to have forgotten that we have other business.*

"I haven't forgotten," said Fenella grimly.

Then why are we here, getting me a medical exam we both know I don't need? Shouldn't we be watching your family? Comparing notes on the ways in which they feel safe? Making a plan?

Fenella shrugged.

Ryland's tone sharpened, as if he sensed what she was thinking. *You can't possibly imagine you can do this without me. My sister is right about that, even if she's wrong about so much else.*

Fenella was curious. "What's she wrong about?"

Never mind, he said dismissively. *Politics. It doesn't concern you.*

"But you started to tell me."

I didn't mean to say that. I'm not used to censoring what I say in my own head.

"Well," Fenella said provocatively, "you might call it politics, but everyone knows you're jealous of your sister."

The cat snarled. *I'm not! Listen, keep your thoughts about her and me to yourself—unless you really don't want my help after all.*

"But she said you *had* to help me. Isn't that true?"

Yes, snapped the cat.

"Good," said Fenella pleasantly. "Not that you've been particularly helpful so far. Did you start that fight?"

It was self-defense.

"Really?"

The wise defense is a good offense.

"Is that so?"

The cat eyed her. *We've moved away from the main topic, which is: What are we doing here? Why aren't we back with your family figuring out how to destroy their safety?*

"I wanted to get out of there," Fenella replied honestly. "It was overwhelming."

Behind the wire mesh of the carrier door, Ryland's almond-shaped eyes met Fenella's. He blinked slowly.

Oh.

They looked at each other.

His mental voice, when he did finally use it again, was mild. *Let me out of this cage?*

Fenella unlatched the door. Ryland stepped daintily onto the counter. Standing at chest level to Fenella, he stretched, arching his fluffy white body and extending his front paws. Coming out of the stretch, he caught sight of himself in the mirror on the wall behind the counter. He snarled.

Fenella looked at the cat's mirrored image. "You don't like your black heart?"

My sister has a juvenile sense of humor. The cat twisted before the mirror, checking his appearance in one angle after another. He shot out his claws experimentally and with satisfaction. He raised his beautiful, white, fan-like tail. Then, facing Fenella, he sat down on his haunches and commenced to groom and to talk.

So. You've got cold feet. His tone was pragmatic. *You're trying to run away.*

"No," Fenella said bleakly. "I know I can't. I agreed. And I want—what I want. There is no other way for me."

The cat continued to groom. *You're distractible too. A male. Who'd have thought it of you, after Padraig? I understand, however. He's a healthy, strapping young fellow. He takes care of animals! How sensitive!*

Fenella glared.

With a delicate tongue, the cat licked his paw and used it to smooth out the fur on his chest. *The heart is growing on me. Don't you think it makes me look sensitive too? See, if it's a sensitive little friend you want, here I am. Pretend that I am as I appear.*

"I am not," said Fenella between her teeth, "good at pretending."

Really? Then why are we talking about the attractive young animal doctor instead of our plan?

"You brought him up, not me."

I was making an observation about your behavior, in case you hadn't noticed it yourself.

"I noticed."

Excellent. So, to return to the main subject. Having now

met your happy, welcoming family, have you decided to give up? Will you go voluntarily back to Padraig rather than hurt them?

"No. I can't." Fenella reached behind herself with one hand. She caught hold of the single chair that the room was furnished with, and sat down on it. Too heavily; the chair skittered on the smooth floor, bumping up against the wall. She looked down, flummoxed, and after staring hard, identified the problem. The chair was on little wheels. How bizarre. What purpose was served by wheels on a chair?

"I won't give up," she said, though her voice shook. "I cannot fail this time."

"Fail at what?"

Startled, Fenella looked up to find the door to the office open. Of course, it was Walker. He smiled at her as if it wasn't odd to find her talking to her cat. And he didn't seem to mind when she ducked her head without answering him.

He said, "So, I have this pamphlet for you. It explains why we recommend neutering."

Notice his nose, Fenella. Somebody flattened him once. I can understand. He's annoying.

Fenella took the pamphlet. "Thank you."

Walker moved past Fenella. "You let Ryland out, good."

Ryland displayed pointed incisors to Walker.

Walker put on a pair of thick gloves. Ryland stood stock-still, visibly tolerating the human while Walker examined his fur, his body, his legs, his mouth and teeth. He even tolerated getting shots, a medical process which Fenella watched with great interest, while thinking again about Minnie. It was only when Walker took up the nail clippers and held the cat down that Ryland let loose again with creative invective aimed into Fenella's mind.

"This is a healthy cat," Walker said at last. "A good weight. Good teeth and gums." He looked over his shoulder at Fenella. "Where did you get him?"

Someone gave me to you, said Ryland sourly. *A woman who said she couldn't keep me.*

Fenella repeated it.

"Really? Near here? Where?"

You don't really remember.

Fenella repeated this too.

"Oh." Walker frowned.

Fenella said firmly, "He's my cat now." As Walker removed his gloves, she stood up and stepped close to the counter, and then picked Ryland up in her arms. The cat settled down against her chest, nuzzling close. She found that, automatically, she was stroking him. His fur was lush and soft, and her fingers sank in and disappeared.

She was going ahead. Of course she was going ahead.

And she'd be a fool not to use Ryland's help as best she could.

"Can you drive us back to the house now?" she asked Walker.

"Yeah, sure, of course." He looked frustrated. "I'm just worried about Ryland getting along with Pierre. We have boarding here. Maybe you could leave Ryland for a day or two? There's a discount I can get you—"

No, thank you. We'll manage.

"We'll manage," said Fenella. "But thank you."

In her arms, the cat purred.

And so, in the end, it was Pierre who went off to board, an hour later. "Only for a few days, sweetheart," Lucy crooned to the visibly unhappy poodle as she prepared to take him outside to Walker's truck. "This way, Walker can check your eye and make sure everything is healing the way it should."

Once Pierre was gone, Fenella released Ryland from his carrier. She picked him up. He closed his eyes, as if he had instantly gone to sleep in her arms, but she could feel he was awake, alert, and monitoring everything.

Zach shrugged awkwardly. "Don't worry, Fenella. Pierre likes the kennel fine. They have a fenced backyard, and the dogs are allowed to mingle. Pierre always makes friends. And when he comes back . . ." He glanced at the cat in

Fenella's arms. "By the time Pierre comes back, we'll have figured out some way for him and your cat to get along. Or how to separate them reliably. I have no idea how, exactly, but we will." He paused. "Like, maybe there's some perfume we can buy to make the cat smell better."

"The cat smells bad?" Fenella sniffed at Ryland.

I do not! Ryland said indignantly. *I'm very clean!*

"To Pierre he does," said Zach. "We could concoct something attractive. Essence of hamburger."

"What?" said Fenella blankly.

"But we don't want Pierre to *eat* the cat," Lucy joked as she came back in.

Zach pulled her against him. "Just my first idea. I have plenty more. Is there something like catnip, only for dogs?"

"Could we cage them side by side? To desensitize them?"

"While we read to them from *The Little Prince*."

"Yes, good! The part about the rose."

Fenella felt as if Lucy and Zach were talking in a foreign language.

"I'm sorry," Fenella said. "Pierre is the one who belongs here in this house, not me or Ryland." She swept her gaze around the kitchen to include Soledad and Leo Markowitz. "You're all being so incredibly kind to a stranger. And her smelly cat."

I do not smell!

"You're not a stranger," Lucy said. "A couple of days away won't do Pierre any harm, and it'll help you settle in. That's the most important thing."

"Absolutely," said Leo.

Chapter 10

That night Fenella could not sleep, though she was again exhausted. She put on the borrowed pajamas and climbed into bed. As the rest of the household settled, she kept a small bedside lamp burning against the darkness. Its low electric light illumined not only her own face and hands as she leaned her back against the headboard, but also the second bed on the table's other side. Twin beds, Lucy had called them.

Against the far wall was a bookcase that held great meaning for Lucy. Lucy had demonstrated how the bottom shelf lifted out to reveal a hiding space. She had told a long story—eyes welling up—of a shirt hidden in the space, and a letter from Miranda describing the Scarborough Curse.

Fenella had nodded, pretending attention. In truth, she

had felt desperate to be alone. But now that she was, that too was not much good.

Ryland was sprawled out extravagantly in the center of the second bed, his white fur rising and falling with his breath, his black heart-shaped bib partially obscured by one outflung leg.

She was aware of her family also sleeping, trustfully, in the other rooms of this house. She thought of Lucy's face when she'd said: *We'd make room for all of them!* Then, Soledad's comment: *I think we could manage.*

"Fools," she muttered. What were they *thinking,* accepting her—and the cat!—on faith? How did they manage in the world? Weren't there lots of people who would take advantage of them? They should be more careful! The world might have changed a great deal in four hundred years, but people surely had not. It would do them good when their experience with Fenella taught them to be wary.

From the house tour, Fenella knew where each one of them lay in sleep.

At the farthest end of the upstairs hall, in the largest room, in a bigger bed than Fenella had ever imagined might exist, were Soledad and Leo. Soledad had been apologetic about the room when she showed it to Fenella during the house tour. "The chaos of twenty-five years." She'd gestured at a chair heaped with rumpled clothing, at a cabinet on top of which dozens of family photographs seemed to fight each other for space, and at the bed whose homey, faded coverings had plainly seen better days. "I keep thinking I'm going to sort it all out. Maybe we'll paint the walls a more restful color."

"Dark purple?" Lucy was leaning against the doorframe. "Eggplant?"

"Cream," said Soledad.

"Boring!"

"Yes, exactly."

Fenella had dumped the cat on the floor, barely hearing the muffled thump he made when he landed on his feet. She felt Lucy's eyes follow her as she picked up a photograph. It showed Lucy tumbled carelessly on Zach's lap with the baby—tiny, bald, and wrapped in pink—cuddled up on her shoulder. Zach grinned happily. The little family was crowded into a big soft chair that Fenella recognized from downstairs. Sitting awkwardly on the arm of the chair was a middle-aged woman with long tangled hair as dark as Lucy's. The woman's knees were so knobby that you could see their outlines protruding beneath the thin fabric of her skirt. She held a tall, fragile glass of orange liquid aloft in one hand.

The other hand clutched Lucy's arm as if she could not bear to let go.

"Miranda," Fenella said aloud, softly.

"That picture was taken the day Miranda came back to

us." Lucy moved to Fenella's side. "The doorbell rang, and there was Miranda, on the front porch." Lucy paused. "Not too different from you this morning, Fenella."

"You don't call her Mother." Fenella kept looking at the photograph. Zach's arms were confident and possessive around Lucy and his attention was wholly on her and the baby, while Lucy watched her mother with soft eyes. For her part, Miranda looked straight out of the picture as if she could see Fenella looking in at her, sometime in the future.

"No, I don't," Lucy said. "Soledad is my mom. Miranda doesn't mind. She *picked* Soledad and Leo for me."

Soledad said, "We're both of us your mothers." She added to Fenella, "There's no such thing as too many mothers, especially when there's a baby to take care of."

Lucy laughed. "There's no such thing as too many grand-mothers, either. Dawn has four! Miranda and Soledad, and then Zach's mom—she lives in Arizona. And there's Dawn's biological grandmother too. Her name is Brenda Spencer. She takes care of Dawn at least two days a week."

"Dawn has *five* grandmothers, with Fenella here."

Fenella stiffened.

Soledad was shaking her head in bemusement. "Not that anybody would ever believe it, to look at Fenella."

"It makes me feel like Dawn is really safe," said Lucy. "So many people to take care of her and love her."

The word *safe* had had the impact of a rock pitched at the side of Fenella's head. She felt the cat insinuate himself, rubbing against her ankles.

She put the photograph down and picked up a small one of Zach and Lucy standing in the living room, facing each other, holding hands. They were wearing formal clothes—Lucy in white—and they looked both terrified and transcendent. The dog Pierre stood beside them, with a ribbon around his neck. He was snarling toward someone. That person was not in the picture, but Fenella knew it must be Padraig.

She put the photograph back down. "Your wedding took place here in this house?"

"Yes." A smile curved Lucy's mouth. "We crammed in more people than I could ever have imagined. I thought Mom and Dad had lost it." She pointed at a different photo. "Here I am with my friend Sarah. She was my maid of honor. In the background, you can see how crowded it was."

Fenella looked carefully at the crowd, but Padraig wasn't in this photograph either. She wondered whether Lucy fully appreciated what a narrow escape she had had, or if the safety and ordinariness of her current life had blotted away the reality of the past.

"We can show you the complete set of wedding pictures, if you want," Soledad offered. "There's video too."

Fenella reached for more photos and listened as they

were explained. A solemn young Soledad and Leo standing on the front porch of the house, after they had bought it. A three-year-old Lucy in a high chair with applesauce smeared all over her mouth, looking startlingly like her daughter. Leo with Lucy, aged six, mounted on his shoulders. Soledad crushing a teenaged Lucy in her arms. A twelve-year-old Zach spraying the ten-year-old Lucy with water from a garden hose. A close-up of Leo playing guitar and singing, on Lucy's wedding day. Dawn and Miranda on the floor of the living room, building a decidedly unstable structure out of wooden blocks.

The cat had butted his head insistently against her ankles. *Pick me up.* She'd stooped for him, and he had craned his neck and looked at the pictures too.

What did it mean to destroy safety? How should Fenella know? She had not felt safe in four hundred years.

The night ticked inexorably away. Fenella watched the cat sleep.

She was still thinking about safety as the gray light of early morning filtered into the room and, softly, the door opened. She looked up.

It was Miranda, standing in the doorway holding a suitcase.

Chapter 11

Fenella stared at Miranda and Miranda stared back.

Miranda looked every one of her thirty-eight years and then some. Like her daughter, she'd cut off her previously long brown hair, but in contrast to Lucy's glossy cap, Miranda's hair was so short that it clung tightly to her head and was decidedly more gray than brown. The gray was in keeping with her face. Miranda had been exposed to all weathers during the years she'd done her best to watch over Lucy and the Markowitzes from afar, and her skin had suffered from it, with lines permanently engraved around her eyes and mouth. She was as bony and skinny as ever too. In fact, Miranda looked older than her curvy friend Soledad, who was actually the elder by more than ten years.

Unconsciously, Fenella's hand went to her own smooth cheek. She was the one who ought to be a bent-over crone.

She wished she were. Better to have your experience written plainly on your face and body, so there would be no mistakes. So that certain unexpected temptations—such as appreciation of Walker Dobrez, the apprentice animal doctor—would not happen.

Ryland opened his eyes. *She's home early.*

He jumped lightly down to the floor and vaulted onto Fenella's bed instead of Miranda's. The gesture of courtesy surprised Fenella; then she remembered Ryland's intention of being adored by everyone. But Miranda did not appear to have noticed the cat. She was still frozen in the doorway in complete shock.

Fenella got up, the too-long legs of the borrowed pajama pants falling in folds over her feet. She took an uncertain step. "Hello, Miranda. It's really me."

A knot of disappointment was fast forming in Fenella's throat. Was Miranda not happy to see her? They had been friends and allies and family, in Faerie. It had not been the close friendship Fenella had with Minnie, because Miranda had left to watch her daughter from afar whenever she was permitted—and that was often, for Padraig had not found Miranda much to his taste. But still, the friendship between Miranda and Fenella had been real and true. When Miranda was freed, Fenella had kissed her brow.

"I will be so peaceful in death," Fenella had told her.

"I will always remember and love you," Miranda had said.

"Live your life," Fenella had responded. "Go to Lucy. Be happy, Miranda."

They had cried together, for joy, before parting for what they believed to be forever.

Miranda said, "You're not dead?"

"No. It's something to do with the initial spell Ryland cast. I'm free," she lied. "I get to go on with my life, like you."

When Miranda said nothing, and her face stayed stiff, Fenella made a helpless gesture. "I'm sorry to intrude on your life here. I suppose you don't want a reminder of the past."

Don't apologize, said the cat tartly. *You have every right to be here.*

I do not, thought Fenella.

Miranda dropped her heavy suitcase and wrapped her bony arms around herself. "What aren't you telling me, Fenella? What's wrong?"

"Nothing! I was released from Faerie. I got here yesterday. Where else would I go?" She heard the defensiveness in her own voice. "They—your Lucy, and everybody—have been so kind to me."

Fenella waited tensely as Miranda moved to the second bed and eased herself down to sit on the edge. She looked as if, with a moment's warning, she might run.

"Fenella?" Miranda said at last. "I can smell Faerie on you, and it—it makes me feel queasy."

Fenella was shocked. "You can?"

"Yes."

"I—I don't know what to say. I bathed with hot water last evening in that shower thing. There was lavender soap."

"It's not a bad smell," Miranda said uncertainly. "It's woody, like trees. Maybe like willow, and something else. It's not unpleasant. It's just there. I could never mistake it for anything else." Miranda inhaled again, more fully. Her gaze swiveled to the white cat, lounging on the bed opposite. She stared at him incredulously. "You brought a cat?"

Fenella waited in dread for Miranda to say she could smell enchantment on the cat too.

Ryland stood. He stretched. He stared limpidly into Miranda's eyes and waved his beautiful tail. Then he nimbly leaped across the gap between the beds to land beside Miranda. He butted his head against her arm, glanced up coquettishly, and then settled himself boldly right on her lap.

Mouth curving with surprising sweetness, Miranda petted Ryland, at first cautiously, and then, as he responded, more fully. "You're a pretty one, aren't you?" she said. "Do you want your belly rubbed? Do you?"

Shamelessly, Ryland rolled over and presented his belly,

and when Miranda rubbed it, he purred like the engine of Walker's truck.

All of her nerves were in an uproar, but now that she's touched me, she's calmed down. He sounded grumpy. *I have some ordinary cat magic. Maybe it will help. But remind me: How did I get into this again?*

Fenella couldn't reply, of course. She watched Miranda with the cat, and the cat with Miranda. Sitting down again on her own bed, she drew her legs under herself. She remembered Lucy saying that she worried about Miranda. She realized: Miranda already doesn't feel safe, even surrounded by people who love her.

Safety.

But she couldn't undermine Miranda more. Could she?

After a while, Miranda smiled apologetically across at Fenella. "I'm sorry. It was scary there, for a minute, seeing you. I got cold shakes. I think I had a flashback. I hope you know, Fenella, I'm glad to see you. I'm glad you're okay. You're not dead! You're free, like me? Tell me everything."

Fenella opened her mouth, but Miranda's attention had already splintered back to Ryland. "Where did you get this little fellow?" She listened while Fenella told her the false story about being given him on the street, and then she nodded. "No wonder you couldn't resist him. So soft. So friendly." Miranda slipped her fingers deep into his fur.

"Look at that adorable heart on his chest. You said his name was Ryland? It suits him."

She went on talking about the cat, seemingly unable to stop long enough to let Fenella answer the questions she'd been asked. Fenella was relieved; she didn't want to answer. But at the first opportunity, Fenella said, "What about you, Miranda? How has it been for you in your new life?"

Miranda lowered her face. She stroked the cat some more. "Such a mix," she said at last. "It's a dream come true in so many ways. My dear friends, Soledad and Leo. My daughter and granddaughter and son-in-law. This home to live in. I used to dream about this house, back in Faerie. Well, you know. I lived here before, when I was pregnant with Lucy. It's always been my ideal of home."

"I know."

"I see my Lucy every day. He's good to her, that boy she married. And she's good to him. They have a hard road in some ways, being so young with a child to care for, and needing to figure out how to earn money and be adults in the world. But they have so much help. They're doing well. I'm proud of them. Do you have a comb for this cat?"

Fenella fetched a comb, which had been provided by Walker. She reseated herself and watched as Miranda pulled the comb through the cat's thick fur. The cat lay supine on her lap, his eyes slit with voluptuous pleasure.

She digs in just enough. Ahhhhh.

Miranda kept her face averted from Fenella. "I adore Dawn. Sometimes when I'm taking care of her, though, I pretend she's Lucy and I'm eighteen again."

Fenella winced.

"Is that horrible? I pretend that none of it ever happened. Soledad says it's normal to have those thoughts, and maybe it is. But I don't know if it's good. I hate it when I come out of the dream. I wish I could appreciate the present. But I'm always on alert. I always expect something terrible to happen." Miranda paused. "I guess that's why I'm—I mean, why I *was*—so scared to see you again, Fenella. I'm sorry." She inhaled. "I don't smell anything now. I must have imagined it. I do that sometimes."

Guilt stabbed at Fenella. But she had choices and she wouldn't hurt Miranda. She would be careful, and thoughtful, about what she chose to do. She would be.

Nobody would be hurt unnecessarily. She swore it.

"I understand," she said.

"Thanks." Miranda pulled a vast quantity of cat hair out of the comb and formed it into a ball that she set aside. The cat rolled over obligingly, and she started combing him on the other side.

"Then there's the whole enormous business of making a new life. I want to contribute, and not live off others. But

I'm not doing so well with that. Some days, I don't even want to leave this house. Soledad says it's early yet. I know I'm useful at home, helping with Dawn."

"Are you . . ." Fenella paused delicately as an unexpected question arose in her mind. "In this new life, is there a human lover for you, perhaps? Or do you think there might be, someday?"

Don't ask her hurtful questions! Ryland's anger came at Fenella like a blast. *I've only just got her calmed down!*

Fenella blinked, surprised.

But Miranda answered, simply and immediately, as if she had dealt with this question before and it contained no pain.

"Oh, Fenella. No. I can't imagine that. It would be enough for me to manage a job of some kind." She tilted her head at Fenella. "Let me ask you the same thing. Would *you* want a real lover?"

"I had a real lover once," Fenella said sharply. "Robert."

"I mean now. Can you imagine being with someone new, someone that you choose freely?"

Walker Dobrez's shy sideways glance drifted into Fenella's memory. She spoke quickly. "No. Never. That part of me is dead."

Miranda nodded. "Exactly. Dead."

"Yes," said Fenella.

"It's too bad, though, don't you think? Lucy says it's like Padraig keeps on winning."

"What?" said Fenella. "No, he doesn't. Why would she think our not falling in love again means that?"

"People always think their own way is the right way," said Miranda. "And that's what Lucy did. She says it's the way to go on with your own life. Loving."

"It's not the *only* way."

"I agree. Especially as I don't think it's possible for me. What's your way going to be, then, Fenella? Now that you're here? What will you do with your life?"

I'm going to die, Fenella thought. She said, "I don't know."

Miranda nodded. "Me neither." She bent to comb the cat some more.

Chapter 12

In the days that followed, Fenella tried to settle into her pretend life with the Markowitz-Greenfield-Scarborough clan. But all the while she was watching and thinking.

At first the household seemed like it was made of pure chaos. There was all manner of movement and noise: phones trilling; doors opening and closing; computers beeping; floors creaking. Neighbors and friends frequently stopped by without warning; suddenly you would hear a strange voice call out, "Hello? Is anybody home?" and then another person would be there amongst them all, and this stranger too would be talking.

Always the talking, the exhausting talking. Nobody was ever quiet for long in this house.

In the middle of it all was the child. Dawn waved her hands and made burbling and cooing sounds. She cried and she laughed. She was into one thing and then into another. Even though she was really getting too big for it, everybody was always picking her up—usually a split second after she toddled into something she should not.

Everything revolved around the child. Where she was and what was she doing. Who could be with her, and when. What she was supposed to do, where she was supposed to be, and with whom. Fenella wondered if it would be better or worse when the child finally decided to start talking.

In any event, Fenella hoped that in the rush of things, nobody noticed how she kept herself as far away from Dawn as possible.

Threaded in among the constant household noise was music. Much of it had to do with Leo and his musician friends, but not all. Leo was teaching Zach to play the banjo, and Lucy tended to break randomly into song, including silly songs that she made up spontaneously. Miranda and Soledad sang too, more conventionally, in the evenings when the men played instruments. The two older women had strong alto voices that contrasted with Lucy's pretty soprano, and the three could harmonize so angelically that, if you had a heart, the sound would have broken it.

There was also mechanical music that came out of the little personal devices that everyone carried around. This modern recorded music was strange to Fenella; fast, with insistent rhythms and lyrics and sometimes sections that were spoken or shouted instead of sung. It could be compelling. One morning Fenella stood frozen in the kitchen listening to a recording by a musician named Solange. Fenella could understand only a word here and there—rage, fire, and a chorus that accused someone of "just waiting." Fenella wasn't sure what it was all about, and yet, when the song ended, the music had wrung tears from her.

After that, Fenella hardened her heart against music. Music was something the fey used. Indeed, Padraig had used music against her, weaving it into the original curse. Music was her enemy now, she felt instinctively. Even at its angriest, music created rather than destroyed. Music was the enemy of destruction. Music was the enemy of death.

Eventually, the family's seemingly chaotic movements resolved into patterns. On weekdays, Soledad went to her job at the hospital. Miranda remained home and took care of Dawn. Leo, Zach, and Lucy had complicated, ever-changing schedules consisting variously of gigs, classes, and employment that earned money. Zach got these schedules from the others on Sundays and posted everything for the week on the refrigerator. Even the child had appointments: She went to daycare two weekday mornings a week and was collected from there by her paternal biological grandmother, Brenda

Spencer. There was also a weekly rotation of responsibility for shopping, cleaning, laundry, and cooking.

Fenella sometimes found herself in the kitchen looking at the complicated weekly plan with its neat little squares of assignments. Did the plan make everybody feel safe? If so, was there a piece in this pattern that she could simply remove, the way you might pull out one of Dawn's toy blocks and topple down an entire structure?

One day Fenella asked to help with cooking, and Lucy took her into the kitchen. There, cautiously, following Lucy's instructions, Fenella turned the dial that ignited the front left-hand burner on the stove.

She recoiled instinctively as a blue flame burst into being.

"So, there's a pipe that feeds gas into the house," Lucy explained. "When you turn the dial for one of the burners, the gas is released into the stove and it ignites to become fire for cooking." Confidently, Lucy twisted the dial, explaining more while Fenella listened closely.

"Gas?" she asked. "This blue fire runs on the same fuel as a car?"

Lucy shook her head. "No. The gas for a car is liquid. Gasoline, it's called. Actually, some cars use other fuels, alternative fuels—"

"What? Why?"

"Well, gasoline is derived from a natural resource called

oil that's running out. So there are experiments with using electricity, and hydrogen, and, I don't know. Other stuff. But anyway, the house is heated with another kind of gas. Natural gas."

Fenella listened intently.

"Natural gas is, uh, it's a gas. Like air. It's invisible. You can set it on fire and it burns, and then you cook with it. You turn it off when you're done."

"It's not invisible." Fenella pointed at the stove. "It's blue."

Lucy pursed her lips. "Okay. Yeah. The gas fire is blue after it's ignited. I don't really know why."

"But—"

"Fenella? I know how to turn on the stove and cook on it. Period. Wait—gas has a smell, even when it's invisible." Lucy sniffed, her brow furrowing. "It's sort of metallic. Can you smell it?"

Fenella nodded.

"I could maybe explain it better if I'd paid closer attention at school. In science classes." Lucy twisted the stove knob and the blue flames flickered lower and died. "But I didn't." She turned away. "Let's start cooking, okay? But first I need that big pot."

Fenella stared at the empty burner. There was nothing to show a fire had been burning there a second ago. No ashes. No smoke. But it wasn't magic. It was a fuel from the earth, put to use via principles of science. Not unlike the way the old watermill wheel had worked, churning power out of the river, back when Fenella was a child. Fenella reached out—

Lucy was beside her, grabbing her wrist. "Don't! It's hot still!"

Fenella froze.

Lucy let go. "Sorry. You wouldn't touch a wood fire that you'd just put out, either. It's the same. A gas fire is danger-ous—in the ordinary way—like an ordinary fire."

Irrationally, Fenella felt like she wanted to touch the burner even more now. Would her flesh burn if she did? Yes, of course, but then she would heal, as she had healed from the knife in Faerie. Why, this whole house could go up in flames, with everyone in it, and still Fenella would survive. She sighed.

Then her stomach did a nasty little flip.

"Explain to me again how it works?" said Fenella, urgently. "All the details?"

Lucy shook her head. "Tell you what, Dad can show you the apparatus in the basement. There're pipes and a boiler and, well, I don't actually know what's down there, but it's a mechanical system. Also, we have a book somewhere that explains everything."

"A book? Oh, good." Consulting a book always made

Fenella feel closer to Minnie. Also, she liked the sound of the words *mechanical system*.

"Yes. It doesn't only explain gas heating systems. It explains how every kind of system works, including cars. And there are pictures."

"I'd *love* to read that book," said Fenella sincerely.

"I should have thought of it before." Lucy paused. "Don't take this the wrong way, Fenella, but you remind me of Dawn. We need to be careful with you too. Accidents could happen, simply because you don't know what to be afraid of."

Fenella felt Ryland at her feet. He twined around her ankles.

"But I'm not a child," Fenella said steadily. "Don't worry, Lucy. I'll be careful. I'll make sure I know *exactly* what I'm doing."

Chapter 13

Fenella bided her time, holding her idea closely to herself, not even confiding in Ryland. "When I'm ready," she told him brusquely. She explained to the cat that she needed to fit into the household and be above suspicion, so that, on the other side of the first task, she would still be a welcome member of the family. "I'll be more prepared for the next tasks, whatever they are, if I first take the time to understand my family."

So long as you let me help with planning before you do anything. If you don't let me advise you, you could make a bad mistake.

"Of course," Fenella said.

Don't forget that we only have three months. Seven days are already gone.

"I haven't forgotten. Don't worry. I've got this." It was a phrase she had recently learned from Zach.

Fenella's idea excited her. If she did it right, she would fully meet the requirements of the first task. She would destroy her family's safety, but nobody would be hurt.

She read the book Lucy gave her and felt her excitement grow. The book was called *The Way Things Work*, and the only problem was that it was so full of fascinating information that she found herself distracted from gas heating systems. One beautiful October morning she took the book out to the driveway, opened the hood of the family car, and identified all the parts of its engine.

She also learned what she needed to know about the gas heating system. She listened intently when Leo, as promised, took her to the basement to explain the intricacies of furnaces. "Does that make sense?" he asked when he'd finished.

Her eyes on the metal box that encased the central workings of the heating system, Fenella nodded.

"But you have a question."

"Not a question." Fenella shrugged. She couldn't explain her sudden urge. "May I touch it?"

"The furnace casing? Sure."

Fenella put both hands flat against the metal box. Then she stepped closer and impulsively laid her cheek against it as well. She was going to betray the machine, she thought. Betray its desire to do its job properly. She was conscious of Leo watching her. She tried to smile at him.

She knew she ought to step away from the furnace. She knew her behavior was strange, even for her. But she couldn't make herself move. I'm sorry, she thought to the machine, and then she had to squeeze her eyes shut tight.

When she opened them, she startled. Leo was right beside her, inches away, facing her, mirroring her, with both his hands and his cheek also on the furnace casing.

He held her eyes.

He said, "It's not just a machine, is it? It's like a heart. It sings when it's doing its job. Right now we can hear the hiss of the steam in the water tank. But this winter, when we heat the house, there'll be other sounds. Different music."

Like a child asking for a bedtime story, Fenella found herself whispering, "Music?"

"Yes. It's music of its own kind. You'll hear a series of clicks, when you first call for more heat. Sometimes you hear banging, as the pipes convey the gas. It's comforting. Every time you turn up the thermostat, you hear these reassuring sounds and murmurs, bangs and clangs. They tell you, yes, the heat is coming. The warmth is coming." Leo smiled at Fenella. "You'll see. It *is* music."

"Oh," said Fenella. She felt obscurely lulled—and then, the swift sure knowledge that Leo was someone she would have *chosen* for family was abruptly unendurable. Fenella pushed away from the furnace. Her voice came out shrill. "I've got to go now."

She fled upstairs, but she felt Leo's compassionate gaze on her back all the way. Her stomach knotting, she presented herself to Soledad and asked to help out with cooking.

To her relief, however, she was turned down. Soledad said firmly, "It's too early for responsibilities, Fenella. Get accustomed to life here. It's enough for you to tag along with Miranda to the grocery store or the library. There's so much new *stuff* for you to learn." She waved a hand vaguely. "We'll carry you, don't worry. It's what family is for. Next week we'll have family meeting and discuss how you're feeling."

"Family meeting?" Fenella was beginning to recover from the rush of sadness she'd felt in the basement.

"We get together and talk once a month. One thing we need to talk about is how we'll get identification for you. Zach says he has an idea, but I'm afraid to hear what it is."

"Why?" Fenella was curious. "What do you mean by identification?"

"Oh, never mind. It's just, you know, a future worry." Soledad changed the subject. "Also, money is tight, so that's one thing we usually discuss at family meeting. Do you understand about money?"

"Oh, yes," said Fenella. Nearly every Scarborough girl in history had lacked money. Minnie had described going hungry as a child; she had had to scrounge for financial help for nursing school. "Money is how you trade for the things that you need. A few people have lots of it. Most people have little."

"I suppose money is one of those things that never really changes." Soledad put another piece of paper on the refrigerator. *Monthly Food Budget,* it said. Fenella looked without comprehension at the number at the top of the page, and then turned away.

In general, Ryland was behaving himself, at least. Most days, he padded behind Fenella from room to room, watching and listening attentively and acting cat-like. He was adorable, as he had promised, but Fenella was privy to his thoughts, which were not adorable. He poked fun at the ragged way Leo dressed, opined that Soledad was too bossy and that Dawn was spoiled, and, moreover, if the child didn't begin to talk soon, he would wonder about her intelligence. He also let Fenella know what his sharp ears had picked up about Lucy and Zach. *She sings to him in bed. She makes up ridiculous songs about—*

"Too much information!" Fenella had picked up this useful phrase from Lucy.

Actually, it's not. We don't know yet what will and won't be useful.

"I suppose."

Fenella had to admit that in the absence of the dog Pierre, Ryland was blending well into the household. He bestowed irresistibly silky ankle caresses on everyone, was praised for his neatness at the litter box, and especially endeared himself by being sweet and patient when Dawn petted him too enthusiastically. Also, though nobody but Fenella knew about it, he managed to keep away from the yarn in Soledad's knitting basket.

I deserve a medal. I wonder if my sister knew I was going to be beset by all the normal cat urges.

At this, Fenella smiled despite herself. She didn't think the cat's obsession with yarn was entirely normal. She was grateful for his presence, though, she realized. Watching Ryland insinuate his way into the good graces of the family while she listened to his acid commentary helped her to maintain the assessing distance she badly needed.

She could not afford to love them. She needed to be hard as stone. She needed to remember she was not one of them.

The next evening, in the living room, something happened to help. Leo had his guitar, and Lucy was singing. Then suddenly the two of them exchanged glances, nodded at each other, and launched into a new song. It was a ballad called "Tam Lin," and it was plain that this moment was planned.

Fenella knew "Tam Lin." She knew it very well indeed.

Her fist clenched as Lucy sang the familiar opening, in which a young girl named Janet is warned against meddling with handsome Tam Lin.

Of course Janet does not listen.

Ryland was on Fenella's lap. She felt him turning his head to stare at her as her entire body stiffened. She thought about pushing the cat away, about making an excuse and leaving the room. Leaving the song. But instead she sat, thrown back in time by the music, waiting with dread for the moment in which it would become clear to Janet that her hot new lover, Tam Lin, was the property of the faeries.

Then she knew she could not stand to hear it.

"Stop!" she shouted. "Stop this song right now!"

The music ceased so abruptly that Fenella's ears seemed to ring.

Everyone was staring, but it was Leo who spoke. "It's not 'Scarborough Fair.' It's a different Child ballad. We thought—we hoped—that it would be all right."

"It's not," said Fenella. She turned jerkily to Miranda. "Miranda, you don't want to hear this either, do you?"

She was shaking. In her inner ear, the song continued inexorably, the verses spinning onward.

Janet holding up her head before all the knights and ladies in her father's castle and proudly declaring her pregnancy. Janet listening to Tam Lin's precise and clear instructions for how she could use that pregnancy to save him from the faeries on All Hallows' Night.

Oh, yes, Fenella thought. It had all worked out fabulously for plucky, lucky Lady Janet.

"Fenella?" It was Leo again. "Of course we'll stop. I'm sorry. Lucy and I thought we could give the old music its place back in our lives. We used to love the Child ballads and we thought maybe we could reclaim this one at least. Let the music wash through us and heal us. But we won't try, not if it hurts too much."

Lucy leaned forward. "Fenella, do you realize? 'Tam Lin' is so different from 'Scarborough Fair.' Janet outsmarts the faeries."

"Like you did?" Fenella snarled.

There was a moment of shocked silence. "I didn't mean—" Lucy began.

Fenella cut in. "I know. I'm sorry."

More silence.

"All right," said Lucy finally.

"Maybe another time," Soledad said. "With another song. A different ballad."

"Maybe," said Lucy.

"Or not," said Leo. Fenella felt him trying to catch her eye, but she didn't want to look at him. Tension continued to fill the air.

Then Ryland, on the floor near Fenella, made a terrible noise. The noise went on and on, drawing all eyes, until it transformed into hacking, and Ryland deposited a small hairball on the carpet.

"That's my signal," Fenella said. She picked up the hairball and regarded it dubiously. "Ick. I'm going to bed now." She escaped, throwing the hairball into the trash as she left.

The next day, Fenella declined to go with Miranda and Dawn on their daily stroll. The moment the door shut and they were alone, Ryland came into the living room and nudged her ankles.

About last night, he said. *What's your exact problem with that song, "Tam Lin"?*

"It's nothing," Fenella said. "What does it matter, anyway? It's only music. I have other things to think about, more important things, and you know it."

As the words left her lips, Fenella realized that she was no longer alone with the cat. She looked up.

"Sorry." Walker Dobrez was in the archway of the living room, inside the front door, looking at her.

Chapter 14

"Is it okay that I just showed up?" Walker held a dog leash in one hand, but there was no dog on it. He was bigger than Fenella remembered. He wore jeans and a dark green T-shirt with long sleeves pushed up to reveal strong brown forearms. His long hair was gathered back neatly into a horse's tail.

The cat muttered something.

"Hello." Fenella felt her cheeks burn. How much had he heard?

Walker's gaze was intent on Fenella, and curious too, and also . . . well. He had that look in his eyes, the one that said he found Fenella attractive. Then the look disappeared, and Fenella was conscious that she hadn't paid much attention when she got dressed this morning. She had pulled on a pair of baggy gray sweatpants and a tight, faded, rose-colored T-shirt that she had received from Lucy. The T-shirt said, *Don't let the pigeon drive the bus,* advice that Fenella felt was sound. The modern clothing was soft and she liked how it felt on her body. She was even beginning to understand the appeal of pants for girls.

But she probably did not look pretty. She curled her bare toes self-consciously on the floor. She also realized that she had not put on her new female harness. She had been told that women should not be seen in public without one on beneath their clothes. A bra, it was called, and it was considered both modest and practical to wear one.

Why did this family run the kind of house where people felt free to wander in without knocking? It was not right!

Walker made no mention of the conversation he had probably heard Fenella having with the cat, and he ignored Fenella's scowl too. "I brought Pierre home. He's in the backyard."

Ryland jumped down from the chair arm and stood next to Fenella, his tail low, his fur on end. *No!*

Fenella sighed. Ryland was right; the dog absolutely couldn't return. "Nobody told me Pierre was coming back today."

Walker looked at Ryland and then back at Fenella. "I was thinking we could try Pierre with your cat again. They'll have to get along eventually, right? I talked to Soledad this morning and she thought it was a good idea. To try it, that is."

Fenella crossed her arms in front of her chest. "Soledad didn't check with me."

"Well, see, I called her at work only half an hour ago." Walker cleared his throat. "My boss gave me a few hours off, and she said you were here, so I thought I'd come on over. Uh. But I see this is too much of a surprise. Still, the thing is, Pierre's fenced in the backyard feeling glad to be at home, and your cat is safely in the house." He glanced again at Ryland, who was still visibly bristling. "Could I take you to lunch? There's a place on Moody Street that has sandwiches and ice cream." He met Fenella's gaze.

That look, that unmistakable look, was back on his face. Perhaps there was nothing wrong with how she was dressed after all.

But Ryland's voice was caustic in Fenella's head. *We do not have time for this lovesick dog in man form. Still less do we have time for the actual dog. Fenella, look this idiot straight in the eye. Say no. Then tell him to take the dog away.*

Fenella's gaze fastened itself on the square of bare skin at the base of Walker's throat, which was located above the round collar of his shirt. She watched the smooth way his Adam's apple moved up and down.

Say it, Fenella. Turn him down. The quick cut is the best, and most merciful too.

Fenella looked into Walker's eyes. "My cat's still settling in."

"Yes, but we could try it."

"I don't want to take the risk."

Good! Now, dismiss him. Say, "Go away and take the dog with you." Then turn your back and walk upstairs. He won't follow.

Fenella knew Ryland was right. She said to Walker, "I don't want lunch. What I want is to learn to drive your truck."

She didn't know which noise came next: Ryland's infuriated snort, or Walker's laugh.

When Walker laughed, his skin crinkled up around his brown eyes. "Okay. Put on some shoes and we'll go. Listen, a small truck like mine isn't much different from a car. It's not like a big rig. You'll be able to drive it easily. Wait. You've driven a manual transmission before? Or have you only driven an automatic?"

Fenella gave a noncommittal smile. She had read about manual and automatic transmissions in the book about how things worked. Of course, she had never driven a car, period, but that only meant she didn't have any bad habits to unlearn. "I'll be right back," she said.

She ran upstairs, Ryland beside her, his paws thudding softly on the stairs, his voice yelling in her head. Once they were safely in her bedroom, she whirled on him and whispered, "I know what I'm doing."

No, you don't. What's going on? How can you drive that truck?

"I just want to. I'm sure I can do it. I read the book. I watch when others drive." Fenella fished her bra out of the bureau and yanked it into place. "It doesn't look difficult."

It's complicated. Even I only know how to drive an automatic.

"You can drive?" Fenella stopped what she was doing for a moment to stare. "How did that happen?"

The cat scowled. *When I was on my mission last year. I was in human form. It was when my sister was messing up. Don't ask.*

Fenella shrugged. She finished dressing and then tied sneakers on her feet. Before leaving, she engaged in one last staring contest with the cat.

Fine. Go. The cat's eyes narrowed.

"I am." She hurtled down the stairs. She was going to drive the truck!

"Have you driven a manual before?" Walker asked her again.

"No, but I understand the principle involved." Fenella walked confidently to the driver's side of the truck.

Since that first day with Walker, Fenella had ridden in

other vehicles. Most of the family shared a car, and Leo had a big van that was often filled up with instruments. She liked the feeling of movement in both the car and the van, but neither had induced in her the joy and exhilaration that she had felt while sitting next to Walker in his truck, or the deep interest she had felt looking under the hood of the family car and identifying the parts of the engine.

Nonetheless, when they went out in the family vehicles, she often asked to sit in front. She watched closely to learn how the vehicles were controlled. And of course, *The Way Things Work* had an excellent section on automobiles.

She knew she could drive. She knew it.

But Walker shook his head. "If you're used to an automatic, it'll take a while to get the hang of things with a manual. Like, several lessons. Which is fine." He looked quite cheerful. "Tell you what. I'll drive us somewhere out of the way where you can practice without any other cars around."

Fenella bit her lip, disappointed not to take the wheel immediately. "Okay."

"There's this place about forty minutes up Route 2. It's not, like, a Sunday morning when I can find an empty parking lot here in the city."

"I see."

"I'll call Soledad and tell her where we are, in case she worries."

"Good idea." Fenella got into the truck on the passenger side, buckled herself in professionally, and watched Walker drive. He used his right hand to execute the manual shifting of gears that the book had described. This shifting was not necessary with an automatic transmission, the book said, but some drivers preferred manual shifting because it gave you more control over your vehicle.

More control. More power. Fenella liked that. Her hands and feet itched to take over.

They were on a highway now and going fast. It was still a populated area, but trees grew thickly on both sides of the road, so that it felt almost as if the highway was cut through a forest. Fenella smiled, thinking of her friends the tree fey.

"I was born to drive," she said impulsively.

Walker laughed. Such a warm sound, Fenella thought. Warm and lovely.

He said, "How long have you had your license? Two years? Massachusetts lets you get it at sixteen, isn't that right?"

"I don't really know," Fenella said vaguely. "I'm from England."

"You don't have a British accent."

"I guess I don't."

"Are you used to driving on the other side of the road? Or did you never drive in England, only here in the U.S.?"

"Oh," said Fenella. "I can drive here."

Walker said, "Me, I've been driving a long time. I drove farm equipment before I got my legal license. My family has a farm. Also, it's less complex to drive where there isn't much traffic, where I'm from. Plus, Boston drivers are crazy. At home, everybody follows the rules. Here, you never know."

Fenella was feeling relaxed; she'd gotten through his question about a driver's license without an outright lie. She watched the thick green trees along the highway. "I like the trees here," she said. "I like that there are so many of them."

"Eastern hardwood forest," said Walker, nodding. "Beautiful. The land here was cleared a couple hundred years ago for crop farming, but the trees are coming back strong. It's a relief to see how the land can restore itself, isn't it? Also, these are terrific trees. Out west, where I'm from, we don't have this diversity. We have a lot of conifers, not so much hardwood."

"Where are you from?" Fenella asked.

"Southeastern Washington state, near the Idaho and Oregon borders."

"That's far." Fenella often consulted an atlas that the family kept, marveling at the largeness and variety of the human world. "Your family has a farm, you said?"

"Yeah, a tree farm. Christmas trees are a big crop for us."

Fenella straightened in her seat. "A tree farm."

"Right. Most people don't think of trees needing to be farmed, but my family's been taking care of trees for generations. Trees are in our blood, my dad says." He laughed. "You know, I was originally going to go to forestry school, like my sisters did. I have two older sisters. I'm still not sure how I ended up choosing vet school instead. Or how I ended up on the East Coast." He stole a look at her. "It just seemed right."

Chapter 15

Fenella felt the tiny hairs on the back of her neck rise. She had to control the impulse to lean over and sniff deeply at Walker's neck. Trees were in his blood? Even though he was human? She inhaled cautiously instead, trying to discern that subtle greenish scent she knew so well.

But Walker smelled of nothing but soap, and dog hair, and himself; the personal, chemical mixture of salt and sweat on his skin. He had been speaking metaphorically, not literally.

Of course.

She said, almost accusingly, "You decided to take care of animals, not trees."

"Well, I like animals a lot." Walker spoke thoughtfully. "I miss living in the forest, and nearer to wilder places. But I also like it out here. It's complicated, I guess. I made the choice I needed to make for myself, when I left home for college. But I'm only twenty-three. I think life ought to take twists and turns, don't you? And you ought to try different things. And be open to, you know, whatever happens."

Fenella watched his profile and heard the confidence in his voice. So human, she thought wistfully. Thinking that any day, life would grab you and catch you up into an exhilarating dance.

But the truth was that, while you might get grabbed and caught, it wouldn't be a good thing. You wouldn't know what had trapped you, or how, until it was too late and your pathetic life was no longer your own. Until all you wanted was for it to be over.

Twenty-three, he said he was. He might as well be an infant, with his hopes and dreams, and what he thought was a complicated life story. Complicated! If ever she told him her story, which of course she never would, *then* he would understand the meaning of complicated.

Walker squinted at a road sign. "This exit, I think." He steered the truck off the highway. "Yeah, this is it." Soon they were traveling at a more moderate speed down a narrow road, with the trees crowded even more thickly alongside.

Fenella put down the truck's window. Oak, birch, aspen, maple, pine. Ordinary trees only, not fey, but she was still glad to see them. This wasn't unbroken forest, of course;

there were mailboxes along the road, and houses that she could glimpse through the screen of trees. Still, it was a pleasant, peaceful road, quite different from the crowded, thickly populated street on which her family lived. The dwellings here were huge, she noted.

"Who lives here?"

"Rich people. The kind that have horses. I've been doing some training in equine medicine. I helped at a birth last week. It was really, really cool."

He kept on talking as they turned onto a narrower road, still paved. Another little distance, and another turn, and then a sign loomed before them.

RUTHERFORD OFFICE PARK. PRE-CONSTRUCTION PRICES AVAILABLE.

They were on a vast paved space that had been cut cruelly out of the trees. A few large, boxlike, unfinished buildings dominated two sides of the clearing, with a scattering of cars and trucks parked close to them. The large central portion of the pavement was empty, however, save for a painted white grid of lines that divided it into parking spaces.

"We can drive round and round here," Walker said with satisfaction. He stopped the truck right in the center and parked it. "Ready to take the wheel, Fenella-who-was-born-to-drive?"

Fenella unbuckled her seat belt, opened the passenger

door, and was on the ground in an instant. Thirty more seconds and she was behind the wheel on the driver's side, with Walker in her old place as passenger. She hardly listened as he said things about how driving a manual differed from an automatic, and described the various engine noises she was to listen to for clues as to when to shift gears. The truck's engine thrummed to life, and she felt the vibrations within her body. Her feet placed themselves on the gas pedal and the clutch, and her hand positioned itself on the gearshift.

"Transition from neutral to first as you give it gas. All right, good. Up to second as you pick up speed, you never stay long in first, excellent, you're doing great. That noise again—hear it?—tells you the engine's uncomfortable at this speed and so it's time to shift up to third. Good. Practice going in circles, staying in the lower gears and transitioning down to a stop when I tell you. Okay, try the brake, control the car, good, and now shift up again. Listen to the engine—Fenella!"

The gears screamed. The truck rocked to an abrupt, nasty halt as the engine stalled.

"Sorry."

"Yeah, no problem. Everybody does something like that when they're learning. Usually several times at least. I'm actually impressed. But Fenella? This is a parking lot, not a highway. You're overconfident with the gas. Don't go fast here. Move in a circle, and practice stopping and starting. That's all. Nice and smooth. Okay?"

"Okay."

"You're doing good. Start the engine again."

She did. She listened to Walker's voice as he guided her, until she began to anticipate what he was going to say. She went around the parking lot in the sedate circle that Walker had asked for, starting and stopping neatly one time per revolution, shifting up and down, and down and up, and keeping the speed reasonable as he had said she should. The engine began to purr for her, more warmly than Ryland ever did. Spontaneously, Fenella took the truck in a figure eight. Walker chuckled.

Then everything clicked together as she had known it would. Fenella could hear and feel what the engine needed her to do, so that it could cooperate with her wishes. They were akin, she and the truck; they were one.

It was amazing!

She did another figure eight, and then, neatly, parked the car and turned off the engine. She turned to face Walker. Her cheeks were flushed.

"Wow, you were right. You *are* a natural." Walker hesitated and then grinned. "You know what? Let's leave this parking lot. You drive us home. You can do it."

Fenella smiled demurely.

Afterward she hugged to herself the memory of how it had felt to drive the truck down Route 2. The whistle of the mild October wind through the open windows. The smile curving on her mouth, and the shouted roar of Walker's approval. The truck's instantaneous responses to the command of her foot on the accelerator, her hand on the gearshift, and her other hand on the wheel. For a precious length of time, Fenella felt as if she might take wing.

This was a detour on her journey to death; only a small detour. What was the word again? A vacation. But still, it had happened.

In front of the house, she turned off the truck and jumped lightly down. She was at the passenger door before Walker had done more than swing his legs out. A big grin split his face. She went up close to him as he hit the ground. She touched his cheek gently with one hand. Then—to her own surprise—she reached farther up, to the back of his head. She said, "Thank you, Walker Dobrez. Thank you for letting me drive." The next second, she pulled his head down and kissed him softly, her closed lips gentle on his surprised ones.

The moment she realized what she was doing, she jumped back, her face flaming.

Walker's face was alive with wonder. His hand touched her cheek, a mirror to the way she had just touched his.

"No," she said hurriedly. She caught his hand and gently pushed it away. "I wanted to kiss you, I guess, but it can only happen once. You're not for me. I'm not for you."

Walker's expression froze. With the truck immediately behind him, he couldn't move away from her. But it felt as if he had.

Fenella backed farther off. "I—I'm sorry, I have another favor to ask. Could you take the dog away? Please? It's only—it's not the right time for him to come home."

After a second, stiffly, Walker nodded.

"Thank you," Fenella muttered. She turned away from Walker. She raced into the house, her mind a churning mess of confusion and dismay and her body still filled with an irrepressible, irrational happiness.

Chapter 16

On the day that she destroyed her family's safety, Fenella awoke feeling strong and alert. It was October tenth, well into autumn by the calendar, but the morning sky outside the window promised summery, cloudless weather.

Fenella's mind was cloudless too. She was in total control of the first task and nobody was going to be hurt.

She got out of bed. In the next second, the cat was crouched by her feet, his almond-shaped eyes glittering. She nodded at him. They had gone over Fenella's plans meticulously the night before. Ryland had made only one suggestion, and had even said an approving word about her timetable and logic.

She followed the cat's gaze to the bedside clock. "Good morning," she said aloud, impatient.

Miranda answered from the next bed; more grunt than words.

"We need to get up, Miranda," Fenella said. "The race is this morning, you know."

"Ummmph."

Fenella threw a pillow at Miranda and darted down the hall to the bathroom. When Fenella returned, wrapped in a towel, Miranda was sitting on the edge of her bed, feet dangling.

"I'm excited about the race," Fenella said chattily. She really was. The Boston Cream Pie 5K would get everybody in the family—actually, probably the entire neighborhood—out of her way and over to Main Street. "It will be fun to see Lucy and Zach run." She felt a pang because, of course, she was not really going to see them run.

"Then we get a pie," she added, although she doubted that this would actually happen either.

"We'll get at least five pies," Miranda corrected wearily. "Some of the racers turn them down. Calories."

"What are calories? Oh, wait. I remember they were in *The Way Things Work.*"

"Is the bathroom free?" asked Miranda.

"Yes. Everybody else is already up. You need to hurry so you can have breakfast before we leave."

"I'm not hungry." Miranda was never hungry. She shuffled out of the room, shoulders bowed.

She might try to stay home today, warned Ryland. *She*

won't want to be out there in a crowd, with everybody making noise.

"She has to go," said Fenella, suddenly tense. "I'll make her go."

Ryland sniffed.

Fenella turned to get dressed.

The Boston Cream Pie 5K race was a fund-raiser for the local high school track team, open to anybody of any age who lived in a three-town radius. Four hundred pies had been ordered for the finishers, and Lucy, her friend Sarah Hebert, and Fenella had made thirty-six of them yesterday.

It had surprised Fenella, how much fun it had been to hang out with Lucy and Sarah and bake.

Sarah and Fenella did the actual mixing and baking, while Lucy worked on assembly. This involved cutting each circular yellow sponge cake in half horizontally, plopping on a thick layer of custard, and putting the layers back together so they could be iced. Lucy was not good at it; her top layers had a tendency to go on crooked. "Taste, not beauty," Lucy would say before turning haphazardly to the next cake. Behind her back, Fenella edged many a top layer into a better position. Once, while she was doing this, she caught Sarah's eye, and Sarah winked. Shyly, Fenella had winked back.

How happy it would have made Minnie to know that sometime in the future Fenella would be out in the world, with family and friends, making pies. Thinking of this, Fenella paused in the act of tying on her sneakers. Of course, Minnie would have been horrified if she knew what Fenella was doing today.

Fenella shook her head firmly to dispel doubt.

Ryland at her heels, she went down the hall to Dawn's room. The child was not there, thankfully. Still, Fenella tried not to look around much. She quickly knelt by a box in the corner filled with outgrown baby clothes. "Stop squirming," she instructed Ryland.

I hate this, the cat grumbled as Fenella pulled a stretchy flowered T-shirt over his head, inserting his front paws in the sleeves and settling it around his midsection.

"You agreed." Fenella pulled out another garment.

I know, but—wait! Not a hat! The cat tried to run, but Fenella had him firmly under one arm and a few seconds later, he was snarling at her from beneath the brim of a lacy white sunbonnet.

"Don't be rude," she said, tying a double knot under his chin.

Tell me again why this is necessary.

"I want to be sure everybody sees you."

The cat glared. Fenella ducked her head to hide a smile. "Go downstairs. Hide. Anywhere but in the knitting basket."

Soledad tied the lid on it.

"Good."

I could chew through the ties.

"Don't."

Fenella got to her feet, yelled through the bathroom door at Miranda to hurry up, and descended toward the kitchen and the scent of coffee. In the kitchen, Zach was stretching, Lucy was looking for an overripe banana she had hidden somewhere so no one else would eat it, and Soledad wanted to know if anybody else had seen a certain item in the news. "We don't have any milk," said Leo plaintively. Fenella smiled at all of them, even the child, whose nonsense syllables formed a soft, running babble beneath the other voices.

Then she stiffened. Walker Dobrez sat at the table with a mug of coffee in his hands and a piece of half-eaten buttered toast before him. He was wearing clothes for running. He looked at Fenella with an expression that was half wary, half questioning.

Alarm lurched through Fenella. She knew instantly that Walker was not just there for the Boston Cream Pie race. He was also there to find out which to believe: her kiss, or her instruction to go away.

She would make it clear. It would be fine. He was not the sort of young man who would need to be told more than twice. In fact, it spoke volumes that he had put aside his pride to come back this second time.

But she didn't want to be cruel, or to shame him. She liked him. It was just that kissing him had been a terrible mistake. Why had she done it? Then she remembered being with him in his truck, and she knew.

"Fenella? I brought something for you." Walker's voice was shy. He reached into the pocket of his shirt, pulled out a white envelope, and held it out toward Fenella.

A gift? For her? Fenella's gaze fastened on the envelope. She knew she ought to say something dismissive.

Nothing came to mind.

A gift . . .

Walker said defensively, "It's only a little thing. Uh. It was free. I just thought, you know, you might want to do this."

Fenella took the envelope. It held two pieces of paper with writing on them. *New England International Automobile Show.*

"It's next weekend," Walker said, speaking rapidly. "I thought you might want to go. Not necessarily with me. I mean, I'll take you if you want. But you could also go alone, or with someone else. That would be fine. It's up to you. I thought I'd tell you about it and get the tickets. In case. They're free tickets," he repeated. "Anybody can print them."

Fenella stood still.

Zach looked from Fenella, to Walker, to Fenella, and then to Walker again, at which point Lucy elbowed him.

Leo opened a cabinet and stared into it.

Soledad became absorbed in fastening a barrette into Dawn's hair.

Lucy pulled one leg up behind her to stretch it.

There was more writing on the tickets.

*The perfect place to browse hundreds of
the newest vehicles!
The premier showcase of the newest model year!
Imported and domestic vehicles—cars, vans, crossovers, hybrids,
light trucks, and sport utilities!
Factory and dealer representatives will be
on hand to answer your questions!*

"Next weekend?" Fenella said. She was only asking for clarification, but Walker's face lit up.

Miranda came up behind her. "What's that?"

"Auto show tickets," said Lucy. She stretched her other leg. "Fenella's going with Walker."

Fenella tried to hand Miranda the tickets, but Miranda shook her head. "No, I mean the leaf." She took the envelope from Fenella and pulled out a large, glossy green oak leaf, tender and flexible as springtime.

"Pretty," she said, and twirled it on its stem.

Chapter 17

Walker looked astonished. "I didn't realize I put that in there."

Miranda grinned. She handed the leaf to Fenella, and slipped past her into the kitchen. "May I have the rest of the eggs?"

Leo stared at her. Then he seemed to pull himself together. "Nothing would make me happier than to see you eat."

Miranda heaped a plate with scrambled eggs. "When do we leave for the race?" She opened the refrigerator and took out orange juice. She loaded the toaster with two pieces of bread.

"Twenty minutes." Lucy's gaze—and Leo's—and Soledad's—and Fenella's—followed Miranda around the kitchen. Miranda opened a cabinet. "Is there peanut butter?"

"In the refrigerator," Soledad said. "Third shelf. You'll have to give it a good stir."

"I'll get it for you," said Lucy. "Do you want coffee too?"

"No, just juice." Miranda poured herself a giant glass. She sat down to eggs, peanut butter toast, and juice, as if she ate this amount every morning. Everyone pretended not to watch her eat. Soledad surreptitiously pushed a bowl of apples nearer.

Fenella discovered she was gently rubbing the surface of the oak leaf. She looked down at it. The leaf was unusually large. Its skin felt smooth and subtly cool; its veins stretched out in a symmetrical pattern.

Touching it had a calming effect.

Fenella pictured tree roots, taking nourishment from the soil, and giving it back in the form of falling leaves. She watched Miranda eat. Miranda, who had touched the leaf.

The leaf.

She felt her blood warm. The leaf!

"We need to get ready to leave," said Lucy. "Ten minutes." People scattered on various errands, leaving only Miranda, Walker, and Fenella in the kitchen.

"Eat something," said Miranda generously to Fenella.

Fenella nodded absently. She sat down next to Walker and across from Miranda. She put the leaf down on the table and asked Walker, "Where did you find this?"

"It was on the ground outside my apartment. It caught my eye, maybe because it's so green. Most of the leaves are turning color now. I must have put it in the envelope without realizing. Embarrassing."

"I like it," Fenella said simply. "I'm glad you picked it up. Can I keep it?"

Walker smiled at her. "Yeah."

He said nothing else. Fenella knew he was waiting. She stroked the leaf again and glanced across at Miranda. Miranda put her hand on top of Fenella's, where Fenella was touching the leaf. Miranda too smiled, and it smoothed the lines away from her forehead.

"Fenella's not in a place where she wants to date anybody," Miranda said to Walker, as easily as if she were talking about the weather.

Fenella smiled gratefully at Miranda and then at Walker. "I would like to go to the auto show. But . . ." She lifted a hand.

"I see," said Walker slowly. Then, remarkably, after a few seconds, he said, decisively, "I get it. Okay. Well, let's go to the auto show as friends, then. Because you would really, really like it. Miranda, want to come with us? I can print out another ticket."

Fenella looked at him, impressed.

"Sure. Thanks." Miranda cut her second piece of peanut

butter toast corner to corner, and handed half across to Fenella. "You're not eating. Here."

Fenella took a bite. The silence in the kitchen felt awkward, but not in a bad way. Had her problem with Walker really been solved so easily by Miranda? And was Walker truly taking it well? Yes, he was. She felt a tendril of regret, which she knew she should uproot. She nibbled on her toast. She eyed Walker sidelong—and saw his jaw drop.

Ryland had raced into the kitchen, fully dressed in Dawn's old clothes.

Dawn toddled behind him at remarkable speed. Her outstretched hands brushed the cat's fan tail before Ryland leaped to the top of the kitchen table. For one instant, his jeweled eyes glared at Fenella from beneath the brim of the lacy white baby's bonnet. Then he jumped from the table to the counter.

Dawn screeched with delight. She toddled to the counter and held on, looking up in ecstasy, babbling nonsense syllables.

"I dressed Ryland up for the race," Fenella said as Walker's and Miranda's faces swiveled her way. "I'll push him in the doll carriage. Doesn't he look cute?"

The cat spat.

Miranda put one hand over her mouth. Her shoulders shook with laughter.

"He won't go in the doll carriage," said Walker. "Not unless you tie him down or put him in his carrier."

"He'll go," said Fenella blandly. "He promised me he would. Didn't you, kitty-kitty?" She let herself enjoy a brief fantasy of pushing Ryland in the doll perambulator, dressed in his baby clothes, into a large crowd of people who would all laugh and comment and want to pet him. She could almost hear the furious curses Ryland would direct at her.

It would be so worth it.

"But—" Walker began seriously.

"Kidding," said Fenella. Another new word. "I dressed him up for fun. I know I can't take him."

Walker looked relieved.

On the counter, Ryland sat down on his haunches and clawed at the bonnet with his front paw. He succeeded only in twisting it over one eye. Fenella and Miranda laughed. Dawn screeched and began trying to jump. Walker stood and picked Dawn up, delighting the child, who at first thought he was lifting her toward the cat. When she realized that he was instead taking her out of the kitchen, she yelled her displeasure.

Fenella got up and shooed Ryland to the floor. He stayed close by her ankles as she helped Miranda clear the dishes and put them into the dishwasher. This was another fascinating piece of machinery that worked by pumping heated soapy water in a directed stream across the surfaces within its enclosure. Then clear water. Then there was a drying cycle. Machines were so wonderful.

There would be many vehicles at this automobile show. Fenella wondered how different their engines would be from each other. Would she be allowed to look within them? To touch? Surely. She would study up beforehand, so that she could better appreciate everything.

Fenella?

She met Ryland's eye, the one that was not hidden behind his askew bonnet brim.

Are you ready?

Fenella bit her lip. For a few minutes, she'd gotten lost in pretense. She'd drifted into thinking that she'd go to the race. That she'd watch for Lucy and Zach and Walker, and Lucy's friend Sarah, and cheer wildly as they went running by. That she'd come home afterward and eat pie and study up on engines, so that next week, when she went to the auto show with Walker—

But none of this was going to happen.

She put her hand on the leaf. It vibrated gently. It was alive; it was fey. She knew it. Receiving it felt like encouragement that she was doing the right thing.

She slipped it into her pocket. She nodded at Ryland as the rest of the family crowded back into the kitchen.

"I'm ready," she said.

"Great. Let's go, let's go, let's go!" Leo held the outside door open. "Fenella, do you want a sweater? Soledad, I'm dropping the kids at the start of the race. Then I'll meet you guys—where?"

"Moody Street on the corner by the ice cream shop," said Soledad.

Walker said, "I thought I was going to take Lucy and Zach with me in my truck."

"No, leave your truck and come in the van with us," Lucy said. "That way you don't have to park."

Dawn spotted the cat and began screaming again. Soledad barely managed to keep hold of her. "If we don't go, there won't be any space left for us to stand on the street."

"All right."

"Let's go."

"Where's her binky?"

"I'm coming!"

There was a mad cram. As Fenella had instructed, Ryland slipped through the doorway with everyone else, and lingered out of sight on the porch. Soon Lucy, Zach, Walker, and Leo were in the van, the wailing Dawn had been strapped into her stroller, and Soledad, Miranda, and Fenella began walking toward Moody Street, Soledad pushing the stroller.

Then Ryland ran. He was gloriously visible in his white bonnet and floral top. He raced from the front porch, down the steps, across the small front lawn to the driveway. He wove artfully around the van, and then did a double circle around the stroller, tangling himself briefly around Soledad's feet. He stopped for two seconds where Dawn could see him, long enough for her to scream even louder in delight.

Then he trotted briskly across the street and disappeared into Mrs. Angelakis's bushes.

"I'll grab him and put him in the house," said Fenella. "Go ahead. I'll catch up." She jogged across the street to Mrs. Angelakis's house, calling Ryland's name, poking ostentatiously into the bushes.

There was no time for anybody to argue with her. The van pulled out. The walkers called encouraging things as they moved down the street.

Within a minute, everybody was gone, and even Dawn's screams had faded.

Ryland came out of the bushes next to where Fenella knelt.

They'd have seen me just fine without the baby clothes.

"Maybe. This worked, so why don't you stop criticizing?"

Okay, whatever. It's time to blow up the house. After you get me out of these clothes. The cat turned to go.

Fenella hesitated.

Aren't you ready?

Fenella put her hand in her pocket to touch the leaf. "Yes."

They walked silently back to the house and into the kitchen. Fenella fiddled with the gas line that led to the kitchen stove, and then with the stove controls.

This is the right thing to do, she told herself again. Everybody is away. Nobody will be hurt.

She waited with tense shoulders while the kitchen—and the other rooms downstairs—filled with gas.

The smell of the gas got stronger and stronger. It filled her nostrils and her lungs. She tried to breathe shallowly.

Once, her right hand twitched forward on its own toward the controls of the stove to turn it off. She snatched the hand back and held its wrist fiercely with her other hand, the one holding the matches.

She swallowed the terrible taste of the gas.

Ryland stood on all fours near the kitchen door leading outside. His tail was at half-mast and his whiskers twitched convulsively. As the seconds ticked by, his expression changed from bland to curious to astounded.

You're really doing it.

Fenella nodded. She couldn't speak. She could feel the gas pressing up against the back of her throat as if it were a solid.

"Run now!" she said to the cat. "Now!"

The cat raced from the house.

Then Fenella was too afraid to wait another second, lest she change her mind. Which she couldn't, she *couldn't*. Hands trembling, she struck a match.

A flame burst into being between her fingers.

Then the flames were all around her: blue, purple, yellow. Sucking all the air from her lungs. Exploding in her ears. Melting her skin. Gobbling her eyes.

In the split second before her entire body exploded in flame, Fenella flung her arms wide.

Please, she thought, before she lost consciousness. Please let me die right now.

Chapter 18

She did not die.

A half hour later, on the other side of a portal inside Faerie, Fenella stood unsteadily before Queen Kethalia. She was unsteady because her feet were burned stumps. It was not possible to understand how they held her up at all.

Ryland sat on his haunches a short distance away, cleaning ash from his fur with a fastidious pink tongue. When he glanced at Fenella, there was wary respect in his gaze.

Fenella's damaged lungs were trying to breathe. Her damaged eyes were trying to see. She raised her skeletal arms. They were horrific even to her blurred vision, with blackened crispy edges around flesh melted into a red and yellow lava-like substance. In some areas, her skin had burned away entirely to expose bone.

She could sense pain hovering. It would rush through her, beyond excruciating, once she regenerated sufficient nerve endings to receive it.

"Fenella," said the queen. "Sit down. There is a chair behind you."

She managed to sit, even though that hurt more than standing.

Then the real pain swept through her body and it was worse than she had imagined. If her lungs could have managed screaming, she would have done it.

She endured.

Sometime later, she realized that she must have regrown her eyelids, because they were closed. Despite the glass curtain of pain enveloping her, she opened them.

The female before Fenella had the queen's voice, and her carriage, but she looked like someone else: a human girl with long, silky hair and supple skin. The girl wore jeans and a soft orange cashmere cardigan that was opened two buttons at the throat. The girl's eyes were lovely and deep-set. There was self-confidence and power in them, but also loneliness.

"Why are you staring at me?" said the girl tartly. "You were helpless. I had to drag you into Faerie so that you wouldn't be seen in your current state. It was necessary for me to take human form. Ryland certainly couldn't do it."

This really was the queen, then.

Fenella managed a nod as a new kind of pain swept in. It was the inexorable tide of renewal. Her muscles and skin knit together. Her nose and ears regrew. Smoke began to clear from her throat. Helplessly, she leaned over and retched.

The pain became a terrible itching.

Eventually she sat up.

Naturally, my sister took this particular form, Ryland said to Fenella conversationally. *She would. But the good news is that we've made progress. One task down, two to go. By the way, Fenella? You did well. I'm proud of you.*

Fenella could now bear to rest her forearms on her lap. The pain was nearly gone. She clung to the last few seconds of it as if it were the press of a dying lover's kiss.

"How long do you wear your hair, again?" asked the girl-who-was-the-queen briskly. Only then did Fenella realize the queen was speeding her healing. She put up a hand to her head. She felt the lengths of hair grow and begin to tangle around her fingers. "Stop there," she muttered when her hair tangled at the familiar length around her throat and down her back. The sounds caught roughly in the back of her throat.

The queen nodded. "You may dress."

It took this for Fenella to realize she was naked. The

clothes folded neatly before her were the same ones that she'd been wearing earlier in the day. Their originals would have burned off her body, yet here they were again anyway. She stood up awkwardly and put them on. Then, without thinking, she slipped a hand into her pocket, even though the abrasion hurt the tender skin on the back of her hand.

The leaf was there, soft, vibrating faintly. Alive. Hers. Her gift from Walker and from—she suspected—the tree fey. She sighed in relief, and looked around quickly. But though she saw a few trees, none were fey. She sat down again in the chair and looked at the pretty human girl facing her.

She remembered the stories about the queen that had flooded through Faerie. The queen must be wearing the guise of her alter ego, the teenage girl Mallory Tolliver. *Naturally, she took this particular form,* Ryland had said.

Ryland jumped lightly up into Fenella's lap, where he briskly kneaded his claws through her clothes into the tender new skin of her upper thighs. She winced but did not stop him. He settled himself down like the most ordinary of lap cats, even purring.

So, was he fully reconciled to being her adviser? Now that he had seen that she really would go ahead and destroy?

Fenella felt sick. She wanted to push him off her lap.

She said to the queen uncertainly, "Did I really complete the first task?"

"Yes."

"I've truly destroyed my family's feeling of safety?" As she thought about it, Fenella was dubious. "I'm still not even sure what safety means. It was only a house. They loved it, of course . . ."

The queen nodded. "You must turn your attention to the second task."

The second task would be harder. Fenella couldn't help thinking of the first task that Lucy had performed: making a shirt without needle or seam. It had seemed impossible only at first glance; in fact, it was quite approachable, and other Scarborough girls before Lucy had succeeded at it, including Fenella.

Fenella had woven together thin, flexible green willow branches using her own hands. It had made for an awkward, ugly, and unwearable shirt. Fenella had despaired and taken it apart—only to discover later that it would have been sufficient. She had tried to tell Bronagh that you could be practical, not elegant, in your approach to the tasks.

But she could not, she *would* not, think of Bronagh. She would confine herself to remembering the lesson of that maddeningly easy first task—Minnie had simply used a crochet hook, arguing that this was fair because, properly, it was a hook and not a needle—and that the second task would be harder.

Fenella sat bolt upright. The cat mewed as she jostled him. "Wait," she said urgently to the queen. "About that first task?"

"It's done. Nobody was hurt, as you wished, yet your family's feeling of safety has been destroyed."

"But listen. I just had a thought. Miranda felt unsafe and afraid from the moment she saw me. She said so. She said that she could smell Faerie on me. What if—" Fenella was breathing quickly. "What if I had come to you after I first saw her? What if I had said to you that Miranda felt unsafe simply because I was there? Would that have fulfilled the first task? That alone?"

A pause.

"Why, yes," said the queen. "Absolutely."

Fury gripped Fenella. She grabbed the cat and hurled him from her lap. He landed neatly on his feet. She leaped up and faced him with her fists clenched.

"You were supposed to advise me! You were there! Why didn't you say something?"

I didn't think of that. Ryland gave a furry shrug. *Besides, what you did worked perfectly well. What does it matter?*

Fenella was incredulous. "I was trying to minimize the damage I did. You knew that!"

Even if I had thought of it, you had to figure it out for your-self. That's the rule. Anyway, you were set on your path from the moment you learned about gas heating systems.

"But now my family is homeless, and I caused it. And I didn't have to! There was a better way." Fenella was panting. "It was a trick." She whirled on the queen. "You tricked me! I thought I needed to do something active. Something physical."

"What you do is your choice," said the queen quietly. "Keep in mind that all choices in life are made in blindness to the full range of options. At least now, as you go forward, you will know to search for more . . . metaphysical answers."

Fenella put her hand in her pocket and clutched her leaf.

"If you *are* still going forward?" asked the queen.

"Of course I am," Fenella snapped. "I am not giving myself to Padraig. I shall see him dead. And I still want to die myself."

"Well, then." The queen glanced at her brother. "Perhaps you can take comfort that you were not the only one blind to a more benign path."

Ryland bristled at his sister. He yowled something.

She yowled back.

Fenella wondered if she had been blind because of her own desire to burn in the flames. Even though she had known she would survive. Perhaps she had not quite believed it. All that lovely new technology. The dancing blue gas flames. They had seduced her.

She sat down again, heavily, on her chair.

She had done wrong. So wrong.

The queen rose from her throne and crossed to kneel next to Fenella. "Nobody was hurt. You may still cling to that."

"Their home . . . it can't be undone, and it was unnecessary."

"I want you to see something." The queen raised her hand to her face and licked her palm. She held it out before Fenella.

In the faint wet glistening on the queen's palm, a tiny pattern formed. It was the street on which Fenella's family lived. Little figures ran past; Fenella could see smoke.

"This is real?"

"Yes. This is what is happening now."

There was no sound, only images. A fire truck racing down the street, and then another. Firefighters with hoses facing the house as it collapsed into itself. Crowds forming at a safe distance.

Her family pushing frantically through the crowd.

Leo and Soledad Markowitz standing side by side before the blazing, smoking ruins of their home. Lucy sinking to the ground at their feet, hiding her face, clutching Dawn against her shoulder. Behind her, a bulky, tense figure—Fenella's heart paused—Walker Dobrez? But then the images shifted and he was gone.

Three firemen restrained Zach and Miranda as they argued and pointed. Miranda's face was ravaged and Zach's was gray as the firemen made discouraging gestures. Zach moved away and knelt by his wife and child. He said something. In Lucy's arms, the child's body went rigid. Lucy began rocking her desperately. Zach held them both.

Fenella grabbed the queen's hand and fisted it shut. "This is supposed to make me feel better?"

"Did you see what I saw?" asked the queen. "It is *your* safety that they believe was destroyed. They believe you died in their home, on their watch. An accident." She paused. "Or possibly a suicide."

"What are you saying?" Fenella let go of the queen's hand.

"That they are thinking about you," said the queen steadily. "You and only you. Their home is secondary. Life is the only loss that matters."

"They will change their minds," said Fenella tightly, "once they see that I am fine."

Absolutely, said Ryland cheerfully.

"Yes," said the queen. "You're correct about that."

Fenella lifted her chin. She said, "All right. The second task."

If it is the destruction of life, she thought, I will not do it. I will go back to Padraig instead. The decision was sudden, but it felt good and it felt right. It gave her strength. She put her hand in her pocket to touch the leaf again.

"What must I destroy next?" she asked.

"Love," said the queen.

"Love?" said Fenella incredulously.

"Love."

Chapter 19

We had better get back to your family quickly, Ryland said, once they exited Faerie.

"I'm not ready yet." Fenella touched the bark of a nearby tree, and put her other hand in her pocket to feel the soothing vibrations of the oak leaf.

Ryland paused, one paw still extended, the other three firmly on the ground. He turned his furry head to look at her.

"I'm thinking," said Fenella.

The longer you delay, the more suspicious—

"This won't take long. I have a question about the destruction of love." Fenella's hands trembled on the leaf. "My presence alone made Miranda feel unsafe. So: Can my presence alone fulfill the second task too? If my family feels unsafe and afraid because of me—and we know they will—then they won't love me anymore. Destruction of love. Done. Right?"

She held her breath.

Love must first exist, said Ryland. *In order to be destroyed.*

"Miranda loves me." Fenella's voice was uncertain, though. "The others—I don't know. But Miranda. At least, she loved me once. When we were together in Faerie."

This is so not my area, complained Ryland.

"I'm only asking you about the logic."

I understand. I don't know. Let's go see your family. Then you can tell me if Miranda, or anybody else, loves you. If you think so, you can ask my sister if you can simply do nothing and call the second task complete. He paused. *I doubt it, okay?*

So did Fenella. But she held on to hope nonetheless.

She came running up to the ruins of the house with the cat in her arms. Most of the crowd had dispersed; only the firefighters, the immediate neighbors, and Fenella's family were left.

No Walker Dobrez. But she could not afford to think about him.

She called out. Her family—Lucy, and Zach, and Soledad, and Leo, and Miranda—turned. Their mouths dropped open. Shock filled their eyes. Shock and relief.

Then—within seconds—another emotion crept in.

They surrounded her, though. There were exclamations.

There were hugs. There were even nods of understanding, as Fenella explained that she had gone off to the parade; that she had looked and looked for everybody there; that she had not at first thought the sounds of the fire engines had anything to do with her.

"But then," Fenella said, "I heard somebody say the name of the street. And I ran . . . What happened?"

It was Miranda who said, after the tick of three long seconds, "They're saying that it was a gas explosion."

"Oh," said Fenella.

Miranda said nothing more.

No one did.

They looked at her.

Fenella said, "I read about explosions. I read it in my book." She immediately knew that this had been a mistake. But then, anything she said would probably have been a mistake.

There was silence in the circle around her. Lucy glanced at Zach. Zach half turned and looked at the smoldering house, and so did Soledad. Leo had already stepped fully away. He was holding the child and looking only at her. In that moment Fenella realized that, in fact, Leo had not been among those who had hugged her.

Yes, Fenella had certainly destroyed safety, and not just for Miranda, but for them all.

Miranda was the only one who met Fenella's eyes. She did it only for the barest moment.

"We need to figure out what to do next," said Lucy, at last. "The police told us about the homeless shelter. They would have room for all of us, for a few days. Or we could go to Sarah's. Only thing is, there's only one guest room there. They have some air mattresses, though. Also, Walker said he has a sofa bed."

Walker, thought Fenella. She had the wild urge to speak up, to say that she could go sleep on Walker's sofa bed—it would get her away from her family, which suddenly she desired more than anything. She did not belong here, with them.

But she had a job to do. She could not leave that job.

If she did leave, she would be not with Walker, but with Padraig . . .

She bit her lip, frozen, bewildered—and terrified. She felt as if walls had started to close in on her.

Zach said, "Brenda Spencer has a nursery already set up for Dawn. We could go there, Lucy and Dawn and I."

"There's my friend Jacqueline," said Soledad thoughtfully. "She has a pull-out bed."

"Mrs. Angelakis offered us a room too," said Leo. "Listen, let's get ourselves situated somewhere for tonight, wherever we can, however we can. We can regroup in the morning."

There was silence.

Don't worry, Fenella, said Ryland. *They can hardly throw you out. They wouldn't, anyway. They're suspicious, but they haven't even talked among themselves yet. They have more important things to think of than you.*

"We really have to split up?" asked Lucy.

Leo nodded. "Probably. For tonight. Until we figure out a plan."

"I don't want us to split up," said Lucy. "I'd rather we all be together at the shelter. Let's call everyone we know first, and ask for help."

"Yeah," said Zach. "Somebody might have space for all of us. Or know somebody who does."

"But we need three bedrooms," said Miranda.

"Two bedrooms and part of a basement, or a sofa."

"Let's go over to Mrs. Angelakis's and talk," said Soledad. "See? There she is."

Fenella saw the neighbor waving from her front steps. She was holding her door open and gesturing at a platter that she was also holding.

"Look at that," Zach said. "Mrs. Angelakis has a Boston cream pie." It wasn't much of a laugh he gave then, more of a chuckle.

Then, somehow, for no reason, all of them burst out laughing. Laughing and crying, really, but mostly laughing. All of them except Fenella. Then they were all moving across the street in a great big group, clumped together, holding hands and shoulders. Leo was even calling something out cheerfully to Mrs. Angelakis about the pie.

Fenella trailed behind, feet dragging, Ryland in her arms. She watched Miranda's straight back in front of her.

They're fine, see? Ryland spoke impatiently. *They're going to eat pie. I bet they have shelter for the whole family figured out by suppertime. Including for you. It's just like you hoped. Cheer up!*

It was all true.

But Fenella felt terrible, wrong, doomed.

Chapter 20

It was past midnight at the start of a new day, the first day after the fire. Ryland's prediction had come true; the family was still more or less together, in a temporary apartment belonging to Soledad's friend Jacqueline's church. Fenella was even still sharing a room with Miranda.

The apartment had once been a large garage and still showed signs of its previous incarnation; one wall of the lower level was a double garage door. This downstairs section contained a kitchen with a table and a sitting area with a sofa bed. The upstairs, reached by a spiral staircase, held a bedroom for Miranda and Fenella, along with a small bathroom. Soledad and Leo were in a bedroom in the church rectory next door.

They would be able to stay here for a few days.

Fenella knelt in the dark on the cool white tile of the upstairs bathroom. She was eavesdropping on Lucy and Zach, using a spyhole Ryland had found. It was where the pipe of an old-fashioned radiator entered the bathroom from downstairs. Sound traveled right up the pipe. Also, because the hole was wider than the pipe, it afforded Fenella a partial view of the room below.

There, in the dim light of a floor lamp, Lucy and Zach sat facing each other on the thin mattress of the sofa bed. Dawn lay on the bed with her parents, her arms flung outward, surrounded by pillows.

"You should try to sleep," Lucy whispered to Zach.

Zach's voice was tense. "I don't want to. I need to keep watch. I want to keep the light on, and keep Dawn near, where I can grab her in one second flat. Not to mention you."

Lucy took a deep breath. "It's going to be all right, isn't it?"

A pause. "Yeah. It's only *things* that were lost. Nobody was hurt. We're together. We've been through worse, you know we have."

Fenella felt Ryland nudge her.

"But it was our *home*! It's not only our things. It's also, well, I've never belonged anywhere else."

"Oh, Luce. Come here. Home isn't a building. Home is us."

Yes, thought Fenella fiercely. Please.

"Yes and no." Lucy's voice was muffled against Zach's chest. "At least Pierre was safe at the kennel. What if he'd been in the basement?"

"Everybody is all right, including Pierre."

The two figures below moved closer, clinging. Fenella's fingers curled tightly into her palms. She hoped they wouldn't make love. If they did, she'd pull Ryland forcibly away from the peephole.

No. Lucy was crying. Crying with great big hiccups. Zach stroked her back and murmured something too softly for Fenella to hear.

Out of nowhere, rage bloomed in Fenella. Lucy was getting comforted! Lucy with her loving husband and her lively, curious daughter, whom she would never have to worry about losing—her daughter, whom she could plan on seeing grow up, day by day, year by year. Lucy would get to watch Dawn become an adult and choose a life for herself. Lucy would not have to watch her daughter be destroyed.

Lucy could afford to lose her home! She could afford to lose more.

Open your eyes, Fenella.

Fenella hadn't realized she'd shut them. She looked down again reluctantly. She saw how Lucy leaned into Zach. How his arms tightened around her, and hers around him. She saw how Lucy instinctively reached out one bare foot and nestled it gently alongside her child, to feel Dawn's breathing. Fenella winced.

They were talking again, their soft voices rising easily up the pipe.

"I heard Dad calling the insurance agent. His face just sort of changed while he listened."

"Changed in a bad way?" asked Zach.

"Yes. Maybe we can't replace the house? Maybe there isn't enough insurance money?"

"Money." Zach shrugged. "We'll do whatever we have to. Our parents have been carrying us for a long time. Maybe this is a big wake-up call. I can work full-time and do college part-time."

"Me too. Or I could quit school for a while."

"I think I should be the one to do that. Look. We have to stay positive. We have options. There are six adults involved here. You can look at it as six people who need to be supported, or you can look at it as six people all pitching in to take care of each other."

There was a pause. "You're counting Miranda in the six adults?" Lucy asked. Another, longer pause. "And *Fenella*?"

Fenella's stomach tightened.

"Yeah, well," said Zach carefully. "Obviously Fenella hasn't been able to help much so far."

Another pause, this one longer. When Lucy spoke at last, Fenella had to strain her ears to hear. "Zach? About Fenella . . ."

Utter silence below. The couple had pulled apart. They were on their sides, facing each other, bodies still touching. Lucy had tilted her head so that she could see into Zach's face, and he was looking back down seriously into hers.

I can't stand it. Lovers who think they can read each other's minds.

Shut up, Ryland, Fenella thought. She dug her nails into her palms.

"The firefighters said it was a gas explosion."

"They're still investigating the accident. *Accident,* Luce."

"But *you* wonder too, I know you do. Fenella was all over the basement looking at the plumbing and electrical and heating systems. She followed the path of every pipe. She pored over that book until it fell open to the right pages automatically. I swear she understood everything."

"I was even having a fantasy that she'd be able to get a job doing stuff like that."

"Jobs like that can pay really well."

"Yeah. I was thinking she could go to school for it."

"Me too. I was excited for her. And . . . and also sad for Miranda. I was wondering if she would feel bad if Fenella sort of, you know, bounced like a rubber ball after everything she's been through. Went to school, got a job, was earning great money. And even . . ."

"Even what?"

"Well, Walker likes her. Twice, she's gone off with him alone. Also, she looks at him when he's around. You know, under her lashes."

Fenella glanced involuntarily at the cat, but he was peering down through the hole, his tail twitching slightly, and he said nothing.

Lucy's breath was ragged again. "We've drifted off the subject. I guess neither of us wants to say it out loud. But you're thinking it too, right? At first, when we saw the house—I thought maybe she had killed herself. But then there she was, just fine, and now I wonder—"

"Me too. But why would she blow up the house?"

"I don't know."

Another pause.

Zach said, "Maybe the investigation will turn up a problem. A gas leak. Something."

"How can they be sure? They whole house is gone. The pipes are gone. Zach, she was all over the basement."

"Coincidence. Or maybe when she was looking at everything, she pulled something loose. Accidentally."

"Wouldn't we have smelled gas?"

"From a small, slow leak?"

Silence.

"But either way . . ." Lucy's voice was firmer. "Either way, don't you see, we can't trust her. There are too many questions."

Slowly: "Yeah."

Lucy said, "We've been trying to treat her like Miranda. But she's not the same. She's not really one of us. We don't know her."

"No," said Zach. "Even Miranda says that now. She doesn't know her."

There it was. Fenella's answer. She was not known. She was certainly not loved.

The second task would not be easy after all.

Chapter 2-1

When morning came, Fenella crept out of bed and slipped from the room. Miranda was either still sleeping or pretending to, with her back turned. Ryland silently paced down the stairs beside Fenella, an inch from her left foot.

Fenella moved quietly past the sleepers on the sofa bed, and into the kitchen area. There she paused. She looked around the strange room. Memories of things from the old home attacked her: Soledad's knitting basket. Leo's piano and his guitars. The schedule on the refrigerator. The worn kitchen table.

She whirled as she felt someone watching her. Lucy was leaning up against the wall three feet away. She wore the same clothes in which she had run the race yesterday. There was a crease on her face from a bedsheet.

"I was thinking of the house," Fenella blurted. "Everything gone. It must feel so horrible."

"Have some juice," said Lucy. She turned away.

Over the next ten minutes, the others slowly, silently, filtered in. During breakfast, Fenella could feel everyone watching her. After breakfast, Lucy disappeared with Soledad, and when they returned, Fenella was not surprised that Soledad abruptly announced that she, Lucy, and Fenella needed to go food shopping.

They're going to question you, said Ryland. *Don't go. You shouldn't be with them when I can't be there to advise you.*

Fenella ignored him. She stood. "All right."

Fine, muttered Ryland, sullenly.

The grocery store was only a few blocks away. Fenella found herself walking between Lucy and Soledad. She kept one hand in her pocket, touching her leaf.

She slid a quick look sideways at Lucy. She saw the furrow across her forehead, and the firm set of her chin, and the world of questions in her eyes. She remembered how on that first day, Lucy had reached out to Fenella, her whole body alive with joy and welcome. Now Lucy's arms hung by her sides. Her hands were fisted.

Any second, the questions would begin. Fenella would have to lie. But if only—

She felt desperate to make Lucy understand . . . understand *something*. She couldn't tell Lucy and Soledad what she was doing, of course. She couldn't explain about the three tasks. But maybe if she told about Padraig—if she explained what had happened to her—

Because if the problem was that they didn't know her, if they needed to know her to love her, then maybe they could learn to know her.

Fenella still had a hand on her leaf. With the other, she impulsively reached out and took Lucy's hand, uncurling the fingers. Lucy stiffened.

"I have to tell you something," Fenella said. "Please."

Lucy's face was wary.

"I have to tell you about Padraig," Fenella said.

She saw the shock and surprise in Lucy's widening eyes.

Fenella gripped her leaf. She turned to include Soledad as well as Lucy. Then the story came ripping out of her.

⌀

All the trouble began because of Fenella's laugh.

Once upon a time, Fenella laughed often. Her laugh would begin with a creaky wheeze that turned into a snicker. Then the snicker would get louder, transforming into a noise perilously close to a horse's whinny. A horse that had been crossed with a duck, because the whinnying was interspersed with a certain amount of what could only be called quacking.

Fenella had a laugh that could make everyone in a crowded marketplace turn their heads and stare. As a small girl, her laughter had embarrassed Fenella so much that she would clap her hand to her mouth to try to keep it inside. But this only compounded the problem; she'd have to clutch her stomach and sway back and forth with her red hair flying over her face. If the laughter escaped anyway, which it often did, why, then, Fenella would find herself stamping her left foot while she whinnied and quacked and, yes, snorted. Because when Fenella Scarborough laughed, her whole body was involved.

By the time she was a young woman, she had gotten over her embarrassment and it hadn't required much to set her off.

Look, young Fenella's in one of her fits again, other folk would say in the marketplace, nearly four hundred years ago, and as they watched, smiles would tug their mouths, and soon they'd be roaring too.

Fenella's laughter was so noticeable that the joy of it had penetrated into Faerie one day in 1627, when she was seventeen. On that day, Padraig heard her.

It was a warm afternoon in May. Fenella was walking her father's donkey, Dando, home from market. Earlier, she had woven daisies into a wreath for Dando, but the wreath was too big and dangled down below his long ears. It made Fenella grin to see the silly floral arrangement on the temperamental old donkey, but that wasn't the only thing that made her smile. Every so often, she rested her hand on one of Dando's bulging saddlebags, aware of the length of fabric that was folded up within. She had done extra work for a long time to commission a fine, soft worsted from the weaver, dyed a pretty apple green.

Two slashes on the sleeves, Fenella thought. Could she have puffs on the sleeves, also? She would have to decide quickly.

The dress was for her wedding day.

Fenella's sweetheart, Robert Ennis, had a sister, Agnes, who was defter than Fenella with her needle. Agnes had promised to make the dress. One thing Fenella knew: The overskirt would split over the underskirt so that it could easily be looped up on the sides. Fenella wanted the ability to loop up her skirt in case she needed to investigate something at the mill.

After all, she had to be realistic. This would be her wedding dress, but inevitably, later in its life, it would be needed in a more workaday way. Fenella was going to be a miller's wife!

The road was rutted, and she had a few miles to go, but the soles of her bare feet were tough and callused, so Fenella barely noticed the road as she walked and daydreamed about Robert, and about their future, and, this particular day, about her new dress and how appealing she planned to look in it.

Under the skirt, Fenella would wear a farthingale to make the skirt stand out from the waist. At her bodice, her stomacher would pull in tightly to plump out her breasts just so above the square neckline. She'd cover up with her fichu, of course, for she knew what was right and proper, especially for her wedding day.

Later on, though, when she was private with Robert, he would take the fichu off.

Robert!

Their wedding wasn't far off, but that very night, there were plans. She and Robert would sneak out and meet. They had been teasing each other for quite long enough. They would meet outside the mill at one hour past twilight.

Not that they were fooling anybody. Not that sneaking was necessary. It wasn't as if their families didn't know, and approve, and smile behind their hands.

But sneaking was fun.

At seventeen, Fenella was full young for marriage. Most girls and boys of Fenella's station could not afford to marry until their mid-twenties. But as the son of the miller, Robert was already part of a thriving business, and it wasn't too much to say that Fenella was part of it too.

From when she was a small girl, Fenella had liked to sit by the river and watch the big watermill churn. She couldn't remember learning how the wheel's machinery worked; it had seemed to her quite obvious. So, one day, when the great wheel ground to a halt that had everyone flummoxed,

Fenella had boldly approached Robert's father. With a small finger, she pointed to exactly where the mechanism had snagged, and explained in a high piping voice the obstruction that she knew was inside the wheel, even though it couldn't be seen.

When Robert, then twelve, crawled sure-footedly out onto the wheel to locate and pull the obstruction out, Fenella—five years younger—had been right on his heels. Robert had been livid that she'd followed him onto the dangerous wheel. In fact, Fenella liked to tease him that he had not gotten over it until he was nineteen and she turned fourteen and her figure bloomed.

She and Robert would run the mill together. There would be other things they'd do together too. Fenella patted the saddlebag containing her fabric and grinned again. She had bought the extra fabric that Agnes demanded for putting in the seams of the dress. The seams could then be let out as needed. For who knew how soon there might be a new baby?

This very topic of children had been the subject of merriment today at market, when Fenella got her fabric. The weaver's wife had much to say on the subject of babies, particularly early babies; holding forth as was her way. Fenella had laughed, not because the weaver's wife was so witty, but because it pleased Fenella to see how the woman's cheeks pinked with pleasure at being thought so.

Everybody enjoyed hearing Fenella Scarborough laugh and everybody tried to make it happen. They would elbow each other and say, "Will the girl burst this time, do you think?"

Today at market, she'd laughed her hardest because, well . . . Tonight. Robert! The sneaking! Her peals had reached out to the sky and beyond. The entire marketplace had rung with them, and the cows and the goats and the geese had joined in and howled right along.

All alone on the road now, Fenella let loose her laughter again. But this time, old Dando did not bray with her. Instead, his ears flickered uneasily, and then the donkey came to an abrupt halt in the middle of the road.

One moment there was a shimmer in the air. The next, a tall, dark-haired man stood in the road before Fenella. He was dressed in clothes grander than anything Fenella had ever seen, silks and velvets, with an astonishing seven slits to his billowing sleeve, and fine lace beneath the sleeve as well as at his throat. He had tight boots of soft leather to his knees, and they bore no dust whatsoever.

His blue eyes glittered.

He bowed deeply, doffing a red silk cap with a long white feather. "Why, it's the laughing girl," he said. "Well met."

His eyes swept her up, and then they swept her down.

Fenella's laughter died in her throat.

Chapter 22

Fenella came abruptly back into the present. She was sitting on the crumpled autumn leaves and fading grass of a small park. She was leaning against the trunk of a tree, with Lucy and Soledad close, holding on to her, listening to her.

She remembered that the two of them had put their arms around her, walked her there, and made her sit, while she talked and talked and talked.

A short distance away, a play area was filled with small children and their caretakers. Raucous shouts drifted to her ears, but seemed unreal. She tried to smile. Lucy, looking at her, shook her head.

"It's all right," Lucy said. "We're here."

Fenella said hoarsely, "Thank you."

How had she gotten so lost in the past? She slowly let go of her leaf, which she discovered she had been clutching in her lap. It uncurled and lay on her knee, unharmed. "I have to stop talking."

Lucy put a gentle hand on Fenella's forearm. "Take all the time you need."

Soledad put her elbows on her knees and buried her hands in her hair. "I knew Padraig too. While he was hunting Lucy, he interfered in all of our lives. I even hired him at the hospital. I invited him into our home—"

Lucy interrupted. "Mom, don't start blaming yourself again for that. How could you know? He was charming and he used magic on you."

Fenella was thoughtful. "In the old days, only the Scarborough girl would see him. Then at some point, he got bolder. "

"He had a whole life set up here in Boston," Soledad said. "An apartment and a job. A bank account! For all I know, he even dated. Certainly lots of women at the hospital noticed him."

Fenella thought of what an outcast Padraig had been in Faerie. No wonder that, more and more, he had enjoyed strutting around in the human realm . . .

"So he changed his ways over time." Lucy's eyes were narrow. She moved even closer to Fenella and put her arm around her. "Maybe he got more powerful here in the human realm, as time passed? The more successful he was? But we defeated him. He's gone. He can't hurt any of us again."

Fenella swallowed. He can't hurt you, she thought. Only me. Then another thought: But *I* can hurt you. I already have.

She got up. "We need to go to the grocery store."

"But you were talking—"

"I don't want to go on right now," said Fenella.

"All right," said Lucy gently. "Later, you can tell us more."

It wasn't until she was in the market, pushing a cart heavy with milk and produce and cereal, that Fenella remembered that Lucy and Soledad had been planning to question her about the fire. She had successfully distracted them.

She was so shocked, she stopped pushing the cart.

They would still want answers. But her breakdown had changed the moment. When they came, the questions would be gentle and accompanied by a predisposition to believe Fenella. She had in fact used the truth to manipulate them.

But she had not done it on purpose. She had thought— she had thought—

What had she thought? That she could make them sorry for her, and so love her? Did love work that way? Fenella stared blindly at a package of unsalted butter.

At checkout, Fenella bagged groceries beside Lucy. She loaded the bags into the little wheeled cart that they had also bought and would push home, and accepted two bags that she would carry by hand. "No, they're not too heavy," she said to Lucy. Her voice sounded overly cheerful in her ears, but Lucy didn't appear to notice anything wrong. "I can take another bag. I'm strong."

There was no room on the sidewalk for three to walk abreast, and Fenella took care to be the one who walked alone, behind the others, holding her bags. She let them get yards ahead, though from time to time when they asked, she called out that she was fine, she was right there. She longed to be alone, to sit down. To hold her leaf. To— something.

She didn't want to see Ryland. He would want to know what had happened with Lucy and Soledad. He would pester her about the second task.

Meanwhile, she could feel more memories of Padraig flooding her mind, pushing at her throat, wanting to be told.

They reached the church. There in the street was Walker Dobrez's truck. And there, inside it, was Walker. He had his head down; he was reading something.

Perhaps it was because she had so recently been remembering Robert. Perhaps it was that she had felt, in memory, the way it had been when she'd been planning to sneak out to be with Robert for the first time. Perhaps it was simply that she felt so alone. For whatever reason, Fenella's heart squeezed inside her chest.

Walker looked up. His gaze skimmed over Lucy, then Soledad, and then landed on Fenella. He got out of the truck.

In the next moment, he was taking the grocery bags from Fenella's arms.

Fenella heard him saying all the right things. She went with everyone indoors, where she managed a smile for Miranda, who was feeding Dawn at the table. She did not see Ryland anywhere and was glad. She helped with the grocery unpacking. She found her hand again in her pocket, touching the leaf.

Then Walker turned again toward her, and Fenella caught his eye and held it.

Not letting herself think, she walked back outside. Walker followed her. She had known he would. She moved to the far side of his truck, where they would be somewhat sheltered from being seen by the others. She turned to face him.

Then she flung herself against his chest and burrowed there, clinging.

Walker's surprise—and hesitation—manifested as tension in his entire body.

But then he gave in. His big arms cradled her, one

strongly around her waist. A hand cupped the back of her head. Under Fenella's cheek, his chest moved as he exhaled. She could feel his lips, brushing softly against the top of her head. She could feel his breath warm in her hair as his fingers entangled themselves in its strands. "It's okay," he murmured.

She knew she should not do this. But oh, she wanted to. She rubbed her cheek against Walker's shirt. She whispered, "It's not okay."

Walker's arms tightened around her. "Yeah, I know. But I'm here."

Fenella pressed closer. She sobbed against Walker's shirt, and her tears were real. He backed up, leaning against the door of his truck, and she went with him. She slid her hands up his back, under his shirt. His skin was so warm. His back was so smooth, so muscled, human and alive. "Just look," she choked out, too low to be heard. "Look at what I've become. I hate it. I hate myself."

"What?"

She turned her head and spoke distinctly through her tears. "It's terrible."

"The house. Yeah." Walker's touch was so gentle on her hair. He pulled her head back and wiped at her tears with a careful finger. Fenella had never seen anything so tender as his expression. "Terrible. I was so relieved when I heard that you were okay. I would have come earlier, but I didn't want to intrude."

"You heard I was okay?"

"Miranda called me."

"Oh," Fenella said.

"Nobody was hurt in the fire, Fenella. It's all right."

"Is it?"

"Yeah." Walker's lips came down on Fenella's brow. Soft. Strong. Tentative. "It's all right. It is."

It was not. Fenella exhaled anyway, wishing to believe it for a moment. She closed her eyes. Instinctively, she tipped back her head.

His lips came to hers, still tentative until she kissed him back, moving her body closer. She felt his breath come more quickly. His heart pounded fast against her.

Her heart had sped up too. She nestled closer, wrapping her arms around his waist. His body was warm, but not as warm as his lips and his breath.

Too soon, too soon, he lifted his mouth. Hers felt cold and abandoned, but at least his arms were still around her, and his body was close. He murmured against her temple, "Also, I've got an offer for you guys, a possible apartment you can move into. *Also* also, Lucy's friend Sarah can take Pierre."

Fenella went quite still in Walker's arms. "Pierre."

"Yes. There's a nice yard at Sarah's house. He'll like it. Everyone can visit him there."

The dog, Fenella thought slowly, as an image of Pierre formed in her head. Of course, the dog. The beloved dog.

Abruptly, she pushed herself away from Walker.

To destroy love, she should murder the dog.

Chapter 23

The dog was old, the dog was sick. The dog would surely die anyway in a year or so. It would be awful, but not *too* awful. She could do it. Couldn't she?

It would be far better than trying to make Lucy and the others love her. Anyway, she had no idea how to make them love her. All she knew how to do was to fish for their pity— and awkwardly, at the cost of exhuming her own memories. Pity was not love.

What was love? She didn't know. She had loved Robert, and Minnie, and—and Bronagh. But none of them had asked for her love. She had given it, freely, instinctively.

Who had loved Fenella? Her mother, perhaps, though that woman had died before Fenella could remember her. Her father. Robert. Minnie. Miranda, once? It was hard to understand why they had loved her, though.

Bronagh had not loved her. Bronagh had screamed at Fenella. Fenella had brought nothing but evil and terror into Bronagh's life. It was all Fenella's fault, from beginning to end.

"Fenella?" said Walker. She had thrown herself against him again, burrowing. His body was warm. His arms around her were strong, even if he was trying—oh so gently—to push her away.

Fenella pulled away from him. The dog, she thought. The dog. It was an easy answer. She peered up at Walker from under her lashes. His short, neat ponytail had a severity that emphasized his features. She couldn't help herself; she grabbed both his hands in hers and squeezed them desperately.

Walker's expression was happy, but now some caution entered. "Uh, I'm wondering . . . does this mean you've changed your mind about me?"

"I guess so." Fenella wanted to hold Walker's warm hands and look at him and feel the reprieve of having thought of a not-too-bad answer to the second task. Even if it was, again, a physical answer.

He was talking. "The thing is, maybe it's just the fire. A shock like that can change how you feel. But you might change your mind again. I'm thinking this is too quick. For now, let's go back to the idea of being friends."

Oh, he was nice. Robert had been nice too. Nothing mean in him, nothing underhanded, nothing conniving or manipulative. You could relax with a man like that. You did not have to be wary or afraid.

Fenella reached up and pulled Walker's ponytail. She moved in close again, brushing her body against his, satisfied to hear how his breath quickened, to feel how his hands went instinctively to hold her waist, to see how his face flushed. With part of her mind, she was amazed. She *wanted* to be close to Walker. Who would have thought that? It felt good, having his hands on her, feeling his breath on her face. She could practically hear her blood humming.

Where had this come from, all at once? She didn't care. She didn't care!

"You're too good to let get away," Fenella murmured, and heard Walker laugh. He pulled her closer.

"I'm not trying to get away. Not since I first met you. You were the one who was running. You might still. And that's okay."

"I forget what I was thinking."

"You wanted my truck, not me."

"I still want your truck."

"Show me where to sign it over to you. No, stop, listen. We should go back in. I want to tell everybody about this apartment. It's in the same building as mine. The people who live there are moving out tomorrow. And you and I already have a date for the auto show. There's no need to go fast. We have as much time as we want."

Fenella knew that wasn't true. She pulled away, however. "All right."

She held Walker's hand as they went back inside, and he held hers. It took only a few seconds for the others to notice. Ryland noticed too, when he slunk down the staircase and twined himself underfoot. But nobody said anything.

Not then.

That night in their bedroom, however, Miranda kept the light on. The bedroom was small, with bunk beds. Miranda had slept in the upper bunk the night before, but now she sat at the foot of the lower bunk, with Fenella facing her. With her voice pitched low so that Lucy, Zach, and Dawn were not disturbed downstairs, Miranda said, "What's up with you and Walker?"

Ryland narrowed his eyes accusingly. *Yes, please do tell us.* He climbed into Miranda's lap and settled there.

"You called Walker," said Fenella. "To tell him I was okay."

"Yes. I had to. Fenella—you should have seen his face, when he thought you had died in the fire."

"Oh," said Fenella. "I see."

Miranda petted the cat with her eyes on Fenella's face.

Fenella said honestly, "I don't really know what I'm doing

with Walker, except that it's exactly what I feel like doing."

Miranda said nothing. Her eyes held something. Blame? Fenella found herself remembering the conversation she'd had with Miranda after she arrived, about love and the impossibility of imagining that kind of healing.

Fenella did not look at her leaf, but she knew where it was on the bedside table. "Something happened today, Miranda." With her eyes on Miranda, and not Ryland, she spoke stumblingly about how she had had an impulse to tell Lucy and Soledad about the first time she'd seen Padraig. That she had talked and they had listened.

"It was after that, then, that you felt like holding hands with Walker?" interrupted Miranda. "Presto, abracadabra, you're healed?" Her voice dripped sarcasm.

Ryland snorted agreement.

"Well, no. I'm not healed. It's only that I . . ." Fenella stopped.

"You what?"

You wanted to bury your troubles in some good sexual tension? Ryland put in with interest. *Is that it? I can understand.*

"I wanted to tell the story of what happened with Padraig. I only told the beginning of it. But I want to tell it all." Her hands were trembling. Only once before had she tried to tell the whole story, and that had been to Bronagh, who had not cared, who had said it was no excuse.

—You ruined my life!

—Bronagh, I know, but it wasn't on purpose. I couldn't help it—I was no older then than you are—

—I don't care if it was on purpose or not!

Fenella had not tried again to tell the story. Not even with Minnie.

"It's not that I expect telling to do any good," she said. "It's not about, you know, healing. When I told you before that it was too late for me, I meant that. I held Walker's hand, and guess what?" Fenella thrust out her chin defiantly. "I kissed him too. And he kissed me. And I liked it. But ultimately, I don't expect any of that to do me any good."

She had burned down the house. She was going to kill the dog. Then she would do some third terrible thing. But after that, Padraig would be destroyed, finally and completely. Then Fenella would die, like Bronagh had. Like she deserved to.

Like Bronagh had wished her to.

But before she died, Fenella would tell her story. Suddenly, for no reason at all—not to gain love, not to gain pity—she wanted to tell. For the sake of telling, she wanted to tell.

"Telling solves nothing. It changes nothing," Fenella said slowly. "But I want to do it. I want to tell everything that I can . . . I want to explain . . ."

Maybe it was that Lucy and Soledad had been willing to listen. Maybe it was as simple as that.

Miranda was staring at her. So was Ryland.

"So tell," said Miranda softly, at last.

Then, from up the bathroom pipe, came Lucy's voice. "Yes, Fenella," Lucy said. "Come down here and tell us more. I'm texting my parents to come and listen too. We all need to know, as much as you need to tell.

"What happened next, after Padraig appeared?"

Chapter 24

"*You've disturbed my nap* this day." The beautiful man smiled, showing gleaming teeth, and nodded toward the small grassy knoll that rose beside the road. "Twice."

Fenella could not look away. Her thoughts buzzed in her head like a trapped fly. Despite his fashionable garb, this man was no ordinary lord. She had never met one of the fair folk before, but she had heard stories and songs all her life. His nod at the hillside alone told her what he was.

She managed to drop a wary curtsy as the faerie lord's eyes took in Fenella from the top of her silky red head to her dusty bare toes. It was a slow gaze, and it grew appreciative as it moved.

"Yours is a large laugh," he remarked, "to come from such a small creature."

To hide their trembling, Fenella fisted her hands in the

fabric of her faded homespun skirt. "I am sorry, sir. My humblest apologies, sir, and it will not happen again."

"You'll never laugh again?" The lord raised his smooth, elegant brows. His eyes brimmed with charm that Fenella could see but did not feel. She pictured Robert's plain, shrewd face with its snub nose and shy warm eyes, and his quick-moving, wiry body and work-roughened hands. Robert was hers and she was his. They had picked each other.

"No, sir. Not if you dislike it, sir."

"I don't dislike it," said the lord pensively, his gaze on Fenella's mouth. "At least, I think not. I've never heard anything like it before. Laugh again, girl. I wish to better judge the music of it."

Fenella pulled her elbows in tightly against her sides. "I am sorry, but my laughter is not mine to command. It comes as it chooses."

"Surely you can summon a small laugh."

Fenella shook her head.

"No? Even if I were to plead? I might do that. Your laugh seemed to me as if it could conjure a celebration." The lord took a step closer to Fenella. His expression was intent. "Would it surprise you to learn that I have had little to celebrate in life so far? I see you would not believe me. Believe this, then: It would please me to hear your laughter, and all sorts of good things might happen, if you were to please me.

I have enough power for that. Power enough to reward one pretty human girl."

Fenella found his barrage of words confusing. She clung to her refusal. "I cannot."

The lord looked thoughtful. "Laughter comes from amusement, but also from enjoyment. Perhaps if you were to enjoy yourself? What if I took you to a grand soiree? Would you laugh for me then?"

Fenella frowned, not understanding.

"A party," explained the lord lightly. "I could invite you to a court ball. It would be like nothing you've ever known, or even dreamed. A village maid like you, who knows nothing, has seen nothing. You would love it, I am sure. You would be impressed and happy." The faerie lord touched Dando's saddlebag, and lingered there. "Even a highborn lady could not command such a dress as I would give to you. It would be my gift, in exchange for your laughter." He paused and then added, almost gently, "And only for your laughter. This I swear. I would take nothing from you that you do not give."

He looked sincere, so sincere that if Fenella had been a fool, she would have believed him. But she was no fool. And though he might be a faerie lord, still she knew his kind. It flared her anger. There were human men like this too, who thought a girl could be bought.

How dare he try to tempt her with a party and a pretty

dress? Yes, she'd been dreaming of dresses, and perhaps somehow he knew it. But she would not risk her future at a handsome man's whim, and still less for a dress. As for a party, what was a celebration without the people you loved nearby? What was laughter without beloved faces around you, laughing in return?

Fenella chose her words carefully. "I'm sorry, sir. Such a dress would be above my station. Nor would it become me."

"Your station will be what I say," said the faerie lord arrogantly. "And the dress will be chosen to sing out the glory of your hair and skin. You have no idea how beautiful you will look." His glance skimmed her figure again, lingered on the crossed neckline of her fichu and her throat above it, and came again to her face and eyes.

"Only laugh," he said again coaxingly. "Such wondrous, joyful music. I have the strangest feeling that it would change everything, if you would but laugh with me." He hesitated and then added, with an odd diffidence, "My offers are not made lightly. I could change your world. You would live like a queen, in comparison with how you live now."

He stood up tall then, and straight, as if he were making a vow. Tension seemed to ripple through him.

Fenella took in a careful breath. She did not *want* her world to change.

The tales and the songs said that you lost your wits at the

beauty of the fey. The tales and the songs said that when one of them beckoned to you, you would helplessly follow. The tales and the songs spoke of faerie celebrations, rites at which you would dance and feast and make wild love. Human decades would slip by in one faerie night, unnoticed.

But the tales and the songs were largely about men, not women. Fenella was not feeling it; or at least, she was not feeling it for this particular faerie lord.

Perhaps it was simply that her heart was already given.

"I repeat: I cannot laugh on command, sir. I must be amused. I must feel joy."

"You think I can do neither for you?"

She had not seen him move, but the lord was nearer. Much nearer.

"Won't you let me try?" Was that pleading in his voice? Surely not.

"The things that amuse me are small and unimportant, my lord. They are not worth your time. Neither am I." She tried another, deeper, curtsy, and as she dipped, she took a large step away from him.

Immediately she knew her mistake, for the faerie lord's voice filled with even more interest. "You like what is small and unimportant?"

Now she did not know what to say.

"Let us make a bargain. Come with me to a ball. Just one

ball, and you dressed like the finest lady. This dress you shall keep, in fair trade for your company. At the ball, we will see how much you will enjoy yourself." His voice grew deep. "Perhaps you will surprise yourself. Perhaps you will laugh for me."

"No! I make no bargain!" The tales and the songs were also full of bargains with the fey, and never did the bargains end up benefiting the human. "I will simply be on my way, good sir, and wish you a speedy return to the sleep that I interrupted so rudely."

Fenella laid her hand on Dando's bridle, inches from the elegant hand of the elfin lord. There was something unusual about the lord's hand, she noted, but she had not the leisure to process what it was. She took up the bridle as if she had no doubt that he would let it go, and to her relief, the faerie lord's white fingers released the leather.

At that moment, her brain caught up with her eyes and told her what was wrong with the elfin lord's hands. It was not only that the fingers were so long and so white, or even that the nails were clean and eerily perfect. It was that each finger folded into four segments.

It would not do to run. Fenella moved deliberately as she guided Dando, who trembled as she did. She walked away, passing within a hair's breadth of the lord. She took care not to brush even the hem of her garment against him.

Step. Step. Step.

At last there was distance between them. Her pace quickened.

She did not look back. But as she moved around a bend in the road, she felt his touch on the breeze that spun up, circling round her, wrapping her skirt tightly around her hips and legs.

She kicked herself free. She leaned on Dando. They staggered forward together.

She had not escaped, and she knew it. She had merely been let out at the end of a long rope, as if she were Dando. The faerie lord would be back.

Which meant she needed a plan.

Chapter 25

Fenella looked up into the faces of her family. She drew a shaky breath. She was suddenly aware of the cat on her lap. His eyes were closed as if he was asleep, but she knew he was not.

Padraig probably was sincere that first day, said Ryland. His tone was strangely thoughtful. *He led a lonely life. It makes sense to me, as I listen to your story. He wasn't looking to make mischief or cause pain. Not yet. He wanted a companion.*

I am aware of that now, Fenella thought. Maybe I should have pretended to love him. Maybe that would have saved Robert and Bronagh, at least.

It was almost as if the cat read her mind. *I don't know what you should have done differently.* He sounded surprised, even frustrated. *How could you have known?*

Fenella shrugged. She had been over this in her head a hundred million times. Why did it feel raw again? Was it the speaking aloud? Was it her family's kind eyes? Was it that a member of faerie royalty was listening to her, finally? Or was it the bald fact that the threat of Padraig was renewed, and she had been the one to renew it?

It came to Fenella with horror that she was telling the story of her victimhood, but in truth, she was now the villain. She had destroyed her family's home, and more was ahead.

"You're not going to stop there, are you?" asked Lucy. "You have to go on and tell us how Padraig came to curse our family."

Soledad said thoughtfully, "I'm guessing that the curse had something to do with Padraig discovering you were pregnant by Robert. Were you with Robert that same night, like you originally planned? When you sneaked out?"

"Yes. I knew not to waste any time in getting pregnant." Fenella's gaze skittered to Leo. After a moment, he nodded back gravely, and she knew that he had understood her—and also that he now fully understood why, before, she had not wanted to hear the song about Lady Janet and Tam Lin. She went on: "I had heard of clever girls who outwitted the fey, using ordinary woman's magic, and, well, love."

"You did get pregnant on purpose, then?" Soledad leaned in. Her gaze said that she, too, had made the connection.

Fenella nodded, glancing compulsively back at Leo. "I could only hope, of course. But it was the right time in my cycle. Robert wanted to be careful, but I told him no. I didn't tell him why. I knew he would give in. We were to be married soon anyway." The old memory floated to Fenella: she and Robert, alone, within the four walls of the dwelling Robert was nearly done building for them. There had as yet been no roof, and so the stars had lit the night while she rested in his arms.

They had had only three nights.

Leo's gaze met Fenella's. He said it aloud, plainly. "When you got pregnant? Were you thinking of Janet in the Tam Lin ballad, even then? You knew the ballad?"

Fenella nodded. "I did. I was reaching for whatever I could think of, and I remembered Tam Lin. But you see, Janet was the wrong example for me. For if I had not been pregnant, Padraig could not have cursed anyone but me."

Logical, said the cat, just as Soledad began shaking her head.

"I didn't think about the fact that I was bringing another vulnerable being into the world. I felt strong," Fenella went on compulsively. "I thought I could succeed."

"You *were* strong," Soledad said.

"In all the wrong ways." Fenella sank her fingers into the cat's fur.

"No," said Soledad. "You are not judging yourself fairly. Believe me, Fenella."

Fenella compressed her lips. "I disagree."

"Endurance is strength too," Soledad insisted. "It's another kind of ordinary woman's magic. There were no good choices. You survived. You're moving forward with your life. It's all strength."

Fenella looked into the cat's unblinking eyes, and then at Soledad. "No. Don't argue with me about it."

"All right," said Soledad. "For now. But we'll talk about this again, all of us, because it's important."

Lucy nodded agreement, and Fenella saw her steal a glance at Miranda.

Fenella said, "It's a song. A story! It's not a guide to real life. That was my mistake. It wasn't like I could grab hold of Robert and not let go for an hour, while he turned into one monster after another." She tried to control the bitterness in her voice. "If only it had been that simple."

"Monsters?" asked Zach.

Leo explained: "In the song, Tam Lin was turned into one monster after another, to test Janet's love and resolve."

"Easy for her," Fenella said bitterly.

"Well, you're right," said Lucy, after a moment. "I never

thought about it before. But Janet had clear instructions. Plus, she only had to be brave for an hour."

Fenella said again, "It turned out to be the wrong story for me. The wrong example. But it explains why I did what I did. Why I became pregnant. I thought it would anchor me to Robert and to human life. I thought it would give me my own power."

Miranda had remained quiet this entire time. She said, "None of the rest of us had that choice. We were all forced into pregnancy."

Fenella would have met Miranda's eyes, but Miranda was watching her own knees.

"I realize that," said Fenella gently.

She said this even though she knew it was not completely true. Each of the Scarborough girls had had her own story, and some of them, like Fenella—and like Minnie—had been with lovers they chose. But there was no reason to say anything that might make Miranda feel more alone. Fenella looked away from Miranda, only to have her gaze caught by Lucy. There was a moment of perfect understanding, filled with shared sympathy for Miranda. Then Fenella ducked her head. She could not afford to feel close to Lucy. Or to Leo, who was looking on with gentle eyes.

Or to anyone.

She put a hand to her throat, and swallowed.

Lucy said, "Will you tell us the rest of the story, Fenella?"

You know what? said the cat suddenly. *I thought I had no knowledge of you before. But now I remember. You were in a red dress, and Padraig had dressed to match, in red and black. You were dancing with him at the ball. I was just a cub, but I was there too, that very night.*

Feeling Lucy's gaze still on her, Fenella said, "Miranda? Should I tell more?"

Miranda moved her head in the tiniest of nods.

"I'll go on with my story, then," said Fenella.

Chapter 26

On a soft evening three days later, Fenella brought hay to Dondo. The donkey adored his feed, so when he ceased chewing and lifted his head, ears prickling, eyes going half-wild, she knew. She was ready, however.

"Good evening, laughing girl," the faerie lord said.

Fenella kept a hand on the donkey, though whether it was to calm the animal or herself, she did not inquire. She turned. The lord was but half an arm's length away from her. She dropped a careful curtsy.

There was no preparing for the impact of his beauty, but it was his clothing that made her eyes widen. His slashed doublet was made of red silk and lushly embroidered black satin, and trimmed with a wide collar and cuffs of finest point lace. The slashes in the doublet showed his full, voluminous chemise sleeves to advantage. He had a broad-brimmed hat to his head, tight breeches to his legs, and high-heeled boots of gleaming leather to his feet. He wore a ring on every finger, and more in his earlobes, and they all gleamed red with jewels.

He took off his hat and swept her a bow.

He was like a male bird come courting in springtime, Fenella thought, feathered out colorfully in hopes of luring a mate, while she, the female, was considered desirable even in her drab brown.

But she knew that being quiet and biddable would not serve her.

"I suppose ruffs have gone out of fashion." Fenella eyed the collar, which lay flat over his shoulders.

"Long since, pretty girl." Was that a glint of humor in his eyes? "This type of collar makes it much easier to turn one's head. Do you like it?"

"I have no opinion." It was a lie, and it sounded like one too. The delicacy of the lace drew the eye. She wondered how Robert would look, dressed in such a way. She really could not imagine. Then she wondered what Robert would think, to see the faerie lord come courting her in such finery, trying to impress her, and this made her feel sick.

But he would *not* see, and if all went well, he would never even know—or not know for many a long year, not until they were very old together and their lives were near done.

The important thing was that Robert was safe, two fields away, finishing work on the roof of the dwelling that would soon be their home.

Fenella would miss sleeping with the stars above their heads.

"I mentioned that I wished to invite you to a party," the lord said. "It is a grand ball, tonight."

"Good sir, thank you, but I mentioned that I did not wish to go."

He stared at her, his face impassive, for so long that Fenella dared hope this would put an end to it. Then the air between them was awash with mist. Fenella raised an arm instinctively to protect herself, but an instant later the moisture was gone and she saw that he was holding a bundle of red cloth in his arms.

"Your dress for the party," the lord said. "The spiders were weaving for three full days, since I first saw you. Your dress has a reticella lace collar too. It matches mine, but is smaller and more delicate." He shook the fabric out and held the dress before him.

Fenella was silent from sheer astonishment.

The dress had a silk high-waisted bodice in red, lavishly embroidered, and tabbed skirts and full chemise sleeves.

Its sleeves were gathered into two puffs by a ribbon at the elbow. The lace collar was soft and sheer, and woven so as to depict pomegranates.

"There is a ribbon sash for your waist. I have not decided yet about your jewels. Jewels should always be selected last."

"No," said Fenella.

"You would build a style *beginning* with the jewels?"

"No." Her voice was strong again. "I shall not wear that dress, and no, I shall not go with you. You cannot make me. If I continue to refuse, you must take me at my word." She tightened her hand on Dando. She put her other hand on her flat stomach, for courage.

She hoped it was true that he could not make her.

But the lord only smiled. "Your name is Fenella Scarborough, is it not?"

Fenella's breath caught.

"I have made inquiries. It wasn't difficult. Your laugh is known far and wide." He stroked the fabric of the dress, and she saw how it sprang softly away from his overly segmented fingers.

"Fenella," he said. "You will come with me to this party. It is only one night. This I swear. One night only, and a party only. Then you will be free to leave me if you choose. I give you my word. But come with me this night, you shall."

In the next moment the dress was on her body, the waist

falling into place, the collar settling lovingly onto her shoulders, the ribbon sash tightening around her midriff, and the skirts swishing around her legs and over her bare feet. A breeze ran through her hair, unknotting it from its plaits and then lifting it high, weaving it tightly into a pattern she could feel across her scalp.

The donkey jerked away from Fenella's astonished, frozen hand. He ran across the field as far as the fence would allow.

Fenella stood still.

"And a high-heeled shoe with a ribbon rosette."

Fenella's feet pinched, and she staggered, looking down.

"Or perhaps a flat shoe instead. Do not fret. It is well known that women, being less athletic, cannot manage high heels as well as men. If that does not work, then you may dance barefoot."

"I shall not dance at all!" Fenella spat. She gathered the skirts of her dress in her fists. She looked down at her bodice, but had no idea how to get out of the dress. She saw no fastenings. Could she rip it off her body?

He was smiling at her, and talking, still talking. "Now we come to the jewels. Pearls, I think. Two strands, black and white, entwined."

Fenella felt the weight of the strands encircling her throat. She grabbed at them—these she would tear off, and immediately. But the movement of her hand brought something else to her attention.

On her right thumb sat a ring of gold set with a single pearl the size of a plover egg. The pearl glowed in the last rays of the setting sun. She reeled back in shock. The price of the ring alone would have kept her entire family all of their days.

There was one moment of confusion. One moment when she thought of the winters in which food was scarce. One moment when she thought of how her aunt had died, tired and sick, lines etching her face. One moment when she thought of the years ahead, of how hard she and Robert would have to work to feed their babes, years when the harvest might be poor and the watermill idle.

For that moment, she wondered compulsively if she was being a fool. Perhaps she ought to make a bargain. She would go to the party, give him this one night, in exchange for the ring. Such a small thing to him. So much to her.

The lord held out his hand for her to grasp. "Come."

But then the moment was over.

"No," Fenella said calmly. "And I do not believe you can force me." She held her arms out stiffly at her sides. "I would like my own clothes back."

Another long pause. When the lord spoke at last, his voice was soft. "I am sorry."

She thought she had won at last.

"I am sorry you have made this decision. It is a bad decision. You see, I have not been idle these three days, Fenella. I have found out much about you. Including . . ." The lord paused. "That you are pledged to marry."

Fenella lifted her chin. "It is true. I am pledged. So good sir, again, I say you nay."

"His name was Robert, wasn't it?" The lord smiled. "He was a good enough young man, from what I hear. What is the phrase you humans use? God rest his soul."

For the length of three heartbeats, Fenella stayed still.

Then she whirled. She ran, hiking her skirts up high like Lady Janet from the song, awkward in the pretty, impractical shoes, clawing with one hand at the pearls at her neck. She felt the necklace thread break and then the pearls spill away from her, falling in her wake. She kicked off the shoes.

She ran across one field, and then two. Finally she came to the little house that Robert had been building for them. There she discovered him at the foot of the ladder, crumpled on the ground, with his neck broken.

Chapter 27

The next day, Fenella didn't go with the family to visit the apartment that Walker had mentioned. She told them that she was too tired.

"No wonder," said Lucy.

When they had all left, Fenella climbed the rickety spiral stairs and sat on the edge of her temporary bed. She took out her leaf and held it between her palms. It sent out a low soothing pulse; nothing that could be translated into words.

She truly was exhausted. After talking about Padraig last night, she had lain awake, her heart hammering with remembered pain, even though she had put her leaf on the pillow near her cheek. It had not helped that in the next bed, Miranda was awake as well.

"Did he make you go to the faerie ball?" Miranda asked, into the darkness. "After he killed Robert?"

"Yes."

"How were you—what were you thinking?"

"That he might kill my father. Or Robert's sister, Agnes. He held out his hand again and I went with him. I said nothing. I didn't fight. It didn't matter anymore, did it? At least, I didn't think it did."

"But you were pregnant."

"I didn't know that. I had forgotten that it was even possible."

Fenella remembered nothing between finding Robert's body and then becoming aware of being in Faerie, with Padraig. The pearls that she had broken were back around her neck, tight. The top of her head was tucked beneath Padraig's chin.

He had thought he owned her. He had thought she would be too broken to fight. The curse had come later that same evening, when he learned it would not be so easy.

She said aloud, "It was four hundred years ago."

Miranda had said no more. She remained rigidly still for the rest of the night. Fenella remained awake as well.

In the morning, Fenella had placed her leaf on Miranda's clothing while Miranda showered. Then, even though the shadows beneath Miranda's eyes were dark, Miranda had at least eaten an orange for breakfast before going off with the others.

Can I see that thing? Ryland was on his hind legs, stretching up with his front paws on Fenella's knee, straining toward the oak leaf.

Fenella held the leaf where he could see it.

Let me sniff it.

"No. It's mine."

Come on. I won't hurt it. Or take it from you. I promise. He paused. *Also, I don't think I could. It wants to be near you.*

Fenella put the leaf down on her lap. Ryland jumped up into her lap and sniffed at the leaf delicately with his pink nose.

It carries a small amount of medicinal power. A simple salve for the spirit. He cast Fenella a thoughtful look. *It will only work on those who are open to it.*

"I'm surprised that it works at all, here in the human realm."

Why wouldn't it? Humans have long understood the healing properties of plants, and only sometimes called it magic. Yes?

Slowly, Fenella nodded. "I see."

Ryland settled down next to her. *Talk to me. You befriended the tree fey in Faerie?*

"They befriended me," Fenella corrected. She rubbed her eyes. "I can't say that I understand them. They so rarely talk, and I have no idea what they're thinking. But they were kind." She touched the leaf. "*Are* kind."

I don't understand the plant and tree fey well, either, Ryland admitted. *They have always felt completely apart from me, even though the old queen was part floral.*

"You inherited none of that part of your mother, then?"

The cat's muscles tensed. *No. I did not.*

Several minutes passed during which Fenella sat patiently. She watched Ryland, and when at last he spoke again, his words came in a confused burst, as if they had been imprisoned inside him awaiting their chance for freedom.

Originally, I thought my sister was all animal, like me. But then her crown grew in as plant matter. Having inherited, who knows what my sister is now? She does not say; or at least, not to me. He paused. *The old queen grew a spine of rock, like the dwarves. It happened after they allied with her officially.*

"Are you sorry to be all animal?" Fenella thought of the fey's disdain for those with unmixed blood; of how Padraig's almost entirely human appearance had marked him as inferior. She had not realized that there were other, subtler gradations of caste involved as well. She had not realized that Ryland could possibly feel less-than in any way.

They had called Padraig the Mud Creature.

Ryland drew his tail in tightly around his body. *I am what I am.*

Fenella stroked the leaf.

I am what I am! The cat burst out again. *So I lack plant and earth matter. But I'm older than my sister by hundreds of years, I have far more experience, and most important—isn't it most important?—I did not falter and betray my own people in the crisis. Kethalia was lost, do you understand? She was lost in love and guilt. She was obsessed with her friend, that redheaded girl. My sister could have ruined us all.*

But she didn't, thought Fenella, though she said nothing.

Ryland's furry white chest was heaving. The black heart seemed to inflate and deflate. *You even saw her the other day, Fenella, when she was wearing her human guise. Why? Why is she thinking about humans and not about her own people? What happens when there is another crisis? Would my sister choose a human's welfare over ours, as she once did? Even if she has the flexible blood of a ruler—plant, animal, earth, and stone—isn't it the composition of her mind that matters? Shouldn't the mind of a ruler be unmixed in its loyalties? Shouldn't it be inflexible?*

The cat stood on all four paws, tail high, eyes ablaze. *My mind is unmixed. My loyalties are clear.* He flung his head back and yowled aloud, a long ferocious keening with a shrill cry at its core. The cry was aimed directly at the leaf in Fenella's lap.

When he finally ceased yowling, the cat's white-and-black body seemed abruptly to shrink in upon itself. Fenella found herself tracing the veins on her leaf. The cat's gaze followed her fingertip almost hungrily.

"I thought your words sounded only in my own head," said Fenella at last. "Was that wrong? Do you think perhaps the tree fey can hear you, because of my leaf?"

The cat looked rattled and unsure. But he raised his tail defiantly. *Perhaps not directly. But they are interested in what* you *hear, Fenella. They are interested in what* you *experience, and in what* you *think.*

Fenella thought about this. Then she shook her head. "No. They are only kind to me. They do not value my judgment any more than—well, than Lucy does." She paused, watching doubt flicker again over Ryland's face, leaving him looking curiously vulnerable.

I wonder, he muttered.

Fenella frowned. Had his brief contact with the leaf encouraged Ryland to confide in Fenella? She felt unsettled by the glimpse inside Ryland's head. She did not care who ruled Faerie, and still less did she care about the philosophical question he had raised about the mind of a ruler.

But the tree fey would care, she thought. They would have an opinion. They might even, somehow, have heard him just now.

Also, she had a question of her own.

"Why are you here, Ryland? You seem to truly want to help me now. Did your sister really have the power to force you?"

The cat's chin jerked up. Fenella was sure she had presumed too far, and that he would not reply. But then—because of the leaf?—he answered. *My sister will be sorry she made me come and advise you. She will be sorry because everyone in Faerie— not only the tree fey, but everyone—will see that, once again, I can accomplish what she cannot. When you succeed, it will be because I helped.*

Fenella propped her chin on one hand. "But it seems like she wants you to succeed in helping me. It was her idea in the first place that you come with me." She shrugged. "Of course, she did say you have a talent for destruction. What you will have done is to prove her correct. But . . ." Fenella paused for thought.

The cat glared at her. *But what?*

"Well, the job of the ruler of Faerie is not about destruc- tion. It's about—"

I know what it's about! Don't you lecture me on the balance of the earth! I have creative *powers too!*

"Do you?" asked Fenella curiously. "What have you in- vented, or grown, or nurtured?"

The cat jumped to the floor with an audible plop. He held his tail high as he exited the room.

After a moment, Fenella slipped her leaf back into her

pocket. She stood up and stretched. She wasn't feeling so tired anymore. She wondered what the family was doing. Did they like the apartment? Would they be back soon, and would Walker be with them? Would Miranda be feeling better after being out in the brisk autumn air? What were they thinking about Fenella, now that they had heard so much of her story?

Was there possibly a corn muffin left uneaten in the bakery box in the kitchen?

She went downstairs to look.

Chapter 28

Fenella had only finished half of the corn muffin when Ryland came back to her. He practically spat.

We're going out. My sister wants to talk to you.

"Oh, fine," Fenella muttered. She didn't even have shoes on. What did the queen want? More importantly, why couldn't a human woman numbering four hundred years die in peace? Why did so much have to be involved? Tasks of destruction. Political wrangling. Terrible memories. Oak leaves. Even cats and dogs. It made a woman want to retreat into tinkering with a car engine. But she got up.

Because of the conversation she'd just had with Ryland, Fenella found she was newly interested in watching the siblings interact. She would observe them closely. She would be leaf-like.

Carrying the corn muffin in one hand and shoes in the

other, Fenella moved outdoors into the sunlight with Ryland. She drew the fresh autumn air deeply into her lungs.

She felt newly aware of her body, of her muscles taut and toned and ready. She had burned to death not long ago, she thought. Incredible. She crammed the rest of her muffin into her mouth, and licked butter and crumbs from her fingers. She tensed her legs, feeling that she could run miles. Her body was healthy. It wanted to celebrate its existence. It wanted—

Fenella had a stunning physical flashback to kissing Walker. Walker, not Robert. Walker. Twining her arms around him and pressing her body close. She could feel the contours of his chest, and his muscles beneath the fabric of his shirt. She could feel how he trembled as he responded, and how the big corded muscles of his upper arms tightened deliciously around her. Then there was the lush, enticing curve of his lower lip, and how it had moved against the sensitive nerves of hers. If only they'd been alone, Fenella could have pressed in close—and grinned wickedly up at Walker—

A needle-sharp claw dug into her ankle. *Carry me.*

"Let me get my shoes on." Fenella stamped her feet into her shoes. Luckily the cat could not read her mind. In any case, she and Walker were just going to be friends.

But why was it best to give Walker up? To please Miranda?

Because Ryland said so? Or was it because she herself was going to die? How did those things add up to saying no to Walker? Fenella couldn't remember.

Fenella's hand went without thinking to her pocket to pat the leaf. She thought of Miranda's abject misery, and of how it seemed there was no way to heal it. She thought of the tasks ahead of her and behind her, and of how her family would hate her if they knew how she was working to hurt them. She thought of Padraig regaining possession of her if she failed.

But then, compulsively and irrationally, she thought about kissing Walker again. She took in one long, deep, confused breath.

The cat was staring at her, narrow-eyed. She said briskly, "Where's the portal?"

No portal. We're meeting my sister at a park here in the human realm.

"Really?"

Ryland shrugged. *That's what she wants.*

Fenella scooped up the cat and walked as he directed. They ended up at a park located almost halfway between the old burned house and the temporary church apartment. The park featured a wide grassy expanse with swings, a basketball court, and a corner triangle that was fenced off for toddlers. It had soft sand on the ground, a colorful plastic slide in the shape of a friendly dragon, and swings with seats both small and large. Two small children were playing there while their mothers stood nearby chatting. Fenella glanced at the children and then quickly averted her eyes from them.

A familiar female sat on a swing in the grassy area. The queen, in human guise, pumped her legs to move the swing back and forth. Her long hair drifted in the breeze she created with her movement, and Fenella could hear the creak of the swing's chains.

The queen put down her feet and brought her swing to a halt. Her eye sockets were so deep, and the eyes within them so dark, that for a second in the bright sunlight it almost looked as if she had holes there instead. If the queen was indeed playing political games with her brother, Fenella thought, then she was not enjoying it.

"Hello, Fenella."

Fenella inclined her head and dipped her shoulders in a modest bow. She dumped the cat at the queen's feet.

The queen gestured to the swing next to her. Fenella sat awkwardly, twisting the swing so that she faced the queen.

The queen said, "My brother claims that your mind is wandering away from your mission. Do you have a plan for destroying love?"

Fenella gave Ryland a severe look. "I do."

"What is it?"

"The dog."

The queen blinked.

Ryland scratched expressively at his rear with a hind paw.

"My brother thinks this will not fulfill the conditions," said the queen neutrally.

"I think it will. Lucy loves that dog. He's been with her since she was a little girl. He can never be replaced. Also, no person loves as completely as a dog loves."

The queen said nothing.

"His name is Pierre." Fenella lifted her feet and let the swing untwist itself, so that it faced straight ahead. "He has an enormous heart! He loves his life. He loves his people. They love him. His death would matter."

"It might work," said the queen, though her voice was doubtful.

Ask my sister this. If killing the dog doesn't work, where are you? Can you try again?

Fenella told the queen what Ryland had said.

"No," said the queen. "If you fail at the second task, it's over. So you must be careful what you choose."

Fenella sat in silence.

There are other options, said Ryland. *I can give you a hint. There's an important love story at the heart of that family. A little deception, a little seduction . . . A marriage blows apart.*

"You mean the Markowitzes," Fenella said, deliberately obtuse. "They hold everything together."

You know who I mean.

Lucy and Zach, their fingers interlaced.

Fenella turned to the shadowed eyes of the queen. "Your brother thinks that I should try to destroy Lucy and Zach's marriage. Well, I couldn't. They're bonded by what they've been through together; what they've proven to each other. They'll be together until death. I couldn't pull them apart."

The queen closed her hands around the chains of her swing. She walked her feet backward in the dust and began swinging again, saying nothing.

If you got one to betray the other, there would be a spiral of destruction, mused Ryland. *Fighting over the little girl. Soledad and Leo and Miranda taking sides. Acts of retaliation.*

"I don't have the power to do that." Fenella gripped the metal chains of her swing. "I want to kill the dog. Listen, they have these things, cameras. I could record the dog dying and make Lucy watch."

Ryland's furry little face scrunched. *That's sick.*

Fenella's shoulders slumped. It was. She knew.

For a time only the gentle creaking of the queen's swing sounded. Then the queen spoke.

"I myself," said the queen quietly, "have intentionally done something destructive to someone I loved. So I understand that it is not easy. It may help you, in a perverse way, to know that you will certainly suffer also, both in the doing and long afterward."

Here we go, said Ryland disgustedly. *My sister's guilty vocal stylings about her little friend. I told you, didn't I, Fenella?*

"I can't do what Ryland says," said Fenella to the queen. "I wouldn't even know where to start."

Ryland sniffed.

Don't lie. Not to us, not to yourself. You know how to break up that marriage. There you were, yesterday, pressing right up against Walker.

"Walker—that's different."

Men are all different, and yet they are alike. You know what to do. Padraig made sure of that. The right herbs, the right situation, and you could make Zach unable to resist you.

"No. Zach loves Lucy. She's the only one he wants."

You can make him forget Lucy for long enough. You'd enjoy it too. You crave a man. You're actually pretty frisky, for a girl who wants to die.

"No!" Fenella lashed her voice like a whip at Ryland. "If you're so smart, if you know everything, if you're such a good adviser, then why can't you come up with a *creative* destructive idea! But you can't, can you, Ryland? You haven't got it in you!"

She felt the queen's dark eyes on her. Abruptly, the queen brought her swing to a stop.

"Fenella? I didn't come here today to go over your options with you. There is something new I must tell you. In the breaking of your life-curse, there is more at stake than your own future."

"What do you mean?" said Fenella warily.

"It turns out the two curses are entangled."

Fenella stared at the queen. She knew the feeling that was stealing over her. She knew it well.

She waited for the blow, and then it came.

"Having begun to break the life-curse, you have re-armed the family curse. Now, if you fail to break the life-curse, the family curse will be reinstated. Padraig will have not only you, but also the others. Lucy—and the child, Dawn. It will all come back again.

"So you must not hesitate in your tasks of destruction. You must succeed for your family's sake, as well as your own."

"No," said Fenella.

"Yes."

"But you never said this before." Numbness warred with a sense of betrayal. For some reason, she had trusted the queen. "You must have known!"

The queen shrugged. "Believe what you like, so long as

you believe also what I say now." The queen's voice grew harsh. "Come. You know us. You should have expected a twist along the way."

Fury filled Fenella. "There has already been one twist! This is the second. How do I know there won't be a third? How do I know this will ever end?"

"I promise it will end," said the queen. "When you have completed the third task."

"It will end when I am dead," said Fenella bitterly. "As I have always known."

She jumped from the swing and strode away.

Chapter 29

Late that afternoon, Lucy, Zach, Soledad, Leo, and Miranda returned, talking about moving into the apartment. Or rather, everyone but Miranda was talking. Miranda sat down on the edge of a chair and held her elbows. Her gaze flicked from face to face, but Fenella felt sure she was the one Miranda was watching most.

She tried to ignore her, tried to listen to the others, tried to act as if all she was thinking about was the new apartment, and, perhaps, her past with Padraig.

She felt choked by the new information about the entwined curses. It was all Fenella could do to get out words of one syllable. She stole surreptitious glances at Lucy. She wondered how long it would take Padraig to break her. Perhaps not long at all. Lucy had spent her life surrounded by love; all her strength was rooted in that. Even the queen had said so. If she was torn from her family—if all she had left was Fenella, Fenella who would have personally betrayed her—what would happen?

It would be like Bronagh, all over again.

Dawn was suddenly at Lucy's knee, asking for attention. Fenella jerked her gaze away, to her lap, so she would not have to see the child. She must not fail. That was all there was to it. Whatever it took, she must not fail.

She forced herself to focus on the conversation.

"I think we could manage there," Leo said. "It'll be crowded but fine. The rent is within the range the insurance company will reimburse. It's near the bus."

The apartment was in a wooden three-story house located down the street from the veterinary clinic where Walker worked. There were three bedrooms, one bath, a big kitchen, and a living room. There was parking for Leo's van. Cats were allowed. Dogs were not, but Sarah had confirmed that she would indeed take Pierre.

"That seems hard," Fenella managed to say. She needed to participate. She needed to appear engaged and caring. She needed her family's trust. She needed it so that she could betray them, and so save them.

Thank God she would die when she was done.

"A place for Ryland, but none for Pierre," she nattered on madly, forcing herself to look directly at Lucy.

Lucy turned her face away to bounce Dawn in her arms.

"It's only temporary," Leo said. "Just for a few months while we figure things out with the insurance company. Eventually we'll find a house of our own again, with more space and a yard for Pierre."

"But Pierre is old." Having started, Fenella simply could not stop. "What if the new house doesn't happen for a while? How will that feel? Will everybody be okay without him? Lucy? Will you? Could Pierre at least visit?" She knew why she wanted the dog near.

"Shut up, Fenella," said Miranda. "Don't bother Lucy. Don't bother anybody. You're not helping. You never help. You make things worse."

There was silence.

"I'm fine," said Lucy brightly. "Miranda, don't worry. Fenella, it's nice of you to ask."

Soledad added, "One good thing: The downstairs neighbor won't complain if there's noise, like Dawn shrieking. Walker even said he'd be willing to share the Internet bill."

"Walker lives downstairs?" Fenella said.

Lucy slanted the quickest of under-the-lashes looks at Fenella. Her smile peeped out, small but definite. "Didn't you realize?"

"No." But a second later, Fenella remembered; Walker had told her this himself. How could she have forgotten?

On the other hand, it was no wonder she had forgotten.

Despair rocked her again. How could she complete her tasks with Walker there?

And what if Ryland was correct and she could not satisfy the second task with the dog? What if she had to do . . . something else?

So far, she had not even looked at Zach. She still didn't want to look at him, but she forced herself to do it. He stood behind Lucy with his phone out. He was scanning its surface with a thumb. He wore jeans that fit his hips and legs tightly, and a T-shirt that was loose, hanging from broad shoulders. His hair fell into his face. Feeling Fenella's gaze, he looked up, shaking his hair back. He smiled briefly, compassionately, before returning attention to his phone.

Fenella looked down for Ryland. For once the cat was not underfoot, or indeed, anywhere visible. She reached out, hand shaking, for the cup of tea that Soledad had given her earlier. But then she was afraid that she would spill it, so she retracted her hand.

"We could move in quickly," said Soledad. "Maybe this weekend. It's not like we have much stuff."

"We'd have to get some things," said Zach. "Furniture. A computer."

"I'm making a list." Lucy affectionately butted her foster mother's shoulder with her head. "I put yarn on it, Mom."

"Check online, on Freecycle," Leo directed. "Look for anything and everything we need. It's amazing what people give away. I got a French horn last year."

"Which you don't know how to play," said Soledad.

"I was learning." A shade passed over Leo's face.

Fenella sat like a lump, hands clenched in her lap. The French horn too was gone.

"I'll send my list to everybody." Lucy pulled out her phone and worked it with one hand while balancing Dawn on her lap.

Zach said, "They have piles of clothing set aside here for a church sale that they said we could look at. Tonight after work? Anybody?"

"I can't," Leo said apologetically. "The next few days I have gigs booked solid. Soledad is working too."

"I can help you, Zach." Fenella's mouth had opened of its own accord, and the words popped out. They were too loud.

"Good," said Zach, simply, easily. "It's a date."

A date, Fenella thought. A date, a date, a date. Even though her hands were still shaking, she managed to grab the cup of tea and bring it to her lips.

The tea was cold. She drank it all down anyway.

Miranda stood up. "Fenella? Why don't you and I walk over to Moody Street to the thrift shop? See what we can find on Lucy's list." Miranda's voice was high and thin.

Fenella leaped to her feet so quickly, she almost overset her empty teacup. "All right."

"Can you look for kitchen stuff?" asked Lucy. "Dishes, pots and pans, silverware. I put it all on the list."

"Yes," said Fenella, when Miranda didn't answer. She was breathing easier, now that she knew she was leaving the apartment for a while.

Nothing was definite, she told herself. She had some time. She would think. She would think and think.

Love. How could she destroy love?

Leo pulled cash from his wallet. Miranda took it silently.

"Call if you need anything," Leo said, and Fenella felt that this was directed toward her, and was about Miranda. She met Leo's kind eyes and managed to nod. The least she could do was take care of Miranda.

As they walked to town, Miranda didn't speak, and so neither did Fenella. She watched Miranda, who stayed half a step ahead. Twice she jerked her whole body to the left, to keep well away from men who passed near. When they arrived at the door of the thrift shop and Miranda reached to open it, Fenella impulsively slipped her oak leaf into the back pocket of Miranda's jeans.

Having done this, though, she felt remorse and uncertainty. Without her leaf, the weight of the second task seemed to descend even more heavily on her shoulders.

What was she going to do, and how was she going to do it?

She stepped closer to Miranda, hoping the leaf could somehow help them both at once.

The thrift store was a large open space filled with mismatched tables, bookcases, and clothing racks. The various departments were marked by handmade cardboard signs. *Children's Clothing. Men's. Furniture. Books.* Fenella put a gentle hand on Miranda's arm and pointed to a sign toward the back that said *Kitchen.*

They spent some minutes silently sorting through piles. Eventually Miranda held up a plate. It was white with a tiny border of green leaves and belonged to a large matched set. "Service for twelve, twenty bucks. They're microwave safe."

Fenella nodded, even though some of the plates were scratched, and two of the bowls were missing. She liked the leaf pattern. She also liked the color in Miranda's cheeks, and the fact that she spoke without a tremble in her voice. "Let's get it," she said. "But what do you think of these little spoons? Aren't they lovely?"

"They're demitasse spoons," said Miranda dismissively. "Too small to be useful. We'll need some child-sized spoons, but those won't do."

"Oh." Fenella put the little spoons down. She slanted a glance at Miranda, who had begun to pick out forks randomly from a large bin crammed full of silverware. *Ten pieces for $1,* said the sign.

"Let's at least try to match them," Fenella said. She winced at the false cheeriness in her voice.

Miranda shrugged.

Working side by side, they put together seven matching forks, eight matching spoons, and three matching knives before Fenella realized that Miranda was crying, tears dribbling silently down her face.

She put down the spoons she held and slipped an arm around Miranda's waist. "Miranda," she whispered. "What is it?"

Miranda ducked her head down. "I'm afraid," she said, simply, quietly. "I've tried to be happy that you're here. But I'm not. I'm afraid."

The choking feeling returned to Fenella's throat. She managed to say, "The fire . . . ?"

"That didn't help. But—oh, I know it's me. I'm not well, emotionally. I understand that. But at the same time, I still feel what I feel. Every day you're here, it gets worse."

Fenella could say nothing.

"Last night, when you started talking about Padraig? I tried to listen. But every time you said his name, I could feel him. Like he's still out there, waiting. Like you've brought him back."

Miranda swiveled. Her gaze was level and her voice calm, even as she gripped Fenella's wrists. "Padraig's not dead. I can still feel him out there. I know he wants Lucy and Dawn. I know it."

Abruptly, she turned away, dropping Fenella's wrists. "But nobody will believe me. Not even you. I mean, look at you. Holding hands with Walker, learning how to fix cars, talking out your memories. Meanwhile, look at me. Crazy Miranda. Always, crazy Miranda."

Fenella could barely breathe.

"Let's not discuss it anymore," said Miranda evenly. "It's not worth words. It's just the way it is."

"But you can't live in terror." Fenella forced the words out; she hardly even knew what she was saying.

"Of course I can," said Miranda. "And I will too, until I'm dead. Or until everything I fear happens again." She wiped her face matter-of-factly with the back of her hand. "But I'd appreciate one thing."

"What?"

"Don't talk about Padraig in front of me anymore. Don't tell your story. I don't want to hear it. I can't."

"All right," said Fenella uncertainly.

"Thank you," said Miranda. "I mean that." She turned back to the task of matching forks.

Fenella looked down at her own pile of silverware.

So—Miranda knew.

Miranda knew, even if she didn't yet understand that she knew. Traumatized or not, at some point she would speak, and the others, already suspicious of Fenella, would listen.

Which meant Fenella had to act quickly. She would not have the rest of the three months.

Chapter 30

"*The car show* opens at ten," Walker said, in answer to Zach's question. "But I like to get places early."

Zach looked up from fastening Dawn into her car seat. "Whereas Lucy likes to get places late. Just saying." He laughed.

"Five minutes late," Lucy protested. "Five minutes late is always perfect!" She turned to Fenella. "I'll squeeze into the middle next to Dawn, so you get the window, okay?"

The day was not shaping up into the desperately needed one-day vacation with Walker Dobrez that Fenella had hoped for. She pasted on a smile, relieved that at least she would not have to sit next to Dawn in the car.

It was Saturday morning, and they were all going to the auto show. From the backseat of the Markowitz family car, Fenella could see the rubber band that clumped Walker's thick brown ponytail together. If she glanced to the left, she'd have a view of Zach's profile as he drove. Zach looked ready to enjoy a break from all the recent worries too. But seeing him only evoked Ryland's most recent advice.

What a great chance, Fenella. Zach and Lucy coming with you to the car show! Brush up against Zach casually while you walk. Bend over in front of him where he can't help seeing down your shirt. Do you need help to make perfume?

Fenella had promptly changed into a high-necked shirt. She had certainly not concocted the perfume. It was an earthy scent that involved a particular type of lichen. She would go to the auto show smelling of soap. And also slightly of motor oil, because she had not liked how the car engine idled yesterday and had adjusted its timing belt this morning.

It had relieved Fenella when Miranda decided not to come.

Fenella longed to tell Miranda that she wasn't crazy. That Padraig was indeed lurking; that Lucy and Dawn were indeed at risk.

That it was all Fenella's fault.

For hours last night she had lain in bed, still as death, thinking about how Lucy had solved the original tasks. Lucy had talked to her family. She had involved them, and they had worked out solutions together. Could Fenella do that? It had not been forbidden; if Ryland could advise her, why couldn't someone else too? Miranda would not even be surprised. But when Fenella imagined telling them, she quailed.

Not yet, she thought. Not unless she knew she couldn't figure it out herself. Maybe there would still be a way to maneuver cleverly, painlessly. She reminded herself of how easily she might have solved the first task, had she but recognized Miranda's fear in time.

Fenella was beginning to despair about her dog plan. It would seem odd for Fenella to visit Pierre at Sarah's. What would she do then anyway? Poison him? What if, at the last moment, she looked into Pierre's single distrustful eye and couldn't hurt him? Or, worse, suppose Ryland was correct and Pierre's death didn't solve the task?

She was afraid that she couldn't risk it.

She leaned closer to the car window, so that her forehead rested against its coolness. Outside, the wind whipped dead brown leaves along ruthlessly. A few drops of rain spattered against the car window as black clouds moved in overheard.

She reached into her pocket and fingered her oak leaf, which she had quietly reclaimed from Miranda's pocket. She needed it herself. A third of Fenella's time was gone, her family was beginning to figure things out even if they didn't realize they were, and the stakes were higher than ever.

What if Fenella—oh, God. What if she were to kill Miranda? Miranda, who defined maternal love.

No mother in all the history of the Scarborough girls had worked harder to protect her daughter than Miranda. Would this be better—more merciful—than seducing Zach? More practical than killing Pierre? It was even possible Miranda herself would agree, if Fenella could tell her what was going on. Miranda was so unhappy. But then again, Miranda, unlike Fenella, had never declared that she wanted death.

Her thoughts caused bile to press up against the back of Fenella's throat. A vision of Robert's crumpled body came to her, and she slumped in her seat. She could not kill Miranda, or anyone.

Except maybe the dog, because she had to do *something*. And she seemed not to be able to think of an idea that was— what was the queen's word?—metaphysical.

Fenella pulled her hand away from her leaf. She didn't deserve its comfort. She thought of the demand she had thrown so impetuously at Ryland, for creative destruction. Her lower lip curled. She was the worst kind of arrogant, selfish, stupid fool.

Music poured from Lucy's cell phone. "Yes!" Lucy said as she read a text message. "Jim Pearce can help with the move tomorrow. He'll do that furniture pickup in Acton."

Zach asked, "What's in Acton?"

"A queen mattress and headboard. It was from a Free-cycle ad. I hope they'll be okay."

"They'll be fine. They're free. Walker, are you coming to-morrow too?"

"Wouldn't miss it," said Walker. "I'm bringing my truck." He turned to glance toward the backseat. Fenella couldn't resist meeting his gaze. He smiled. She knew he was imag-ining the two of them together in his truck tomorrow, working the move as a team. Maybe it would be so.

But if it was, Fenella would be doing the wrong thing. Leading Walker on. Another destructive act. If only she could get credit for it. Her lips moved in a mirthless smile.

They pulled into a parking garage with walls that were high and thick and gray and hard. They piled out of the car. Lucy unfolded the stroller and set Dawn into it. She pushed the stroller as they walked in a group to a large building by the ocean. An enormous banner hung above the entrance: *New England Auto Show*. The banner shuddered in the wind above throngs of people.

Fenella felt Walker's warm, broad hand on the small of her back. With his other hand, he offered a piece of paper. "Floor map. What are you interested in? Trucks, right? Any-thing else?"

Fenella shrugged.

Just ahead, Zach handed over their tickets, and they

passed through a set of doors and into the main display space.

Fenella blinked. It was a room so wide and tall and long that it was impossible to see the walls or ceiling. It was filled with vehicles, arranged attractively as far as the eye could see, and beyond.

Right in front of them was a sleek red two-seater convertible on a platform. Both of its doors were open, revealing a white leather interior. A smiling woman dressed in silver gave Dawn a balloon with *Aston Martin* printed on it. Dawn pulled the balloon's ribbon to make it bob. She chortled.

Lucy smiled at the woman but barely glanced at the little red car. "I'm interested in the electric vehicles. And maybe the concept cars."

But Zach was not listening. "Bond," Zach said. "James Bond." He moved dreamily toward the red convertible.

"Should we split up?" Walker said. "Fenella and I can go see the trucks. We'll meet you guys maybe later?"

Lucy flicked a quick glance at Fenella, hesitating, and Fenella understood that Lucy had thought the auto show would be a friendly, casual, non-confrontational place in which to ask the long-overdue questions about the fire. But in the next second—how transparent people were sometimes—Fenella saw Lucy decide that it could wait.

She knew then. Lucy didn't want to ask; Lucy was afraid to ask. She would force herself, and soon, because she was the kind of person who did what she had to do. But it would not be today.

"Sure." Lucy looked at Zach, who was talking animatedly to two other guys about the car. "I'll text you."

"Okay." Walker smiled at Fenella. "We're on our own."

Fenella smiled back. She couldn't help it; his face was so open, so warm. She watched Lucy maneuver Dawn's stroller away and all at once began to feel better. Perhaps the day could be a vacation after all.

She had a day with Walker. With Walker and with cars. Cars and trucks. Inanimate objects that did what they were designed to do. That did not trick you or betray you or hurt you. She would enjoy it. Couldn't she do that? Couldn't she have this one day?

She would.

The feeling of relief made her almost giddy. She revolved slowly in a circle, gripping her map. Where to start?

Over there, a clutch of shiny cars were lined up from smallest to largest, their hoods invitingly open; their engines gleamingly clean. An ordinary-looking van was parked in the opposite direction. It was not unlike the one Leo used, but inside its sliding side door, Fenella glimpsed the most preposterous thing: a kitchen, complete with a stove and refrigerator and table for two. She took a step toward it and realized that there was a small sofa in there too. It was a tiny house! A van-house! Well, why not?

There, over to the right in the distance, there were giant tires, higher than her head, holding up—

It penetrated that Walker was saying something about trucks, and pointing beyond the cars with the open hoods.

Words burst from Fenella. "Yes! I want to see the trucks. But let's go look in those engines over there first. And then . . ."

Chapter 3-1

In the late afternoon, the crowds inside the convention center thinned. Lucy and Zach left to take Dawn home, with Zach promising to come back to pick up Fenella and Walker when called. Happy to be even more alone with Walker, Fenella took her pen and crossed out the part of her map that said *Jeep*. She said to Walker, "Toyota next? It says here that they have hybrids."

"Sure." Walker pushed one hand through his loose hair. When he had gone with Fenella to look underneath the electric Mitsubishi MiEV, he had somehow lost the rubber band for his ponytail. "I'm surprised you didn't want to see the hybrids before."

"I needed to focus on gas and electric engines separately, first."

Fenella had spent a delightful day crawling under cars

and poking inside engines. She had read data on emissions, and discussed fuel economy, deep-sea drilling, and long-range oil pipelines with anybody who came near and showed an interest.

She had also had many questions for the car manufacturers' representatives. At a certain point, however, they all became annoyed. She was told, in these exact words: "You don't understand the laws of physics, young lady." She stopped asking after that.

It was maddening. As if she needed to be told that she didn't understand physics. Of course she didn't. Nobody did! You didn't have to spend four hundred years in Faerie to realize that the so-called physical laws were not really laws at all. Human scientists understood this, no problem. One of them, Albert Einstein, who was so acclaimed that he'd come up several times even in Fenella's limited reading, had said it plainly. Yet these car salespeople talked as if there were rigid and incontrovertible rules.

As she studied engines and how they burned fuel, Fenella couldn't help wondering how much further she might push human knowledge, herself, if she had the opportunity to try. There were baseline presumptions in other people's minds involving physical reality that she simply didn't share. If she were to go to school and study; if she were able to talk and learn and experiment with people who *thought* about these things—knowing what she already knew, having experienced what she had already experienced . . . what might happen?

Walker said, "Can we grab something to eat? It's after five o'clock. You only had that pretzel at lunch."

"It was delicious." Fenella consulted her map again. "The food court is in the opposite direction. We only have today. I don't want to miss anything."

"We'll be quick. I'll be happy with a hot dog. I can cram it into my mouth in three bites."

"But—"

"Two bites."

"But what if there are long lines, like at lunch?"

"Hey, look, I promise we won't leave this convention center until you've seen everything you want. Even if we have to hide out here after they close." Walker was grinning.

Fenella smiled too. "In that case, we can sit down to eat."

"My digestion thanks you."

"I don't want you to starve."

"How thoughtful." Walker motioned. "This way."

If only Walker hadn't been joking, Fenella thought. If only they really could spend the night here at the auto show. They could stay in the van-house; she had discovered that the van's sofa folded out into a bed . . .

She quickly steered her mind somewhere safer.

Soon they were settled on one side of a large round table, with hot dogs and drinks and a large pretzel for Fenella, and with their legs aligned side by side beneath the table, not quite touching but not quite apart either. A noisy family group occupied the rest of the table, but it was easy to forget they were there.

Absently, Fenella put her hand on her pocket where her leaf thrummed gently. It was happy, Fenella thought, because she was happy.

She looked frankly at Walker over her pretzel and discovered he was looking back. For no reason, she blushed.

"A penny," he said.

"What?"

"For your thoughts."

It took a second for Fenella to figure out what he was asking. For once, she could answer with the truth. "I'm happy," she said simply.

"Me too." Walker's voice was soft. Fenella leaned closer on the excuse of needing to hear better. Then her face was only inches from his. It seemed natural—inevitable—that he cupped her face between his hands. He kissed the tip of her nose and then withdrew an inch, smiling. She smiled back, and waited for a real kiss, on the lips. But he moved back.

She understood. He thought they had all the time in the

world. So she didn't move in on him, because it was also sweet—well, bittersweet—to be for today what he thought she was.

She offered him half of her pretzel.

"Have you always been interested in engines?" Walker asked.

"Just lately." Fenella hesitated. "I'm sort of fixated on them. You might have noticed. I've been dragging you all over the place today, haven't I? Demanding we see this and that."

"I enjoy it. I invited you here, remember?"

"Yes." It came to Fenella that maybe Walker hadn't actually planned on spending the whole entire day at the auto show, from opening to closing. A few hours had obviously been more than enough for Lucy and Zach. "If you don't want to go look at the Toyota hybrids, we could go do something else," she offered.

Walker had been drinking, and at this, the liquid went down the wrong pipe. Fenella pounded him helpfully on the back. "You can't mean that," he said when he had recovered.

"I do."

"Liar."

"Well, you've indulged me all day long. We should do what you want to do next. That would be fine with me too.

It will still have been the best day that I ever—" Something caught in her throat. "I mean, it's been a really wonderful day. For which I have to, you know." Why was she whispering? "Thank you," Fenella finished, in a raw little rush.

There was a pause.

Now their legs were touching beneath the table, from thigh to knee to calf to ankle to foot.

"Let me clarify," Walker said at last. "I don't particularly care about seeing the hybrids. But I want *you* to see them. And I want to watch you see them."

Walker looked straight into Fenella's eyes. Fenella looked back. He's going to kiss me, Fenella thought. But he didn't.

"I like watching you enjoy yourself." Walker's voice dropped to a near whisper. "I have the feeling that you . . . How to put this? That you haven't enjoyed yourself all that much in your life." He stopped before adding, deliberately, "For a long time."

His eyes were as brown as the mulch of leaves on the ground in the wetness of early spring.

"And—I hope this doesn't offend you, but I have to tell you: I wonder. Why did you leave your past behind and come live with relatives you'd never met? What was your life before? What happened to you? Why did Miranda say you needed time?"

Walker's voice got, if possible, even lower. "What are you

running from? Who are you? There's only one thing I'm sure of, and it's that you have a story. A story and a past."

There was no accusation in Walker's words, and also no demand for an answer. But she had to give him something. She *had* to. She put her hand on her leaf for courage.

"Yes," she said hoarsely. "I do."

"You'll tell me someday," Walker said, with certainty.

Fenella shook her head helplessly.

"No pressure. No worries. There's as much time as you need."

They had until ten o'clock, when the auto show would close. That was all, because tomorrow was moving day.

Also, she had decided.

Tomorrow was the second task. And so, there would be no someday, for she knew what she was going to do.

She said, "No worries."

"Good." Walker got up. "Want to go look at Toyota hybrids?"

"Yes," said Fenella. "I really do."

Chapter 32

Early the next morning, Fenella captured Ryland. Once he understood her purpose, he struggled, trying to scratch and bite, all the while sending a stream of invective-laced thoughts into her head. One curse was particularly creative, having to do with the excretion of a fire ant army that had picnicked on hemlock.

She tried to detach his claws from the rim of the cat carrier's gate. "It's moving day. Everybody will think it's strange if you're not locked safely away."

Ryland stopped struggling. *I suppose so.* He looked sullen, however. Fenella pushed him the rest of the way inside the carrier and clicked the gate shut.

Because of donations from friends and the community, there was a surprising amount of stuff to move. A list on the kitchen table had all the particulars. Fenella wasn't sure how many people and how many trucks were involved with the move; she only knew that everybody was meeting here for breakfast at seven a.m.

Zach was always awake early, before Lucy, before everybody.

Fenella stared pensively at Ryland. He scowled back.

I hate this cage. Also, I don't think you're putting me in here because of the move. I think you're up to something, and you don't want me to know.

"Not at all," said Fenella gruffly. "I'm taking the good advice you already gave me. Seduction, remember?"

She met the cat's stare through the bars of the cage.

But you need me to coach you through it.

"You told me that I already know what to do. It's true."

Do you have the perfume?

Fenella nodded. She had arisen last night and slipped outside for the key ingredient. "Can't you smell it?"

Did you tune it to Zach, specifically?

"Of course I did." Although in fact she had forgotten.

Ryland paused for so short a time that it could have been Fenella's imagination. Then he nodded. *It really is best. Other things* might *work, but this definitely will. I only hope it won't be too painful for you.*

Fenella was taken aback. Compassion? For her? From Ryland? Surely not.

He curled up on the bottom of the carrier. She placed it in the apartment's downstairs bathroom and went into the kitchen. She felt fine. Not nervous. Calm.

This would not be like the fire. There would be no deniability and no doubt about what she had done. There would be no family afterward. Not for her, and possibly not for any of them, either.

But maybe later they would heal. If any family could, it would be this one.

She hoped.

Fenella pulled at the top of the coffeemaker. There was a hidden compartment in which the coffee should be placed, but she couldn't find it. She hit the machine with her fist.

"Hey, Fenella. Morning. Let me do the coffee, okay?"

It was Zach, behind her. Her shoulders tensed. Perhaps she wasn't ready after all.

She moved a few inches to the left and watched as Zach opened the coffeemaker. He reached for filters and coffee.

When precisely do you think you will be ready?

The snide voice wasn't Ryland, of course; he was locked away. It was her own internal voice, telling her what he would say.

Because this was a good time. Zach was up. Lucy probably was stirring too, as this was moving day. She might walk into the kitchen at any moment.

Zach was still dressed for sleeping, in sweatpants and a faded, ragged T-shirt. His feet were bare, and his hair was tousled, and his eyes looked tired. Still hesitating, Fenella watched him measure coffee. He had strong forearms nicely roped with muscle and arteries.

Fenella had envied Lucy before. Now she felt nothing except the bleak necessity of going forward.

She stepped close. She brushed up against Zach, and saw him glance down at her, startled at the contact. She smiled up at him.

Then she cast out the fragile cobwebs of sexual allure. It was a matter of intention, of eye contact, and finally, of scent. Scent could not be defended against. Scent spoke directly, animal to animal. Scent undermined and weakened and convinced.

A hundred small signs told Fenella that her message had been received. The minute warming of Zach's skin. The involuntary change in his own scent. And of course the fact that—you didn't need Faerie training to perceive this—for a few shocked seconds he ceased to breathe.

Fenella leaned forward, pretending great interest in the coffeemaker. If Zach looked down, he would see inside the gaping front of her shirt, where she was not wearing the harness called a bra.

He looked down.

She possessed nothing that Lucy didn't also have, but what mattered, in the sexual trance, was that she was a different version. Different in shape and weight and texture. Softer in some places, harder in others. Her skin had a different tone and her sweat a different taste. The enticement, the promise, of the differences . . . all wrapped up in the scent.

The scent.

Zach's hands jerked and the coffee grinds spilled all over the counter.

Fenella slipped her body between Zach and the counter. She put her hands on his hips and held him unmistakably against her.

For a long moment, neither of them moved.

Then, to Fenella's surprise, Zach broke away. A second later, he was all the way across the kitchen. His face was flushed. He looked horribly confused, and guilty, and angry. And lustful.

Fenella smiled at him knowingly. He was still linked to her; she could smell it.

Odd that he'd had the strength to break away. But it didn't matter, she told herself, so long as she kept her resolve. If she couldn't seduce him right here and now, on the kitchen floor, then it would be soon. She would have lost the element of surprise, but it would be made up for by the strength of his imagination. She had sent the poison into his system. He might struggle, but he wouldn't escape if she acted soon. He would fantasize meanwhile.

Zach had his spine pressed up against the refrigerator. "We'll forget this," he whispered.

He'd have backed right out of the room, Fenella thought, except that he wasn't sure at the moment where the door was located.

She shook her head. "I won't forget."

Deliberately, she turned her back. She bent to clear up the spilled coffee grinds, aware of his gaze still on her body, aware of the exact second he managed to flee the room.

Or had she let him go?

No.

Surely not.

She finished making the pot of coffee. After a while, the first volunteers arrived.

Chapter 33

The morning wore on. Fenella said no more to Zach. She glanced at him from time to time, as if casually, while people moved boxes and furniture in preparation for the move. He did not look back, and he did not look well, and he kept as far away from Fenella as he could.

Nonetheless, awareness ran between them, taut and thick.

She felt disembodied. Watching herself watch Zach. Watching Zach watch Lucy. Once, she put her hand into her pocket, where she had placed the leaf. She felt its tendrils of calm, but they too seemed distant. The leaf could not, or did not, tell her what to do.

I must go ahead, she told herself. I must. It will save Lucy from Padraig. She knew it was true. But she tasted bile in her throat just the same, pushing up through an unholy stew of shame and despair, of anger and fear.

However, the stew contained something else, as well: hope that she was making the right choice—the least bad choice.

She clung to this like moss to bark.

Zach tried to stay near Lucy, which was not easy because Lucy was always on the move. She had a pair of sunglasses perched on her nose and a Boston Red Sox cap on her head. Once all the boxes were gathered outside, she whistled—startlingly loudly, with two fingers in her mouth.

"Miranda, let's see, could you just take Dawn to the park? Jacqueline and Soledad are driving to the new apartment in Jacqueline's car. You'll be cleaning and then unpacking the kitchen stuff, and making the beds. Fenella, you and I will be based here for a couple hours, directing traffic. Amy and Mark, I think you said you were willing to go to Somerville to get those beds, right? Zach, I have you and Sarah taking her parents' van up to Portsmouth for the kitchen set. Then you'll stop in Newbury for the TV and bookshelves, and then in Lexington for the toddler clothing. God, that's a lot you and Sarah are doing—is it okay?"

Zach hovered close to Lucy. "Why don't you come with me instead of Sarah?"

"I need to to clean up here and direct things."

"Can't Fenella do that? With Sarah instead of you?" Zach didn't look at Fenella.

Lucy shook her head. "I want to do it." She consulted her list. "Dad?"

"What?" said Leo, who'd been out on a gig until late. He leaned against Soledad and issued a loud, fake snore.

"As soon as Walker gets here, you're going with him in his truck."

Walker's truck. Walker. Ferocious longing caught Fenella unprepared. It seared through her, anchoring her again in her body. Walker—that was healthy, that was right. Her whole body knew it. Whereas this . . . this *thing* she was doing—

She summoned back the disconnected feeling of floating. She reminded herself of the consequences of failure.

"You could nap for a few minutes, love," Soledad was saying to Leo.

"No, our daughter won't let me."

"I could go with Zach," said Fenella abruptly, loudly. "Lucy, Sarah could be here with you."

Zach's eyes flared. "Um, I, well," he stuttered.

Then he said, simply, "Lucy."

Fenella was astonished that Lucy didn't hear how his voice caught as he spoke.

But Lucy was nodding abstractly, "Okay, fine, thanks, Fenella. Zach, Fenella's with you. Sarah's with me."

Zach went pale. For a fraction of an instant, he looked across and met Fenella's eyes.

And he gave up. She felt it happen. The darkest part of Zach was in thrall to her. It was the impulse of chaos; and because he was so young, it was a part of him that he had little knowledge of, and absolutely no experience controlling.

When it was over, Fenella knew, Zach would blame not only her, but himself. He would spiral down relentlessly into the darkness . . .

She knew what would happen. She could see it.

Zach confessing to Lucy. Lucy's horror. How she'd run to her parents. Their reaction. Zach being asked to move out. Dawn's bewilderment at the disappearance of her father. It was even possible that Zach, full of self-hatred, would then—

Yes. The ripples of destruction would spread outward and destroy them all, shattering the Scarborough-Greenfield-Markowitzes. Even if, eventually, Fenella had an opportunity to explain, it would be too late and it would do little good.

Fenella would not have to watch for long, she told herself. She would be dead. She would get the third task done as quickly as possible and then she would die, so she would feel nothing. Nothing—

Walker was there.

The floating feeling that had protected Fenella dissolved completely. Her body tensed with awareness. Walker was close behind her, so close she could reach out a hand and lay it flat against his chest. It seemed to her that his presence filled the entire room. She turned to look at him; she had to.

"No, no," Walker said. He had never looked happier. "Send Leo with Zach. Fenella can come with me." He had Fenella's elbow cupped warmly in his hand. She turned with him. She moved with him. She let him steer her toward his truck.

And—deliberately or not, she was never sure—she let the thread of power between her and Zach snap.

She stumbled. She would have fallen except for Walker's arm coming around her in support. "You okay?"

Fenella didn't answer. They had reached the passenger side of the truck. The seat was already occupied. The dog Pierre stood on the seat with his head hanging out the open window, his one good eye fixed yearningly on Lucy, who had just come outside too.

The dog barked.

Across the yard, Lucy looked up, saw him, and smiled. The dog scrambled through the open window of the truck, leaped down, and raced to her.

Pierre.

Her alternative plan formed instantly in Fenella's head.

She looked up at Walker. "Can I drive?"

"I'd better do it today."

"Come on. You know I'm competent. I'll enjoy it so much."

He held out for a few seconds more, looking down into her eyes. Then he grinned. "All right."

"Great. I need to get something from the house first—I'll be right back."

Fenella passed Lucy and Pierre on her way in, and then again on her way out. The dog was up on his hind legs, licking Lucy's face. Lucy had her arms around him. She was ruffling his head and laughing.

Lucy loves that dog, Fenella reassured herself. That dog loves her. It will count. It *must* count.

Please, oh, please.

Nobody was looking when Fenella climbed behind the wheel of the truck, and Walker got in on the passenger side. Nobody watched while Fenella adjusted the mirrors. Nobody paid attention as she started the engine and backed competently out of the wide driveway of the church.

She paused, then, foot on the brake.

Everyone—Zach, Soledad, Leo, Miranda holding Dawn, and the crew of volunteers—was listening to Lucy. Pierre lay contentedly on the ground with his chin resting on the toe of Lucy's sneaker.

Walker said, "Fenella, turn left at the end of the street and then—"

He never finished his sentence. As he spoke, the cat slipped around the door of the apartment, which Fenella had left ajar. Ryland raced directly toward Pierre, making the kind of noise an ordinary cat might make if he were being boiled alive.

The dog leaped to his feet. Dog and cat collided into each other, amid snarling and barking. A whirling dervish of tumbling fur moved across the fading autumn grass so quickly that it was difficult to recognize where one animal began and the other ended.

The sharpest possible gaze, however, might have noticed that it was the cat controlling the direction of their combined movement.

Into the road.

Walker swore, reaching to unlatch his seat belt. Before his fingers could connect, the mass of frenzied fur rolled in front of the truck.

Fenella shifted gears and stomped on the accelerator.

Chapter 34

She didn't want to see; she couldn't bear to watch. As the truck jolted forward, Fenella closed her eyes.

She heard Walker yell her name. She felt his hand grab hers on the gearshift. But she was already in second gear, heading toward where the dog would be.

Simultaneously, however, Fenella's other hand moved, on the wheel of the truck. It moved independently of both her brain and her will.

She jerked the wheel hard to the left, to avoid the dog.

It was too late. She knew it within a second. The impact of the collision was unmistakable.

Fenella slammed on the brakes. The truck rocked to a halt. She tasted salt in her mouth.

She could hear screaming. It was a woman's voice.

Maybe she would never open her eyes again.

The salt in her mouth was from blood; she had bitten into her lower lip.

She could hear Walker's urgent voice but she couldn't comprehend what he was saying. He forced her numb right hand away from the stick shift. His foot kicked hers away from the floor controls. He did something else and the truck engine died.

A single fact penetrated slowly into Fenella's mind. The dog was alive. Pierre was barking, a frenzied healthy barking that was edging into a full-throated howl. The barking was intermingled with the screaming.

The dog was alive and well, yet the truck had hit *something*. Something heavy. Heavier than Pierre?

Fenella could understand the voices now, hear what they were saying.

"Oh my God, oh my God!"

"Call 9-1-1!"

Who did I hit? Fenella thought. Who?

She was frozen with dread.

Then came a keening even worse than the dog's, a human keening. It was a special kind of noise—Fenella knew it well. She had made it herself, once.

It was the sound that a woman makes over the dead body of her lover.

Please, Fenella prayed. Not Zach. I know death must

come for him and Lucy someday. But please not while they're so young.

Let me not have done this.

Let him live.

In that moment she knew: It would have been better if she had seduced Zach. At least, then, there would have been the possibility of healing, of forgiveness, of renewal.

Death ended those possibilities. Death ended all possibility.

How could this have happened? This was the one thing she had sworn she would not do.

Shakily, Fenella reached into her pocket for the oak leaf, desperate for its comforting pulse. She curled her fingers around the leaf.

It did not pulse.

It had abandoned her, she thought. She straightened her fingers and let the leaf fall from them. She buried her face in her hands.

Beside her, the truck door was wrenched open from the outside. Walker grabbed her arm and pulled her down, out. Whatever he was saying still did not penetrate, though his urgency did.

Fenella's legs were weak. She fell onto her hands and knees beside the truck. Walker did not catch her. He was no longer there at all; she felt his absence.

Of course he had gone. Walker would hate her now too. They all would.

What had she done, what had she done, what had she done?

Screaming tore through Fenella's head like a hundred steel blades. It was inside and outside her head. Sirens were shrilling, coming closer. There was hard pavement beneath her hands and knees. She pushed herself into a sitting position. She grabbed her knees and pressed her body against her thighs, curling small. She rocked back and forth, eyes shut.

Then came the brush of soft fur against her side.

Fenella.

It was Ryland. Fenella managed to move her lips. "What's going on? Who—" She swallowed. "Who did I hit?"

You didn't do it on purpose?

"No. No! It was—I changed my mind—it was an accident."

Silence.

"I'm begging you," she whispered. "Tell me. I can't bear to look. It's Zach, isn't it? I've killed Lucy's husband."

Finally, Ryland spoke again in her head, his tone quite dispassionate.

It's not Zach. It's Leo. He ran into the road. I suppose he was hoping to grab the dog in time. But then you swerved and hit him *instead.*

Fenella felt at first a shameful rush of relief. Not Zach. But then—

"Leo's dead?" she said numbly.

She could envision Leo Markowitz's face, intent, leaning over a guitar. She could almost hear his voice, lifted in song. And now she recognized that the woman's voice she heard, the voice whose keening had turned into a low whimper, was Soledad's.

She did not need to open her eyes to know that Soledad was beside Leo's body. Cradling her husband in her arms. Begging him to wake up.

She had done the same for Robert.

Ryland said: *Your veterinarian friend is doing what he can. But it doesn't look good.*

"I didn't mean it," whispered Fenella. "I was trying to hit the dog."

You're not making sense. You swerved away from the dog.

"I know."

After all my work too. I did what you told me to. You're sure you didn't see Leo coming, and improvise? You didn't simply realize that hitting him was a better solution?

"No. No! Leo shouldn't have been there. It was a mistake. Also, I—I had my eyes closed."

A pause. Then: *You are an extremely frustrating young woman.*

Fenella did not reply. She listened to Soledad's keening.

The good news, said the cat, finally, *is that you have succeeded at the second task. You have destroyed love.*

At this, Fenella opened her eyes. She looked straight on at the destruction she had wrought. She looked at her family. Lucy and Zach and Soledad and Miranda. And yes, Walker. They all had their backs to her.

As they should.

It had only been a few minutes since the accident. The sirens sounded closer. Help would be here soon. Eventually they would remember her. Then Walker would tell them that it had been Fenella in the driver's seat.

She thought of her dead leaf, fallen in the cab of Walker's truck.

"Ryland?" she whispered.

What?

"Can you please, please, please get me out of here?"

Yes, said the cat. *Let's go see my sister and find out about the third task.*

Chapter 35

A fire truck, an ambulance, and two police cars roared down the street. The vehicles pulled between Fenella and Ryland and the accident.

Fenella managed to push to her feet and totter after the cat. Ryland paused by a leafy rhododendron bush. He gestured with his head for Fenella to slip behind the bush. He twined himself around Fenella's ankles and then they were in mist.

Three steps forward, then two to the left.

The mist drifted off on a gentle breeze.

They stood on a winding, worn stone path that lay inside the archway of a private little walled garden. Beyond the garden's low walls, covered with delicate new ivy, Fenella could see a green forest and, farther away, the purple outlines of mountains.

The garden itself seemed designed to please a domestically minded human woman. It was both pretty and cozy, with riotous flowerbeds. On the garden wall, a magpie preened its long tail. Above, the sun shone down benevolently from a lovely blue sky.

Fenella looked toward the forest. Were any of the tree fey present? Her hand crept into her pocket to touch the leaf that was no longer there.

This place again, Ryland complained. *I hate this garden. My sister should stay away, but she likes to torture herself. Look, there she is. At least she's not pretending to be Mallory Tolliver.*

In the small stone clearing at the center of the garden, under a tall oak, stood a chair formed from flowering vines and the roots of the living tree. Queen Kethalia sat in it.

Seeing Fenella and Ryland, the queen rose. Her strong hawk's wings flared out behind her and she lifted a clawed hand in an ambiguous gesture that could have been either waving or beckoning.

With Ryland slinking beside her, Fenella moved to the queen. The queen reached out her clawed hands, as if she wanted Fenella to take them. Fenella barely touched the hands. She stood awkwardly.

"How are you, Fenella?"

"I did it," Fenella said heavily. "At least, Ryland thinks so."

"Yes. The second task is complete. I can feel the difference in your body. You are nearly free." The queen's tone was neutral. "But you don't look happy."

"He was a nice man, the man I killed. Leo Markowitz." Fenella paused, and then words came out in a rush. "You would have liked his music. They—my family—will miss him terribly. He was Lucy's father, the only one she ever knew. And his wife—they were married many years—her name is Soledad. She—they—everybody was so kind to me."

She felt pressure behind her eyes and in her throat. But murderers had no right to tears.

"You have indeed destroyed love," said the queen, almost gently.

"There is no going back." Fenella's voice was strangely high.

The spotted lizard crawled out from the mass of the queen's hair. She stroked him gently with one finger. "Have your feelings changed?"

"Which feelings do you mean?"

The queen scratched her lizard's back with a careful claw. "Do you still want to die?"

Fenella exploded, incredulous. "More than ever! Especially now, I deserve—" She stopped speaking. Her eyes flickered.

"What?"

"I *deserve* death," Fenella said. "Not as reward. As punishment. No. Death is too good for me."

The queen made a gesture, inviting Fenella to sit on the living chair that was formed of tree roots and vines. The branches of the seat accommodated themselves to Fenella's shape, cradling her.

Fenella put her head in her hands. "I thought I was trapped before. I was willing to do anything to free myself. But now I have killed, and—it was an accident. Killing Leo, completing the second task. I have done two terrible things. To my own family! There will be a third task ahead. And I must do it—for their sake now, not mine. To save Lucy and the child."

"Yes." The queen restored the lizard to her shoulder. "You must go forward."

Fenella took in the multitude of shades of green and brown and orange that composed the flowing mix of hair and fur and feather cascading from the queen's head and the nape of her neck, noted the way the cascade melted into the feathers of the queen's wings. So beautiful; so alien. Yet the queen looked kind, even sad.

"You warned me at the start. I should never have accepted the tasks."

"I understand," the queen said. "I too have walked the path of destruction, and seen no way out."

Fenella asked sharply, "You didn't *choose* to pursue destruction, though, did you?"

"No. But destruction was where I found myself. I played my role."

"It wasn't the same," said Fenella. "I know about this. You went into your mission with the goal of saving others. Your intentions were honorable."

"Do you think, then, that good intention excuses bad action?" asked the queen. "Do you think it is allowable to destroy one person in order to save many?"

Fenella slipped from the tree chair onto her knees. She looked all the way up into the queen's face. "I can't do anything else to them! I can't complete the third task."

"You are declaring defeat, then? You will belong to Padraig, and you will condemn Lucy and her child to this as well?"

Fenella thought of Walker, and of how he had looked at her. "Someday," he'd said. Walker would not want that someday anymore. At this moment he would be denouncing her to her family.

"I wish I had never agreed to this," Fenella said hopelessly. "No matter the outcome, I have done too much harm."

"There can be healing, though. On the other side of pain and suffering."

Fenella shook her head. "I don't believe it."

The queen persisted. "People can recover from even the worst blows. They mend and go on with their lives."

Fenella thought of how her family had rallied after the loss of their home. She thought of how Lucy and Zach had fought through great terror together. But—

"These are tasks of destruction! By definition, they do terrible, irrecoverable harm. Even when people mend, they've changed. They're damaged."

"Doesn't the regular process of life, and all its normal tragedies, change people anyway? Didn't you say so at the beginning of all this?"

"This is different," said Fenella.

"How?"

"Because I'm the one doing the damage."

"That matters to you now?"

Fenella glanced down at Ryland, who was sitting sphinx-like on the ground, small head alert. The queen did not look at her brother at all.

Fenella's voice was sharper. "I've become an arsonist and a murderer. Do you think I like that?"

The queen snapped back, "So it's all about you, not your family? You don't like giving up your vision of yourself as a poor little tortured martyr? You'd rather return to having no agency at all?"

Fenella gasped.

"It is not bad," said the queen, more calmly, "that you decided to be active. That you wanted to take control of your life, to pursue what you desired."

"But I chose destruction."

"You also chose change."

Fenella was silent for a moment. "I don't understand. Is change always destructive?"

"How else is room made in the world for the new?"

"But . . . but . . . do you *approve* of what I'm doing? Is that what you're saying? I killed a man! A good man! All because I would not stay quiet and accept my lot."

"I did not say I approved. Or that I disapproved. Neither of which matters, by the way. This is your own path."

"I'm confused," said Fenella tightly.

"And angry," said the queen.

Fenella tilted her chin. "And angry."

The queen looked beyond Fenella, finally, at Ryland. He got up and stretched. He trotted over to the edge of the clearing, turned a disdainful back to them, and sat down— still well within earshot. The queen laughed then, low.

Fenella said, "At the beginning, you told me Ryland was good only at destruction."

"I did," said the queen neutrally.

"And now you say destruction has its place."

"I do."

"You also told me you wouldn't speak in riddles!" said Fenella with frustration. "But you do. First destruction is bad. Then destruction is change, and it's maybe good, or at least inevitable. And the tasks themselves—they have turned out to be riddles too."

There was a silence.

"I am new at my job," said the queen. "Choices in life are indeed riddles. And creation is all mixed up with destruction. You cannot have one without the other. I don't think I fully understood that before either." She paused. "What I also now see is that riddles are sometimes the only way to express truth."

Nonsense, Ryland said. He had moved when she was not looking and was now at Fenella's feet. *Ask her about the third task already.*

Fenella nodded grimly. She would do the third task. She would do it as quickly and as mercifully as she could, but she would do it. She would see Lucy and her daughter safe from Padraig before she died. She had to.

She turned to the queen again.

The queen said, "The last task is the destruction of hope."

Chapter 36

Queen Kethalia slipped away. Fenella was left alone with Ryland.

"Hope?" Fenella said uncertainly. "The answer to this one *has* to be metaphysical, then? It doesn't seem as if it could be violent."

At least, she hoped so.

That depends on your definition of violence.

"Violence is what I just did," Fenella snapped. Bile rose in her throat again, and she swallowed it. "I won't go there again."

The cat flicked his tail. *You can't afford to wallow in misery over what you've done. Or be too picky over what you do next. My advice is to get it over with.*

He leaped to the top of the stone wall, turned around three times, and then sat. *This will be the hardest of all.*

There's no more getting close to your family and surprising them.

Fenella wrapped her arms around herself. "My family will also be speculating about a faerie reason for what I did. They'll be angry, as well as deep in grief. Miranda knows a lot about Faerie. She and Lucy and Zach were already suspicious after the fire. Lucy will be relentless. Miranda will share her suspicions. Also, Zach will tell them . . ."

That you tried to seduce him?

"Nothing happened." Perhaps it was wrong to feel grateful for that, given that she had then done something even more terrible. But it was all Fenella had. She said, "I wouldn't be surprised if they were hunting for me this minute."

They might guess you're in Faerie, said Ryland. *But it's the police who will be searching for you in the human realm.*

"What? Who?" For a moment Fenella was confused. Then she remembered Lucy mentioning the police, after the fire.

Ryland said patiently, *The police are the authorities charged with keeping the peace and controlling criminals. If we hadn't slipped away when we did, they would surely have taken you away with them to be questioned. They arrived as we left. Remember hearing the sirens?* Ryland paused thoughtfully. *Maybe they took your veterinarian friend away already.*

"Walker? But I was the one who hit Leo, not Walker."

It was his vehicle. It might be his responsibility too. I'm not sure how their laws work in a situation like this. There could be a criminal charge against him.

"Oh," said Fenella blankly. "Why didn't you warn me how complicated all of this would be, with police and everything?"

Ryland was snide. *I thought you were going to kill the dog, remember? Or seduce Zach.*

Fenella scowled. She said nothing.

Anyway, here we are now. We'll have to keep you away from the police, or you'll be locked up. And soon they'd find out that you don't exist legally, and we'd be in the soup even more. You would never get a chance to perform the third task.

Fenella discovered she was sitting on the ground again. She pulled her knees up to her chest and wrapped her arms around her legs. She was a murderer. She accepted that. But had she inadvertently destroyed Walker too? It seemed there was no way to control the ripples of destruction.

Compulsively, she imagined Walker telling her family how Fenella had begged to learn to drive his truck. How she had kissed him, then spurned him, and then turned to him again. Zach had his story to tell too. Maybe they would all decide together that her behavior with Walker had been part of her plan.

She was truly guilty of so much, and yet the thought of this one injustice stabbed so deep, it felt almost like physical pain. Her time with Walker had been the one small pleasure she had. Now she had ruined that too.

On top of being an arsonist and a murderer.

She said to Ryland, "If I went to my family and told them it was all Padraig's fault, would they believe me? Would that buy me time for the third task?"

What do you think?

Fenella didn't believe they would listen to her for a millisecond. But she tried to convince herself. "If I told them that hitting Leo was an accident—which it *was*—maybe they'd take me in again for a short time. Long enough for me to destroy hope."

Do you have a plan for that? Ryland tilted his head curiously.

"No." The truth was that Fenella couldn't imagine ever having another plan. Her head felt like it was full of sand.

But to encourage herself, she said, "After the third task, when I'm mortal again and they are safe, I'll kill myself in the human realm. I'll make sure they find my dead body. It'll be like a gift to them."

On top of the wall, Ryland said nothing.

Fenella went on wildly. "But it would be best if I could figure out the third task without needing to see them." She bit her fingers hard. "Ryland?" She hated the plea in her voice. "Could I stay here in Faerie to figure out the third task? Then I'd pop out and—and destroy hope. Quickly. Somehow."

"But you hate it in Faerie," said a new voice.

The voice was behind Fenella.

It was a voice that made her skin shrivel and her throat clench and her blood turn icy. Even though she had succeeded in two out of three tasks; even though she could hear that the voice was only a thread of sound.

The Mud Creature! said Ryland, annoyed. *What is my sister thinking, to release him here now? She knows we have work to do. Tell him to go away, Fenella.*

Fenella could guess what the queen had been thinking. That this would stiffen Fenella's resolve to go forward. That seeing Padraig would push her into action.

That she needed the reminder.

Padraig went on. "You hated Faerie from the first moment I brought you here. You were my guest at the ball. Remember, my sweet? It wasn't the night either of us had planned. Nothing has gone as planned, since that night. But now you want to linger here. I hope the irony doesn't escape you. Dare I hope that you're changing your mind about living here in the future? With me? Dare I hope that you will restore everything back to the way it was?"

Fenella did not look. She breathed.

She remembered.

Why aren't you talking? Are you still afraid of that weak nitwit? Ryland's voice was incredulous. *Look at him! Just look!*

Padraig said, "My Fenella. Still so pretty. Yes, keep your eyes downcast. That's how it should be."

Fenella? Ryland said again.

Fenella scrambled to her feet. She turned. Ryland was also on his feet atop the wall. He was beside her as she faced Padraig.

See? See the Mud Creature now?

Fenella's eyes widened. This was not the same Padraig that she had seen at the start of her tasks.

He was able, as ever, to read her expression. "It's because you have accomplished two tasks," Padraig said to her.

His gaze was as of old: a storm of malicious, beautiful blue. Nothing else was the same, though. His face was shrunken and his skin was gray. His beautiful thick hair had gone completely lank. And his frame was skeletal, his tattered, once-elegant clothes falling in deep folds over sharp bones. He had not even the strength to keep himself upright. He leaned heavily upon a cane.

"But it only looks like you're winning," Padraig rasped. "You'll fail at last. I know why, and so do you."

Ryland yowled aloud, furiously.

Padraig directed a bow in Ryland's direction. His tone grew a shade more courteous. "I don't mean that as a slur on you, Lord Ryland. Even with your help, however, Fenella will fail." He smirked, his teeth yellow. "Don't you see what has happened? There she was, trying to destroy love for them. But in the process, she fell in love *with* them. I knew she would."

Fenella said nothing.

"Her love will paralyze her. She won't be able to destroy anything else. Not to save herself, not to save them. Even while they hate her!"

He laughed.

Ryland yowled again. *This ignoramus doesn't speak cat,* he said to Fenella contemptuously. *He can't understand me. So tell him from me that it's not so. You will stand firm.*

Fenella said nothing.

Fenella?

"You know the truth when you hear it, Fenella." Though only a whisper, Padraig's voice held the sureness of an experienced vulture winging at prey.

Fenella, Ryland said irritably. *Tell him no.*

But Fenella could not say a word. Padraig was not done talking. She must not say anything before he was done, because he hated being interrupted, and if she and Lucy and

Dawn were indeed all to be returned into his power—

"When we are together this time," Padraig said, "it will be good. You know why, don't you? This time, you will have reinstated the curse yourself. All the girls will hate you. Which means there will be nobody else for you to love but me."

Leaning heavily on his stick, with Fenella still silent, Padraig limped away.

Chapter 37

What was that? The cat spat onto the wall. *Why were you standing there like a lump?*

Fenella continued to stand like a lump.

Fenella? Ryland stepped delicately closer. He put out a paw toward Fenella. She didn't react. He crouched, leaped, and landed on her chest, hanging precariously by his claws from the fabric of her T-shirt until, reflexively, she raised a single arm to hold him.

Her other hand scrabbled in her pocket for the leaf that wasn't there.

The cat's cold nose touched hers. *Fenella.*

Her eyes were open but saw nothing. He said her name again. He said something else too, but Fenella couldn't understand what it was, even though she recognized all the individual words.

The cat butted her nose with his head, hard. The momentary pain brought Fenella back into her body.

"What?" she said.

I said, what was that? Ryland was again nose to nose with her. *The Mud Creature is a liar,* he announced. *He is nobody in Faerie.*

She looked at him straight on. "So am I nobody."

The cat blinked. "Yes, but you have your tasks. And they're my tasks too. I'll be humiliated if you don't finish them."

That was all that was on the line for Ryland, Fenella thought. Humiliation. And whatever was going on between him and his sister.

Was the Mud Creature correct? the cat said impatiently. *Do you love your family?*

Love is nothing but a trap, Fenella thought. Again and again in her life, she had loved, and yet the only relationship that had lasted was the one formed by hate. The irony was that Padraig wanted her to love him. Maybe she should have. Maybe that would have destroyed him centuries ago. She laughed, a bitter little bark that was nothing like the laughter she once had reveled in. "No wonder I was given these tasks," she said. "My existence has destroyed everyone I ever loved."

Do you love your family now? The cat stared at her from two inches away.

"How can I love anybody? I'm dead. I've been dead since—since Robert was murdered."

But you loved that girl you keep talking about. The smart one. Minnie. That wasn't so long ago. So you're still capable—

"I'm trying to stop," Fenella burst out. "Don't you see? When I'm dead, that will stop it. I won't love anybody, and there won't be any more pain."

The cat was silent. Fenella put him back down on the wall. She wrapped her arms around herself and thought about what Padraig had said. Love had paralyzed her before. It was true. She had been trying to protect Robert, and so she had not warned him.

For a flash of a second, she thought of her own baby, Bronagh. Seeing Bronagh destroyed—no, she would not remember it. No!

I remember when the Mud Creature brought you to the ball, the cat announced. *It was after he killed your lover, Robert. Right?*

Fenella nodded.

That was the same night he cursed your family.

"Yes."

What happened? Tell me, in your own words.

"What does it matter?" Fenella was impatient. "It's the past. I have to figure out how to destroy hope. How hard can it be? Hope makes no sense in this world anyway." She gave the bitter bark of a laugh again. "Probably Soledad is feeling exactly that way too. Maybe that's my answer, right there. So, let's go. I'll figure something out. Save everybody and then die myself."

Not so fast. First, tell me about the ball.

Fenella tried to stare Ryland down, but the cat didn't blink. She felt the warm sun on her hair. Birds chirped in the distance. Near the horizon, the leaves on the trees moved in the light breeze. "Fine," she said at last.

She sank onto the ground again, with her back to the stone wall so that she could lean against it. The cat leaped down from the wall and settled beside her, tucking his forepaws under himself. He did not close his eyes, but she closed hers.

"He had to drag me away from Robert," she said tonelessly. "I screamed my throat raw. People were nearby. They should have heard me, they should have come. But nobody heard and nobody came. Then Padraig yanked at me from behind—"

❧

The next thing Fenella knew, she was standing at the edge of a forest clearing, barefoot, in the beautiful dress. The elfin lord held her tightly to his side. Unearthly music filled her ears: the high trill of a flute, the low beat of drums, the intertwining of voices singing in a language she knew not, in a key that should not have existed. Light poured down from the full moon, which glowed larger and brighter than any she had ever known.

Before her, in the clearing itself, hundreds of strange creatures danced.

"See?" The elfin lord's breath was warm in her ear. "See how few of them are like me? But you, you are like me. We belong together. With you as my mate, I will make a place for myself here."

"No." Fenella's lips moved, but if the word was audible, she couldn't hear it.

She was in a nightmare of warring senses and memories. She could still feel the weight of Robert's head in her lap from when she had pulled him desperately into her arms. His body had been warm, but his head flopped unnaturally to one side, and his beloved face held nothing of his personality.

But no, now she was standing in this strange place. Beneath her feet the ground was cold and damp. The handsome elfin lord held her tightly. Her ears rang with the strange, haunting music. Creatures that she did not have the imagination to make up twirled and frolicked and reveled before her.

The dancers were a mixture of animal and plant and human and reptile and bird and even stone. While many were humanoid in the general shapes of their bodies, many others were not. She saw hoofed feet, and leafy backs, and wing-like arms.

"Come," said the elfin lord, and pulled her into the dance.

The steps were nothing like the figures Fenella knew, and of course she had no wish to dance at all. But the music seemed to talk directly to her limbs and her feet and there was no question of refusing its command. She stomped and jumped and revolved, with the bell of her skirt whipping out gracefully. She curtsied and went down the line accompanied by a man with antlers. She swayed left and right and left again in order to weave the dance through a flutter of enormous red-winged bird creatures with ferocious, intelligent eyes. A willow branch caught her waist and twirled her briskly around seven times. A giant snake-like creature writhed forward and back, and she stepped nimbly into the curving pattern of its movements.

The whole time, hardly a step or two away, danced the elfin lord, tense, unsmiling, and expectant.

At one point the music changed and the dancers paired off, and then she was caught close to the lord, forced to take his hand and feel his too-long fingers fold around hers, feel his body curve close to hers. She kept her eyes level with his shoulder, not looking up. Her heart had been pounding so frantically for so long that she had stopped hoping it meant she would soon collapse and die.

He whispered in her ear, "I shall love you forever."

If he had been human, she would have known him for a madman. If there had been people she recognized around her, she would have known how to demand help. If she had not been sunk deep in shock and terror and grief, she would have found some way to break free.

At last the music changed, softened, and Fenella's feet ceased to move. She turned, and so did everyone else. She found herself moving into a perfect circle around a female creature so tall that Fenella had to blink in astonishment. The female wore a crown of flowers on her long hair, hair composed of dozens of colors that were all to be found in nature, though never together. The yellow of a bee's fur; the russet of a fox's pelt; the white of a dandelion gone to seed; the shiny black of a songbird's eye. The female's hair fell in waves that looked alive against her skin, skin that glowed green in the moonlight, skin formed from leaves.

The circle around her bowed as one. The elfin lord jabbed an elbow into Fenella's side. "It's the queen. Dip your head. Curtsy."

Fenella did, belatedly.

Near the queen stood her attendants, equally strange and beautiful. Something drew Fenella's attention to one of the attendants in particular, and a moment later she realized that she was responding to the elfin lord: His gaze kept flickering between the queen and this attendant. It was as if he was trying his best to avoid looking at the attendant, but could not help himself.

He had a strange expression on his face, a mixture of longing and hate.

Compelled, Fenella studied the attendant. She was small, the top of her head as high as Fenella's elbow. She had human limbs and face; she had pale, glimmering skin and floating reddish hair only a shade lighter than Fenella's; she had insect wings that sprouted from her back; and she had the delicate, pointed ears of a fawn. In fact, she looked precisely as a faerie should look, according to the tales.

But there was another striking feature about her, and it was her expression. The half-size faerie had, quite literally, the sweetest, kindest face that Fenella had ever seen.

Then the fawn-faerie turned her head, as if she felt Padraig's gaze on her.

Smiling vaguely, she looked right through him.

Chapter 38

Ah, said Ryland, nodding his furry head. *Yrenne. The Mud Creature's mother. Now, this is where my memory starts to fit in with yours. I remember the Mud Creature pulling you forward in front of the court. I was with the old queen that night too. You don't remember seeing me? I was an extremely cute cub.*

"His mother?" said Fenella, shocked.

Didn't you know? You haven't seen Yrenne since? Odd. She's never been one to miss a party.

"Maybe not, but I am," Fenella snapped. "Anyway, yes, I've seen her since. Although not lately, I suppose. But she's never paid any attention whatsoever—and Padraig never said—his mother? Are you sure?"

Of course I'm sure. Everyone knows.

Fenella said slowly, "I thought she was just another female who had rejected him."

She had felt sure of this, because Padraig spoke often about Yrenne. He said something every time he saw her, as if he couldn't help it. That Yrenne has the brains of a blade of grass, he would say. Or: That Yrenne is certainly looking her age. Or: Someone ought to slap that Yrenne. If there had been any concept of sluttishness in Faerie, he would have spoken about that too. He had certainly been known to comment on how frequently she changed lovers.

She did reject him, said the cat, stretching. *Yrenne left the egg by a mud pond to hatch or not, as it pleased. She never looked back. The Mud Creature raised himself.*

Fenella felt as if her head had been snatched off her body and then restored, backward. Eventually, she managed, "But didn't he at least have a father—or fathers— to take care of him?" She had chosen her least confusing thought to utter.

Ryland's voice was noticeably patient. *No. The Mud Creature is not one of us. Obviously. He must have some human father. Some long-dead half-wit who stumbled on the Midsummer Revels, I would imagine.* He waved a paw. *Don't ask me for the specifics. Only Yrenne would know, and no doubt she has long forgotten.*

Fenella was aghast. It must have showed in her face, because Ryland squinted at her and added: *You humans are so sentimental about young. For what it's worth, I'm sure*

Yrenne—if she thought about it at all—believed her egg would not survive. These mistakes rarely do.

Especially if you abandon them, Fenella thought. "But when he did survive—surely—" She waved a hand aimlessly. "Surely someone should have taken responsibility? For a child?"

Why? Ryland was genuinely puzzled. *Who would want the Mud Creature?*

She could not get over it. "But a child—"

He shrugged. *He should never have been viable. Really, it's rare. At the least he should only have had a human lifespan. Every single year he's lasted has been a surprise, and he's only gotten more annoying over time. Then there was what happened during the crisis. Nobody really minded him stealing power in the old days, but when it was scarce, it was not acceptable. He simply did not conduct himself like one of us.*

"Well, no wonder," Fenella said tartly.

Really, Fenella, this is an excess of concern, especially coming from you. It's not as if the Mud Creature treated you well. The cat stretched out his front paws. *You really didn't see me at the ball? Truly, I was an adorable cub. Everybody said so.*

"No," said Fenella flatly. "I didn't see you." She felt flummoxed. Should she have known about Yrenne? Yet how could she have, if Padraig had not told her? She talked to no one else except the tree fey, and that had been later, and she couldn't imagine them being concerned about Padraig's parentage. Any more, apparently, than Ryland was.

The other point was, however, that she would never have asked Padraig about his parentage, even if she had thought of it. She had never wished to express any curiosity about Padraig at all.

She asked slowly, "When did all of this happen? When was Padraig born?"

Several years before me, in the early reign of the old queen.

"The queen your mother. Who did not abandon you in the mud," Fenella said nastily, she knew not why. Her mind filled with puzzle pieces that she didn't want to fit together. One question pressed at her. "How old was Padraig when he kidnapped me?"

I don't know exactly. The cat's tail crooked irritably.

"But if you were a cub at the ball, and he was born several years before you—was he—was he around my age? Seventeen, eighteen?" She waited tensely.

That would be about right, I suppose.

Fenella inhaled sharply. She had always thought Padraig ancient, steeped in evil. Had he really only been her own age?

Why are you asking these questions? Does it change anything?

"No," said Fenella after a moment. "It changes nothing. He did what he did." She put a hand to her head and rubbed her temples. Fenella thought of all the years of terror. Of Robert and Bronagh and all the Scarborough girls, suffering, dead. "You're correct," she said. "It changes nothing."

Right, Ryland said. *Now, go on with your story. We were at the ball. You noticed the Mud Creature looking at Yrenne, and then, what?*

"He pulled me forward before the court," said Fenella. "Before the queen. There was an argument."

☞

The elfin lord's voice cut across the music, which ceased abruptly and discordantly. He spoke words in a language Fenella did not understand. He yanked Fenella to the center of the clearing before the queen and the fawn-faerie and the others. He held his head high, arrogant.

The faces that turned to them were surprised, and amused, and also scornful. These others said more things that Fenella did not understand, but she felt the elfin lord's hands tighten almost cruelly on her. Those hands were on her shoulders; he held her before him like a prize on display.

The queen said something. She smiled; a dismissive smile.

Quickly, urgently, the elfin lord spoke again. There was something different, portentous, about the timbre of his voice. His hands burned cold, right through the fabric on Fenella's shoulders. Pain shot through her and then dizziness. She would have fallen if he were not holding her.

And then all at once she felt strangely, weirdly, *well*.

The queen's eyes turned to slits. She drew herself up to her full height. Her voice crackled like thunder as she spoke.

The elfin lord seemed angrier now too. Angry and also righteous. He said more words. The queen shook her head. The elfin lord said something else, and the queen shrugged. This went back and forth for some minutes.

Fenella turned her head to follow the conversation, or argument, even though the language was strange to her. She was aware of the queen's attendants looking at her in the same way you would eye apples at market that might prove wormy.

Then the queen looked directly at Fenella and spoke. It took Fenella a few moments to realize she was being addressed in English, and a few more to disentangle clear meaning from the sibilant music of the queen's accent.

"He has brought you here to be his bride. But I perceive you are with child by someone else. In nine months, you will bear a human daughter."

The elfin lord sucked in a shocked breath. Fenella could not see his face, but she felt his rage flame.

Hope flared in her. She was indeed pregnant! And somehow this queen knew that it was a daughter.

"Yes." Her voice came out strong and vibrant. She held herself straight. "It is the child of my true love."

"So you are not here voluntarily?"

"I am not. The lord"—she was unable to interpret the expression on the queen's face at this—"murdered my lover and kidnapped me."

"She belongs to me," interjected the elfin lord. "I took her. I choose her for my bride. Is that not the way of the court? The strongest do whatever they want?"

Fenella held her breath.

She felt the elfin lord holding his as well.

The queen drawled, "No. It is not. The girl must have a chance of escape." She eyed Fenella up and down. "A fair chance. An artful chance. A chance that will entertain us all." Her gaze moved to the elfin lord as she finished. "Devise a riddle! Show us what you can do. We'll even loan you some power to do it, if you haven't enough of your own."

The court laughed.

The elfin lord let go of Fenella. He bowed deeply.

At this point—and this was something Fenella could comprehend in any language—bets were laid, all around.

⌒

"Then," Fenella said, "then Padraig cursed me and my unborn daughter. There was much laughter. Yes, I was quite the center of entertainment at court that night."

Not really you, said the cat mildly. *The Mud Creature.* He smiled, showing his teeth. *Though, as you have already said, knowing that changes nothing in the game you must now play. Does it?*

Fenella rubbed her eyes wearily. "No."

You still must go forward.

"I will." She felt confused, so confused, but at the same time grimly determined. Perhaps the queen had been right, to send Padraig so that Fenella had to see him, talk to him.

There was one more task. She would do it. All the horror would not matter then, because, at long last, she would die.

Chapter 39

In the human realm, it was late afternoon. Half the bright, withering leaves still clung stubbornly to the trees, but the other half had fallen to the ground to be blown about and scuffed underfoot. As Fenella walked, she tried to avoid stepping on the leaves.

Fenella had Ryland draped so that his body lay in her arms while he faced backward over her shoulder. Her only concession to disguise was a shabby gray cap that Ryland had nosed out on the street. She had tucked up her hair under it.

Perhaps she wanted to be found, she thought. But though she had seen one police car, it had driven sedately past her.

Before returning, she had spent an hour discussing the third task with Ryland, but Fenella had not found an obvious solution. Hope was a slippery concept.

Also, the more time passed, the more anxious Fenella became, thinking of her family and of what they were going through. It was unbearable not to know what was happening. Yet now that she was in the human realm, she could not imagine how she might find out.

Part of her wanted simply to go to her family and tell them about the tasks. But her mind went blank when she tried to think out the repercussions. She could hardly ask them to volunteer ideas for ways in which she might destroy them.

She moved slowly down a wide, attractive street lined with maple trees. People were out and about, but she looked to the trees. These maples were not sentient like the tree fey, but perhaps they were aware of her passing. She longed to think so. She put a hand on the bark of an especially large maple. She stroked the tree, running her fingers over its trunk, admiring the ridges that showed how it had grown. This tree was not so very old, perhaps a hundred years, and it was strong and alive and so beautiful.

She thought about taking one of its leaves that had fallen to the ground, of putting it in her pocket. But if she had been worthy of even that small comfort, she would still have her own leaf. So she did not.

She walked on. As twilight fell, she found herself in a town center crowded with stores clustered around a parking lot. It looked familiar; perhaps she had been here before. She had a vague memory of Miranda walking beside her, talking.

To her left, next to the parking lot on an island of green, grew a thick little copse of trees. Instinctively Fenella stepped closer, stooping beneath the low branches. She found herself in a sweetly private bower, big enough only for the empty park bench placed invitingly there.

This was not a private spot, of course. It was at the edge of a parking lot, and when Fenella squinted through the leaves, she could see the lot and its cars outside. She could hear them too. But still, somehow, the screen of trees made the little shelter *feel* private, and she realized it would be difficult, especially in the growing darkness, for people outside to see in.

She sank down thankfully on the bench.

Ryland curled up in her lap with his eyes closed. Fenella stroked him and watched the lights of the cars in the parking lot. Cars came and cars went. Gradually more cars went than arrived, and the lot emptied. The streetlamps came on. The footsteps of the people on the street sounded less frequently. Fenella thought about getting up and moving on, but she still didn't know where she would go or what she would do.

And it felt safe and sheltered on the bench within the

trees. Even peaceful. Absently, she put one hand up behind her and touched the rough bark of the trees. Oak. She let her fingers linger a long moment, caressing.

Full dark settled in. The streetlamps outside the bower gave sufficient light to see by.

Destroy hope?

In her lap, Ryland's body rose and fell with his breath. Maybe he really was asleep.

"As long as there is something that you want, you would still have hope," Fenella muttered aloud. "To have no hope would mean you have no energy left to want anything. How can anybody want nothing? Even when I was with Padraig, there were still things I wanted. Things I hoped for. Even now, at this moment, I want. That means I hope. Doesn't it? Can you want without hope? No. You cannot. When I want death, I hope for death. Right?"

In Fenella's head, Ryland's voice stirred.

"I said to my soul, be still, and wait without hope
For hope would be hope for the wrong thing; wait without love
For love would be love of the wrong thing; there is yet faith
But the faith and the love and the hope are all in the waiting.
Wait without thought, for you are not ready for thought:
So the darkness shall be the light, and the stillness the dancing."

"What?" said Fenella.

Ryland repeated the words.

"But what does it mean?"

She felt Ryland shrug. *Human poetry. A man named T. S. Eliot. Did you think you were the first to ponder these questions?* Ryland's breathing resumed the even tenor of sleep.

Fenella wondered about this poet who had tried to school himself to hopelessness and lovelessness; who had placed all his faith in waiting. *The stillness the dancing.* That sounded quite fey. No wonder Ryland liked it.

But the lines of the poetry did not, to her, sound hopeless. For who could dance and remain entirely without wanting, entirely without hope? This particular poet, perhaps? No, for his poem was an attempt to *instruct* himself in hopelessness. It was not success.

How long she sat on her bench trying to be still and wait without hope, Fenella never knew. At some point she closed her eyes. Feeling shielded by the trees, she might even have slept. But suddenly, someone sat down heavily on the bench beside her.

Instantly her body knew who it was. Her eyes snapped open. Her skin tingled, and her fingers went cold, even buried as they were in Ryland's fur.

She felt afraid to look at Walker Dobrez, but there he was. Beside her. Saying nothing. But she could tell that nothing inside him was quiet.

Eventually, she turned her head to him. There was enough

light to see that his brown hair hung ragged around his ears instead of in its usual neat ponytail. The expression in his eyes was hard. He lifted one large hand and she saw that he held in it an oak leaf. Fenella's hand went to her mouth.

It was her leaf.

He held it out to her.

Ryland, in her lap, was watching Walker too. Walker spared the cat a single glance before returning his attention to Fenella.

"Leave us alone," Fenella said to the cat.

Ryland obeyed, as he must, leaping lightly to the ground and disappearing outside of the little copse of trees.

She took the leaf, careful not to touch Walker. She cupped the leaf in her palm. It was emitting its gentle, soothing pulse. It was alive again! What did this mean?

"I found the leaf in the cab of my truck." Walker drew a hand through his hair. "It wanted me to come here. So I did." He paused, and then burst out: "Who are you, Fenella? *What* are you, that a leaf gives instructions about you to me? Leo— do you *know* what you did to him? It was on purpose, wasn't it?" His anger and bewilderment wound through the words.

Fenella held her whole body tight. She said nothing.

"I told everyone it was an accident. But I know it wasn't. You were planning something all along—you used me for my truck. Didn't you? First you used me to learn to drive.

Then there's the dog. You were after Pierre, right? You were trying to kill a dog! What kind of monster are you? Then you changed your mind and you did—what you did. And then you ran away!"

Fenella bit her lip.

"What does that make you? A user, a liar, a coward, and a murderer." Walker's cheekbones stood out in his face.

"Yes," Fenella said, into the silence. "I did it all. You are completely correct."

Walker ripped his hand through his hair again. "I know I am."

Then he muttered, "And yet. This leaf. And you. I look at you—your face, your eyes, the way you move. I listen to your voice. Something in me can't believe it. I don't want to believe it." He shook his head. "Maybe this is a nightmare and I'll wake up any minute."

Fenella held the oak leaf up to her cheek. "What about Leo?" she asked Walker steadily. "Tell me what happened after I ran away."

"He's on life support at the hospital. They did blood transfusions. They were talking about surgery. But realistically, there's little hope."

Fenella's heart leaped, however. Leo was still alive? There was little hope, Walker had said. But that meant there was *some* hope. The third task was about hope.

Then her mind splintered. If Leo lived, would that mean she had failed at the second task? But even if he died, Soledad and Lucy and Zach would still love him. So how had she destroyed love, exactly? The queen had said she had succeeded. Padraig had been withered. It didn't make sense.

Walker said, "I told the police I was the one driving the truck. I said that I lost control, trying to avoid hitting Pierre. Do you understand, Fenella? I covered for you. I took responsibility before the police and your family. Everyone thinks it was an accident. My fault, my accident. Not yours."

Fenella doubted it. Her family knew things about Fenella that Walker did not.

Still, he had lied for her to the police. Around an obstruction in her throat, Fenella managed a single word. "Why?"

Walker's hands clenched. "You know how I feel about you. Don't pretend you don't." He paused. "But that's not why." He looked down at his hands, and then directly at her. "There's something deeply wrong with you, Fenella."

"Really, you think so? Beyond my being a liar and a murderer and so on?" She didn't know how she'd managed sarcasm, or even why she had bothered. She didn't mean the sarcastic words. She was still amazed. Walker had lied for her!

"I'm talking about you being damaged. I'm talking about

the kind of damage that causes you to do the things you do. That's the only reason I'm here. I think you're mentally ill. You must be. I think you need help."

The oak leaf pulsed in Fenella's hands.

Walker continued steadily, "At the same time, Fenella— and hear this, because I mean every word: *I hate you.*" He stood up. He loomed over her, and the closeness of the trees around them somehow amplified his size. "I was feeling this even while lying to the police and to your family, even while covering for you, even while telling myself that you've got to be mentally ill. Something terrible must have happened in your life before, to hurt you, to make you unstable. Abuse of some kind, maybe."

She sat still and silent, watching him in the dimness. And listening.

"I'm also afraid of you," Walker said starkly. "I'm afraid of what I feel. I'm afraid of what I did. Do you understand? I lied. I lied to the police and to everyone else. For you. I lied for you!"

She nodded; a small movement of her head. It seemed to satisfy him in some way. He sat down again by her side.

"Just now," he said hoarsely, "I followed a *leaf* to find you. A leaf that acted like a compass, and you're the North Pole. So, there you go. You're crazy, you've made me crazy, and you've turned the whole world around me insane. Did you burn that house down too, by the way? Right. I can see by your face that you did."

"I'm sorry," Fenella said.

It was of course entirely the wrong thing to say. He exploded again. "You're sorry? You're *sorry*? God! What am I doing here? I should get in my truck and drive back home alone. I should do it this minute. I will do it! I'll drive away without looking back, and then I'll never think of you for the rest of my life. No! First I'll haul you to the police, *then* I'll walk away. No! Before *that*, I'll force you to face Soledad and Lucy and Zach and Miranda. I'll make you tell them what you've done."

Walker was breathing hard. "Then I'll take you to the police." He snatched her wrists and held them manacled in one hand. "After that, *that's* when I wipe you out of my mind. That's when I walk away forever from the sociopathic, beautiful, leaf-attracting monster that you are. You're sorry, you say. Sorry!"

She could explain until the world came to an end, and he would never believe or understand. He was crushing her wrists. If he broke them and her bones healed themselves before his very eyes, what sort of monster would he call her then? Fenella had a vague curiosity about it. She wondered if he remembered that he had seen her arms heal, instantly, from cat scratches, on the day that they met.

Incidentally, he had also just called her beautiful.

She heard her breath coming hard and fast between her lips. Walker's face was bare inches from hers, his breath smelling faintly of mint.

He was breathing as rapidly as she was.

By her wrists he pulled her closer, right up against him. Heat poured off his body. His gaze pierced her in the darkness, cold and hot at once. "That's what I want. You're going to come with me and—"

Fenella dropped the oak leaf. She scrambled on top of Walker, settling onto his lap on the park bench, her skirt riding up. Her hands were trapped between them by his grip on her wrists. His other hand rose to her shoulder, grasping it, and made to push her away.

She was desperate for contact, for warmth. She tried to push her body against Walker's, but her arms were in the way. That was all right, though, because there were still his legs beneath hers, his thighs long and taut and muscled, and it felt so right to be on his lap.

"Okay," she said. "I'll go with you if you want. But first, this is what *I* want. I have to have it. It's the one thing I want before I die."

She set her mouth on his.

Chapter 40

For a few seconds Walker held Fenella off, so that her mouth could only barely brush his. "You're even crazier than I realized," he said. But then Fenella captured his mouth fully. Long moments later when she let it go, he whispered her name, sounding as tender and desperate and wounded as she felt.

She leaned in again. She bit his mouth, oh so gently.

His hand on her shoulder, which had started out by trying to push her away, went still as she kissed him and felt his response. His entire arm came around her waist, pulling her tightly into his chest. Triumph surged in her. She leaned to take his mouth again and this time he met her halfway.

She squirmed closer.

At last Walker freed his mouth from Fenella's. He was

panting. "You need to be on medication. You're dangerous to others and to yourself."

"Don't think," Fenella said. "Kiss me." She closed her eyes. She turned her face blindly, seeking his mouth, and found it.

But too soon Walker withdrew his mouth again. Fenella laid her head on his shoulder and murmured, "Isn't there somewhere we can go to be truly private? Just for a while? It's night—is anyone at the vet clinic?"

"A few animals that are being boarded . . . No! I'm not going there with you, Fenella. Or anywhere. What if my supervisor saw us? Wait, no, that's not why. It's because it's wrong. It's because—"

"It wouldn't be for long. Just this once. This is the only chance we'll ever, ever have, don't you see that?"

Walker turned his face away. His breathing was ragged in her ear. His chest fell and rose beneath her. "I said no."

"Afterward, I'd go anywhere you said. To my family. To the police. I promise I would."

She could feel him shaking his head. "Your promise is worthless, beloved. You're Lifetime movie material. Some actress could win an award playing you."

Beloved.

"You can tie me up while we're there," Fenella offered. "To make sure I won't escape."

"Or to make sure that you don't try to kill me." Bitterness had leaked again into his voice, and she knew he was remembering Leo.

"I wouldn't hurt you." She blew gently at a spot on his neck where his thick, dark hair fell away from the skin. She longed for the use of her hands so that she could cup his face with them, but he was still holding her wrists. "It truly was an accident with Leo."

"Yeah, right. Because you were after the dog."

"No, I—there's no sense my trying to explain. Let's forget it all for a little while. Just a few hours alone. Even one. One would do."

"I said no, Fenella. I won't be manipulated. I'm not that guy."

She heard his words, but his body was telling her something else. She waited, and he added, "You're so convincing. I almost believe that you want me the way I want you."

Fenella moved against him gently as she whispered into his ear. "I don't want you the way you want me. I want you *more* than you want me."

Beneath her, he returned her movement. "Liar."

Fenella brushed his lips. "How long has it been for you?"

His breath mingled with hers. "None of your business."

"Who was it with? A girlfriend?"

"I'm not telling you anything. I won't give you anything else belonging to me."

They were nose to nose in the dimness.

"Not even her first name?"

"Nothing."

"Did you love her?" Fenella persisted.

"No."

"No, you didn't love her?"

"No, I won't tell you whether I did or not."

Fenella squirmed. "Let my hands go, I want to touch you."

Walker's grip tightened on her wrists. "No. I don't want you to touch me."

"Always no with you." Fenella rocked against him. "No." She moved again. "No."

Sweat had long since broken out on Walker's forehead. A drop worked its slow way down along his temple. She licked it, tasting the acidity of his skin. He made a small noise that might have meant anything in the world, except for no.

"Okay, so I didn't love her." His voice was lower than low, and quite desperate. "My last girlfriend. I liked her, though. I'm liking her better and better by the minute. See, she was *sane.*" As he spoke, his hips moved again, strong, a pulsing counterpoint to hers, and then they were moving together.

But in the next second, Fenella went still. Then so did Walker. His eyes cut to hers.

She said, "If you really want me to slide off you, I will. That's not what I want to do. I want us to finish what we've started. But if you tell me to, I'll stop. You can take me to my family and then to the police or whatever it is you want to do. Now or later."

Another drop of sweat trickled down the side of Walker's face. Again, Fenella leaned in and followed its path with her mouth.

"Shall I stop? Should we go now?" She moved her hips again. "Or should we do this first?"

"This is insane," Walker muttered. "We're in a public place."

Fenella kept her eyes fixed on his. "The trees are protecting us," she murmured, and knew in that instant that it was true, even though these trees were not fey.

"I'm not insane." Walker's voice strengthened. "I won't be insane. I know better."

Fenella knew a long, terrible moment of dread and despair. So, she was to have nothing then, not even a few stolen moments beneath the trees with a man who had called her beloved. Slowly, reluctantly, she began to shift away.

Instantly, Walker's arm tightened full around her to keep her close to him, even though his hand in between their bodies kept its grip on her wrists.

"No," he said. "No! All right. Don't go. Stay. Stay—right—there. Keep doing what you were doing."

Fenella gave him one, two, three seconds to change his mind.

Then she leaned forward. "I will," said Fenella. "I absolutely will." This time when their lips met, his desperation entwined with hers.

It would do. This would do. It would have to, because this moment on Walker's lap, fully clothed, on a park bench shielded by trees, was all she was going to get. This time, this deed, and the single word *beloved*. It was more than Fenella had dared dream of receiving.

Even though Walker would believe nothing she said, she would give him a gift as well. She would give the gift of truth.

She whispered, "Listen to me. I haven't been with a man that I chose for nearly four hundred years. Until tonight."

Walker laughed. He kissed Fenella's neck, small nips that stopped short of bites. "It's been a year for me. It only feels like four hundred."

Then he stilled. "What do you mean, a man you chose?" He yanked his head back. "What are you saying, Fenella? Were you raped?" His gaze searched her face in the dim light from the streetlamps. "Four hundred years? That's crazy talk again. But rape—Fenella—we have to stop, right now, and—"

"Never mind," she said hastily. "I just meant that I choose you and I choose this. I want you. I want you so much."

"Me too," said Walker indistinctly. "Although I need to

point out that we're also choosing possible arrest for public indecency. Not to mention—"

"Quiet." Fenella kissed him. Then, for a blessed time in the night, there were no words and no thoughts, only Fenella and Walker, alone enough.

Chapter 41

A blissful little island can only remain suspended in time and space for a short while, however. Some unknown number of minutes later, a scream from a cat brought them crashing down to earth. Walker reacted immediately, bucking Fenella off his lap fast and hard. She fell onto the ground on her hip. He stood, looking around warily.

The cat screeched again. A minute later, two women, one elderly and holding on to the other's arm, passed under the streetlamp beyond the sheltering trees, but they did not even so much as glance within the bower.

As the women's footfalls died away, the catcall came again. Now it was louder, closer. Ryland, Fenella thought. She supposed he was being as tactful as possible under the circumstances.

The noises of the suburban night penetrated her awareness. A car door slammed. An automatic lock chirped. She heard the croaks and whistles of grackles in a tree overhead, and a murmur of voices accompanied by a drift of music as people exited a nearby restaurant.

Fenella realized the sounds of others had been present all along.

From her position on the ground, she smoothed her skirt, crossed her legs, and leaned back on her hands philosophically. It was too dark to see anything but Walker's outline, and since he had turned his back on her, she had to try to read his emotions by the set of his shoulders.

He mumbled something.

"What is it?" At the last second she kept back the word *beloved,* but only just, and the sweet, sure shape of it seemed to linger in her mouth.

"That wasn't real," Walker said, and swung around.

Fenella sat up. "What?"

His face was completely in shadow. "That wasn't real. Whatever that was—it doesn't matter. It wasn't for real."

It was like the moment when Fenella had felt the queen's sharp, serrated knife enter her body. For whole seconds there was no pain, and then the next, there was nothing but.

"Not *real*?" She scrambled awkwardly to her feet. "We both participated! You said yes, so did I! That's real enough for me."

"Stop shouting! Okay, it was real, in the sense of not imaginary, but still it doesn't count."

"Who's the liar now?"

Walker took a step away. A second later, Fenella felt the cool caress of the cat's fur. Ryland wound himself around her ankles, his long beautiful tail lingering the longest. *You yell like a fishwife,* he said.

Fenella ignored him.

"You seduced me," Walker said, in a cool, measured tone. "You're responsible."

Fenella took a step back too, and put her hands on her hips. "You were willing. Don't claim you didn't enjoy it, because it was evident to me that you did." When he shook his head, she added bitterly, "Listen. You had a very good time. I'm not inexperienced even if you are, so don't think you can deny anything."

Ryland's claws dug sharply into Fenella's ankle, and she yelped.

Stop right there, my friend, Ryland said. *The wise woman does not mock her lover for lack of experience.*

"I wasn't mocking, Ryland, you idiot!" Fenella yelled. "Anyway, what do you care what I say to Walker? You don't even like him!"

The cat's almond-shaped eyes shone in the dimness like a beacon from a strange land. She squatted down in the dirt to glare directly into them. "Also, do you think I don't know what a woman is and isn't supposed to say to any male about his lovemaking? Do you think I don't know what a male creature wants to hear? Do you think I wasn't well trained? When I want your advice, I'll ask for it! Otherwise, nobody tells me what to say or what to do! Not you, not anyone! Never again! Do you hear me? Never!"

The cat's ears flattened. *Fenella,* he said quietly, *it's all right. Calm down. Please. I'm here to help you, remember?*

Fenella pressed the heel of one hand to each eye in turn. Eventually she was able to straighten.

Walker was staring at her. Even in the dark, she could feel the intensity of it.

"I'm sorry about that outburst," Fenella said. "Chalk it up to my craziness. I talk to cats! My own cat, anyway. You know why? It's because he talks to me first. I hear him in my insane little head. He was lecturing me now. About men."

Walker said carefully, "And what did your cat say about men?"

"You really want to know?"

"Yes."

Fenella repeated it.

Walker took it in. "Now tell me again what you said to your cat?"

"You heard me the first time. That I wasn't mocking you."

"But you also said—"

"Forget what else I said."

"But it was—there was something about being 'well trained'? What did that mean?"

"Oh, who knows what insane things I might say?"

Walker shoved his hands down into his pockets. "I want to take back what I said before. You were right. It *was* real. And I wanted it too. Wanted you. I was just trying to say that it was—" He squared his shoulders. ". . . a mistake."

Fenella stood up again, like a soldier. She lifted her chin.

"For me," she said, "it wasn't." For there was no longer any point in such trifles as the preservation of pride or the pretense of indifference.

Walker paused, but only for a moment. "I'm sorry. I don't know what to say."

"Then don't say anything at all."

Silence.

Then Walker said grimly, "Not possible. You told me you'd go with me to tell your family the truth. I'm going to insist on it."

Don't go. Run away! I'll help you run! I'll hide you in Faerie! The cat sounded panicked.

"All right," said Fenella calmly to Walker.

No! Don't you see how that would be fatal?

Fenella looked down into the cat's upturned face. "No. I think—this feels like the right thing to do."

But the third task—

"If you don't shut up, I will put you in a sack and do my level best to drown you. That's a promise."

Ryland shut up.

Fenella sighed. She knelt by the cat. "All right. Sorry. I know you mean to help me. But you also know this is my decision, not yours." She held out her arms. Haughtily, the cat leaped into them. She straightened and turned to Walker.

"Take me to my family. I'll tell them you lied to protect me."

Walker nodded. "Then the police." His face was implacable.

"I'll tell the truth to anyone I need to."

They ducked beneath the trees and emerged next to the parking lot.

Refusing to turn and look back at the little shelter of trees—even though she wanted to—Fenella followed Walker to his truck, which once had delighted her so much. She did not glance at the front of it, lest there be damage. He courteously opened the passenger door for her; he even held Ryland while she climbed in, and then handed her the cat.

He avoided even brushing her fingers with his own.

Chapter 42

Silence ruled during the dark drive; a silence choked with things left unsaid, with one exception.

"Your cat who talks in your head. Can you tell me more about him?"

"Certainly," said Fenella politely. "What would you like to know?"

"Whatever. Anything."

"He's not actually a cat, but a faerie prince."

"A faerie prince."

"Yes. He's under a temporary spell while on assignment from the Faerie Queen, his sister. He's advising me on the completion of three tasks."

"A handsome faerie prince under a spell."

"Not handsome. He's what you'd call a freak."

The cat yowled. Walker's hand jerked on the wheel of the truck.

Fenella said, "Ryland wishes you to know that his natural form is that of a manticore."

"A manticore."

"Yes. Human head, body of a lion, dragon's tail. Wings."

Walker flicked a glance toward Fenella's lap, where Ryland sat sphinx-like, front paws extended, head upright. "Of course. A manticore." He returned his attention to his driving.

Walker hadn't even seemed to take in what she'd said about the three tasks. He had certainly not asked what they were or about Fenella's involvement with them. She found herself compulsively shaping conversational gambits in her head. There were so many things she might say. So much pity she might fish for. So many explanations she might make. And, oh yes, so much begging she might do.

Was there any chance Walker would by some miracle believe her? He had experienced the tangible magic of the oak leaf, which—oh. She groped in her pocket. She remembered holding the leaf on the park bench, and then she had scrambled on top of Walker, and she had no memory of it after that. She sighed heavily, but Walker did not even look her way.

She knew then it was useless.

Fenella closed her eyes, only to see Padraig form instantly in her mind's eye. He was dressed in silk and leather, as of old, and his body was restored to full strength and power. He swept down low in a mocking bow. Rising, he held out a commanding hand. Despite her will, her feet took her to him and she accepted his hand. His long, overly jointed fingers dug into her as he drew her body against his. His honeyed voice poured a long, detailed story into her ear, a favorite of his, about some things he had done to Bronagh.

Then he told her that he was going to do those things to Lucy.

Stop that shaking, Fenella, said the cat, though he sounded panicked himself. *Once Walker tells your family the truth—once you do—you won't be allowed near them. And then he wants to get the police! They'll lock you up. They'll discover you have no identification—that you don't legally exist. So you must do the third task now. Tonight. Or never!*

He paused. *Or you could still buy yourself time. Run and hide. Run the moment the car stops. I'll be right behind you. Because, don't you see, Fenella? Once they know, it's all over.*

Fenella's stomach did a strange little flip.

Once they know, it's all over.

Just like that, she knew what to do. She knew why she

had gotten into the truck and why she was going to tell the truth. She knew her plan. She sat up straight.

"Ryland, I have decided about the third task." Fenella stole a glance at Walker's profile, but only the twitch of the muscle in his cheek acknowledged that he heard her speak to her cat.

The cat stood on his hind legs, his whiskers brushing her cheeks. *What?*

"I can't tell you aloud." Fenella's eyes remained on Walker. "You will have to do what I say. Instantly."

I have to obey you anyway.

"I know."

I hope your idea is a good one. Strange. Ryland sounded like he cared.

Walker said nothing. Of course not. Her talk of faeries and tasks would only have confirmed what he had decided before. She was a crazy, dangerous girl who talked to her cat, a girl soon to be locked up for her terrible deeds. Nonetheless, as they drove, she kept her gaze on him. This was the last time she would be alone with him.

Too soon, they pulled up in front of an unfamiliar building, a three-story house. "The new apartment," Walker said tersely.

Fenella hesitated, her hand on the truck's door handle. "After I hit Leo, they went ahead with the move?"

"The family went to the hospital. Everyone else moved things for them. Then Lucy's friend Sarah and some others set things up here."

"I see."

"Do you? Do you see how thoroughly you've wrecked their lives?"

Fenella stared at the house. She reminded herself that Walker lived on the ground floor. The Scarborough-Greenfield-Markowitzes' apartment was on the next two floors. Electric lights burned from there.

Walker came around to Fenella's side of the truck and opened her door, as if he thought she'd been waiting for that. He did not offer to hold Ryland for her this time, and so she simply dumped the cat on the ground, where he stretched, arching his back. She slid out of the truck.

Who was home? Lucy? Zach? Soledad? Miranda? Someone would be there with the child, who required regular hours and food and sleep.

"Are you sure this is the right time? Won't hearing from me make things worse? What about waiting until morning?"

"There will never be a right time."

"But what if they were to hear that Leo will live after all?"

"What you're really saying is that it would go easier on you, when you confess, if he's alive and doing better."

No. Really she was saying that she didn't want to do the third task.

Walker took her elbow in a firm grip. "Let's go."

Ryland padded lightly along beside Fenella as they moved up the walk to the front door. Inside, a steep staircase turned sharply upward. They climbed, and Walker rapped on a wooden five-panel door.

Lucy called out in response. "Come in."

Chapter 43

"*It's Walker.* Sorry to bother you. I have Fenella with me."

Fenella and Walker entered the living room, which was lit only by a bare electric bulb in the center of the ceiling. The room was of reasonable size and its wide-planked wooden floor felt solid underfoot. But it was hard to imagine it ever feeling anything like the home that was gone. Cardboard boxes were piled high against stark white walls. A broom and dustpan leaned against the wall, next to a window open to the autumn night air. In the far corner stood a portable playpen, with a few totally unfamiliar stuffed toys lined up within. A big shabby sofa was half-covered by a pile of clothing. Two interior doors gaped open to other rooms.

The whole place smelled overpoweringly of fresh paint.

Lucy had risen from the sofa. Her eyes were blank disks. Dawn hung, a dead weight, over her mother's shoulder. The child's eyes were closed. She had two fingers stuffed in her mouth and wore faded white pajamas covered with pictures of frolicking kittens.

"Are you here alone?" Walker asked Lucy.

"Yes."

Ryland, who had followed, jumped lightly up on the sofa behind Lucy, who cast him a quick, unwelcoming look. Ignoring her, Ryland made himself a nest on top of the clothing. "We need to talk," Walker said.

Lucy nodded. She looked only at Walker, though, not Fenella. But Fenella could feel the force of Lucy's awareness of her. "I've only just got Dawn off to sleep. I'll put her down first." Lucy moved into the next room as if wading through hip-deep water.

Fenella felt Walker's bulk heavy behind her, like a jailer. "I'll tell Lucy," she told him. "I said I would and I will."

"Tell me what?" It was Lucy, back in the doorway already, her body tense, her hands fisted before her.

Fenella stepped forward.

Her plan for the third task would work, or it would not. They would all be saved, or they would all be destroyed. It began with telling the truth.

"*I* was driving the truck today, not Walker. I hit Leo.

Also, I burned down the house. But you knew that already, I think."

It was like taking a knife to a knotted mess of string. Fenella only had a moment to exhale in the relief of honesty, and the pain of it.

In the next second Lucy knocked Fenella to the floor and was on top of her, screaming in her face. *"Why? Why?"* Lucy's hands gripped her shoulders, shaking her. There came a slap and a punch and a knee digging into Fenella's stomach, and then Fenella's head was shaken so hard, she felt dizzy.

Fenella didn't struggle. She took her attention away from her body and whatever it felt. It didn't matter. She looked up at the way the skin creased at the corners of Lucy's eyes and mouth. At the way her mouth trembled.

Lucy was crying. Tears ran down her face, her shoulders heaved as she tried again to shake Fenella. This time she failed. She was crying too hard.

Fenella found Lucy's wet cheek with her palm.

"Don't touch me!"

"I'm sorry," Fenella whispered. She truly meant to remove her hand. Instead, carefully, tenderly, she wiped Lucy's tears away with her fingers. "Don't cry. Don't cry, baby. It's going to be all right. I promise. I *promise*."

Lucy froze. She jerked her head back and stared at Fenella.

Fenella was shocked too. The preposterous promise had come from some primal place. It was a mother's promise, the kind made when all hope is lost but the mother refuses to believe it. And she had had no business saying it! It was against everything that she was trying to do.

Lucy had to understand that no, everything was *not* going to be all right. She had to!

As if he'd been far away and had now come closer, Fenella heard Walker. He sounded desperate, crazed, and uncertain. "Lucy—Fenella—stop—we all have to talk—"

"Talk." Lucy heaved herself to her feet. For a moment she stood above Fenella, panting. Her expression was confused. Then, slowly, suspicion and anger returned.

Good, Fenella thought. Don't trust me. Hate me. Fear me.

Step by step, Lucy backed away until she was leaning against the wall. "I guessed about the fire. I suspected about Daddy." Her voice threatened to crack on the childish word.

Walker said, from somewhere to the left, "Fenella says hitting Leo was an accident."

"I don't care," Lucy said.

Fenella shifted to a better position on the floor, so that she could see Lucy, Walker, and also the attentive twitch of Ryland's ears from his perch on the sofa. She laced her hands in her lap. Her heart was racing, racing. It was ready.

So was she.

Lucy was still staring at Fenella. "Walker? Leave Fenella and me alone to talk."

"No. You and Dawn are safer with me here."

"You're here to protect us?" Lucy sounded incredulous.

"Yes. Fenella is not trustworthy." He paused. "She's, uh, insane."

Lucy smiled mirthlessly. "Fenella? Are you insane?"

Always the same question.

"I am no more insane than any Scarborough woman ever was."

Lucy inhaled sharply. "What's *wrong* with me? I should have known. I did know—somewhere in me. I just didn't want to believe it." Then: "Walker, leave now. Now! This is family business."

"But Fenella's crazy. Don't believe her when she says she's not! She thinks her cat talks to her. She says he's a faerie prince under a spell."

Lucy's head swiveled to Ryland. "The cat is a faerie prince?"

Walker said, "Yes, her delusion is that he—"

Lucy grabbed the broom. She leaped. The broom handle descended viciously.

Ryland slithered to the floor barely in time. He dove under the sofa. *She thinks I'm Padraig!*

Lucy dove to the floor too. She stabbed beneath the sofa with the broom handle. "I'll kill him this time!"

With one shoulder she heaved the sofa up on end. Exposed, the cat skittered across the bare floor toward Fenella. He raced round and round her legs.

Fenella yelled, "Lucy, listen! This isn't Padraig. He doesn't even *like* Padraig."

It had come to this. Fenella was defending Ryland against Lucy.

Blessedly, however, Lucy stopped. She swayed on her feet, staring at Ryland, but she didn't move to pursue him further.

"I hate all faeries," she said at last.

Walker fell against the wall with an audible thump.

There was silence for a full minute. Then, cautiously, the cat stuck his head out from behind Fenella's legs. *Fenella? May I suggest proper introductions?*

"Lucy," said Fenella evenly, "meet Ryland. He's the brother of the Faerie Queen."

Ryland waved a front paw.

Lucy narrowed her eyes.

"I'm the only one who can hear what Ryland says," Fenella said. "So I'll have to translate."

"What does he want from us?" said Lucy.

"Nothing. This is not about him, but—"

"Lucy," Walker interrupted. "Playing along with Fenella won't help."

Lucy whirled on him. "Shut up and let me talk to Ryland and Fenella. This is family business. If you don't believe it, you can leave."

Walker could go downstairs and make us all some tea, said Ryland brightly. *I've been dying for a dish of Earl Grey. Cream, no sugar.*

The cat was right, and so was Lucy. It would be easier if Walker was out of the way.

Fenella said, "Ryland thinks we should all have tea."

"The prince wants tea?" Lucy said incredulously.

"Earl Grey, weak, with lots of cream if possible, and milk if not. No sugar."

In a nice wide dish. Not a teacup.

"Served in a soup bowl," said Fenella. "Big enough for his fat head."

There was a pause. Lucy looked at the cat. Then she looked at Fenella.

"Walker?" said Lucy. "Do you have tea downstairs at your place? Because I think it would be soothing for all of us."

Walker was already backing away as his eyes shifted with astonishment from Lucy to Fenella and back again. "Okay," he said. "I'll see what I can do. I can't promise—what was it?—Earl Grey."

"Anything is fine," said Lucy. She moved with Walker to the door, as if he needed an escort.

A moment later, Fenella knew why. Walker had not gone more than a few steps down the stairs when Lucy closed the apartment door. Then she snapped the deadbolt.

Now Fenella and Ryland were locked in with Lucy and the child—exactly as Fenella needed them to be.

Chapter 44

Lucy swiveled back. Her cell phone was in one hand and the broom handle in the other. Fenella blinked in surprise as Zach's tired voice came out of the phone, on speaker. "Lucy?"

"Tolkien," Lucy said tensely. Then the phone was tucked in Lucy's bra and she had both hands on the broom handle, holding it positioned horizontally across her middle as if it were a fighting staff.

And she was standing so as to block the door of the room in which Dawn lay sleeping.

Lucy said, "Zach's on his way, with backup. Just in case your grasp of technology is shaky, he's listening. He can hear everything that happens in this room."

It's all right, Fenella told herself. I can adapt.

Tolkien, said Ryland bemusedly. *They prepared for an*

emergency with a code word. How sweet. But you're the only
one who can hear me.

It was a good point.

"Zach," Lucy said. "Fenella is here with the cat. I have things under control so far. But the cat isn't a cat. He's faerie."

"I understand," said Zach.

"Come as quickly as possible. Fenella, start talking. You burned down our house. You ran Leo down. Why? And what does that faerie cat have to do with it?" Her voice sharpened. "Tell him not to move."

Ryland had poked his head out from behind Fenella.

"The cat can't do anything without my agreement," Fenella said soothingly. "I came here to explain to you what's going on."

"Go ahead."

"I will. Uh, I just wonder why you locked Walker out."

"If I have to attack you, I can't have Walker getting in the way."

"But Walker thinks I'm crazy. He was here to protect you." Fenella had no idea why she was persevering with this instead of proceeding with her planned and necessary confession.

"I won't take the risk. He's in love with you."

"No! Walker hates me." Fenella paused and then added stupidly, "He said so."

Lucy didn't reply. Her grip tightened on her broomstick.

Fenella got hold of herself. She raised her voice to make sure that Zach would hear her.

"I wasn't released from Faerie to freedom. That was a lie. I have been given three new tasks. They aren't like the tasks from before. These are tasks of destruction, and—and all of them had to be aimed against my family. Against you." She swallowed. "I got to pick what to destroy, though. The first two, you already know. But there is the third task still to perform."

Lucy assimilated this. "You could simply pick any three things to destroy? No puzzle, no song? How easy for you!" Her voice sharpened. "Was it fun? Was it more fun than the three tasks that I did when *you* couldn't?"

"Don't judge me! So, you made a shirt and found some land and so on!"

"*You* couldn't do it."

"I could have, if I'd had help like you did! How dare you? You have no idea what you'd do, if you were in my place."

"I know I would not get in a car and—" Lucy's eyes shot poisoned arrows. "Nothing could make me hurt someone else. Nothing!"

"You are very young." Fenella tried to regain control.

"Really? That's my problem? Then I never want to be old!"

"Neither did I! Nobody wants to lose their ideals and their dreams and the certainty that they will always find a way to make things right. But that's what happens when you grow up." Fenella twisted her hands together. "You do all sorts of things you never thought you would. Some of them are—are bad."

Lucy's face was hard.

Fenella cried out with complete sincerity. "You go down a path you never meant to go! If you would only understand why—"

"I'll never understand. Not if I live to be a hundred." Lucy said this like it was impossible. "Tell me anyway. Tell me about these evil tasks of yours."

Fenella looked into Lucy's implacable face. This was how it had to be: Lucy on one side, Fenella on the other.

But it hurt even more than Fenella had thought it would.

She said, "I had to commit three tasks of destruction. The first was to destroy safety."

"Zach?" said Lucy.

"Yeah. I'm listening. Go on, Fenella." Zach used the tone you might use in trying to soothe a wild animal.

Fenella said, "I burned down your house. But I was careful to make sure nobody was there." She swallowed. "Then—you see, the second task was to destroy love. I had other ideas but they didn't work out. I thought maybe the dog, but at the last minute, I couldn't do it and then Leo ran into the road. It was an accident."

Fenella searched Lucy's face, and at the same time, she

listened for anything Zach might say. She hoped he was putting the pieces together. She hoped he remembered those moments between the two of them in the kitchen of the church apartment, and now understood that he had been an alternate answer to the second task.

And that she had backed away from that choice.

She said, "I had to choose. I had to find some way to destroy love within our family."

Silence from Zach.

Lucy's brow knitted. "But until the day I die, I'll love my daddy. Everyone still loves him. Anyway, he's not dead. He's in surgery."

Fenella said, "I've thought of that. But the Faerie Queen— she was the one who explained the tasks—said the second task was complete."

Zach's voice came in. "Maybe the queen is trying to trick you."

My sister is many things, but not a liar! flashed Ryland. *The second task is complete.*

"Ryland says it's not a trick and that the second task is done."

The expression on Lucy's face made it clear what she thought of Ryland's assurance.

Fenella said, "So, only the third task is left." She paused. "Destroying hope."

Lucy looked at her. "Zach? Did you get that? Destroying hope?"

"Yes," said Zach.

Lucy said, "What you still haven't said is why. Why do you have to do these things? Are you still in Padraig's power? Were you forced?"

How Fenella wished she could have said yes. That, Lucy might have understood.

"No. I am not in Padraig's power. You released me when you broke the first curse."

Lucy waited.

"And nobody forced me. I agreed to the tasks."

"You *agreed*? You agreed to destroy your family?"

This was the moment, then.

"So I could die," said Fenella. She met Lucy's disbelieving gaze. "I am under a secondary curse that gives me long life. I am sick of it. I planned to do the tasks in such a way as to minimize your pain, and yet get what I needed.

"I deserve peace. I must have it. I must have death at last, and this is the only way. You won't forgive me, I know. But I must and will complete the third task. I must destroy hope."

She turned to the cat. "Ryland. This is when I need you. Do as I say. Take Dawn to Faerie. I am going to give her to Padraig."

"What?" yelled Lucy. She dropped the broomstick handle.

There was a blur as Ryland raced through Lucy's legs into the room beyond, where Dawn had been placed. Lucy whirled instantly to follow.

Fenella ran faster than she ever had in her life. She arrived in the next room on Lucy's heels, just as Dawn's voice sang out, finally, with the first word she had ever uttered.

"Keekee!"

Kitty, Fenella translated. Dawn couldn't pronounce it, but her intent—and her delight—was perfectly clear.

In the dim of a child's night-lamp, Dawn was sitting upright on her bottom on a small mattress set directly on the floor. Her attention was focused entirely on Ryland. The cat had draped himself over her lap and against her tummy, and Dawn had both little hands ecstatically star-fished in his thick, soft fur.

Lucy leaped toward her daughter, both hands outstretched.

But Fenella was already there too. With one hand on the child and the other on Ryland, she said to the cat, "Go."

Then Fenella, Ryland, and the child were in Faerie, leaving Lucy behind.

Chapter 45

They were once more in the little walled garden in Faerie.

Fenella had never wanted to hold the child. She had managed to avoid it this whole long while. But Dawn pulled in several shallow, frantic breaths as she looked about in this strange land and did not find her mother. Abruptly, she yelled; a single, high, piercing shriek. Fenella knew what was coming.

She picked Dawn up. She cradled her in her arms.

She felt the weight of the child's compact, strong, yet vulnerable body. She smelled the powdery scent of her skin. She was shocked by the softness of the child's hair under her cheek.

Fenella had never held Bronagh. Upon Bronagh's birth, with the three impossible tasks left undone, Fenella had been snatched immediately into Faerie. She had next seen

Bronagh when her daughter came of age. Bronagh was eighteen and Padraig's property.

Fenella had failed to save her.

Dawn tried to fling herself away from Fenella. "Keekee," she wailed.

Fenella held her tightly. "No," she said. "No kitty."

Dawn's frightened gaze caught Fenella's. The child had wide hazel eyes, lightly lashed, with deep, dark, thoughtful pupils. Fenella and Dawn stared at each other for one seemingly endless moment. Fenella felt as if her heart were being squeezed.

Then the child's fist caught Fenella a hard blow on the chin. "Keekee," Dawn said again, dangerously.

Fenella looked belatedly for Ryland. But the fluffy white cat with the lush tail and the black, heart-shaped marking was gone. The manticore stood in his place.

Ryland in his true form was larger than Fenella remembered. The shoulders of his powerfully muscled lion's body came higher than her elbow. His feathered wings were spread and his spiked dragon's tail flickered high. Fenella blinked, trying to match him to the delicate cat she had known.

Dawn had no trouble. "Keekee," she cooed.

It was a shock to hear Ryland speak aloud from his human mouth. "Fenella, you may place the child on my back. Don't worry—she'll love it."

Fenella tightened her arms. "We're fine."

"You don't look fine. You look terrified. I won't hurt her. I see myself more as a babysitter."

"We're fine." Fenella hitched Dawn higher in her arms. Again she inhaled the child's powdery scent. "Where's the queen?" she demanded.

"Here."

Fenella turned. The queen stood in the glade. Her clawed hands were folded before her, and an honor guard of six tree fey surrounded her. The presence of the tree fey made Fenella's chest expand in unexpected relief and gladness.

She took a step toward the queen.

"See?" said Fenella tensely, even as the child strained again in her arms toward Ryland. "I've kidnapped the child. I have destroyed hope."

"Explain," said the queen.

Fenella held the squirming child firmly. "There is nothing worse for a mother than the destruction of her daughter. That's what Lucy is feeling. She believes that I'm giving Dawn to Padraig. This time, Lucy has no way to protect her, no way to save her."

"Keekee!" screamed the child.

Fenella began rocking her.

"Put Dawn on my back," said Ryland patiently. "To quiet her down. Or we won't be able to hear ourselves think."

Fenella cast him a look. "No!"

The manticore took an involuntary step back.

"No!" cried Fenella. "This time I'll protect her!" She whirled back to the queen. "Summon Padraig. Do you hear me? Summon Padraig here. Now!"

The child began crying in earnest. Fenella knew it was because she was holding her too tightly. She managed to loosen her arms. "Don't worry," she murmured. "I'll take care of you. Mommy promises. Be brave. Just a while longer."

She was aware of Ryland sidling up next to his sister. "It was too hard. She's lost her mind after all."

"I have not," Fenella whispered. "I am strong." She gathered her breath and fixed her eyes on the queen's. "Summon Padraig." Her voice cracked. "I need him here now."

The queen nodded to the tree fey. Two of them slipped away, the wind rustling through their leaves.

Fenella found a better way to fit Dawn in her arms. "There," she said. "There, there. I'll love you always." She rocked the child as she held her against her own thudding, terrified heart.

The child's cries gentled to a whimper. Her limbs relaxed. And then, abruptly, she fell asleep, her exhausted head lolling on Fenella's shoulder, her arms curled loosely around Fenella's neck, and her body tucked up against Fenella's breasts.

Fenella held Dawn. She held Bronagh.

She held them both.

"Fenella Scarborough," said Queen Kethalia, softly, after forever. "Attend."

Padraig stepped into the clearing along with the tree fey guard, one to either side, as they made him walk forward. He lifted a thin, shaking hand to his thick dark hair. The gesture was as vain as ever. But as he touched his head, his hair fell away in clumps. Scalp gleamed ghoulishly beneath.

Fenella tilted her chin. She approached. Taking great care not to jostle the child, Fenella faced him.

"I give you this child. Dawn." Her voice was steady.

Padraig did not move. She looked into his eyes. They were hazy.

"Hold out your arms. Take this child from me. You must do it."

Stiffly, like an automaton, Padraig tried to obey, reaching out toward the child. He failed to raise his arms fully, however, until the tree fey's branches bound his arms together to form a safe cradle.

Fenella placed the sleeping child into the cradle. Her breath burned in her throat. She could barely speak.

"I have kidnapped the child. I have taken her from her mother. I have delivered her into the center of the night-mare that all the Scarborough women have dreaded for generations. Her mother will scramble for hope, but in the darkest hour, she will not find it. This I know, for I have done it too. So, the third task, the destruction of hope, is complete."

Fenella stepped away, leaving the child in Padraig's arms.

She felt the gaze of the queen, and of Ryland. The wind whistled through the leaves of the tree fey.

Everything depended on her being right.

She said, "But simultaneously, with the completion of the third task, the life-spell upon me is broken. With its ending, Padraig is destroyed. And therefore Dawn is free."

Fenella turned. She met the gaze of the queen.

The queen nodded.

Fenella exhaled.

Then her body acted so quickly that her mind was left stuttering behind. She darted forward. She grabbed once more for the sleeping child. She snatched her away from Padraig, forever.

She held Dawn safe.

The Mud Creature fell to his knees. "I would have loved you." His voice was a rasp. "The curse was your fault." He attempted his old sharp-toothed smile, but two teeth fell from his gums.

His death came rapidly then. The sockets that held his eyes shrank to bare white skull. Skin sloughed away from his cheeks. How he kept his head upright and his back erect without either muscle or skin, Fenella did not know. Yet the Mud Creature managed, until he had rotted to bone.

With a clatter, his skeleton fell to the earth.

His clothing remained. Fenella recognized the empty knee-length boots of supple leather, the same boots he had worn on the day she had first seen him, four hundred years ago, when she was coming home from market with her donkey.

Chapter 46

When Fenella came back into herself, she was still holding Dawn. A sliver of moon had risen in the sky above, and the stars filled the heavens, more numerous and visible than they could be in the troubled human sky.

She glanced at the queen, who stood with Ryland at her side. On the queen's right, a large copse of the tree fey had appeared. They stood close together, their limbs and leaves and needles and bark whispering. They were black oak and willow, ash and chestnut, magnolia and locust, pine and walnut, birch and hemlock, fir and hawthorne, maple and alder. They were both young and old intermingled. Their numbers seemed endless.

No other fey were present.

"The child must be returned to her mother," Fenella said numbly. "It is my last obligation before I die."

"It shall be done," said the queen. "This I swear."

Then the tree fey seemed to open their arms to Fenella. Her feet took her to them. She leaned against the strong trunk of the central, largest fey. An oak leaf brushed her cheek. She felt old, rough boughs come down and gently encircle her shoulders. Younger boughs touched her waist and lingered there. More caressed the child, supporting her as well.

"I am sorry," she said aloud to them. "I made so many mistakes. I understand that I should have stayed here in Faerie and continued to learn patience. I could have had a life here, with you. There would have been no pain for my family. I was selfish."

You are and will always be our adopted daughter, the oak whispered back to her. It was not an acceptance of her apology, and it was also not a reproof, and it was also not an answer, really, but that was the way of the tree fey. A leaf brushed her skin again, and she remembered the oak leaf that had been sent to her in the human realm. It had given her such comfort and reassurance. "Thank you," she whispered. "For everything."

Then, because she knew what she must do, she moved to stand again on her own. A last question came to her, and she turned impulsively to the queen.

"I remain confused about the second task. Leo Marko-witz is still loved, even if he dies."

"He won't die. His injuries were serious, but the surgery has gone well and he will recover. Perhaps not to full health, but he will be well enough."

Fenella caught her breath. "Really?"

"Yes."

Fenella closed her eyes briefly. This weight had been even more terrible than she had realized, until this moment when it was released.

"I'm glad, but . . . very confused. How *did* I destroy love in my family, then? I didn't think it could be that I destroyed their love for me."

Ryland said, "That's correct. You didn't destroy love in *that* family. You destroyed love in *your* family, precisely according to the terms of your contract."

"But I only have one family," said Fenella blankly.

At this, the tree fey murmured. Their voices, unified, calm, without reproach, formed a braid of sound on a sudden warm wind. *You are our beloved adopted daughter. We are your family. And you are ours.*

Their warmth filled Fenella. But her confusion did not lessen. What had their acceptance of her to do with the second task? She hadn't hit a tree with Walker's truck. Had she weakened the tree fey's love in some other way?

"I still don't understand."

Ryland stretched out his back paws deliberately, first the

right, then the left. "Think, Fenella, you stupid girl."

"She's not stupid," said the queen.

"I mean it affectionately. I like her. She's fond of me too, whether she realizes it or not. We're friends. So, Fenella? You know who stopped loving you the moment you hit Leo with that truck."

Fenella did know. She snarled, "Walker is not family! The destruction had to be aimed at family!"

In her arms, the child stirred. "Shh," Fenella said. "Shh, Dawn, I didn't mean to shout. Sleep."

The little girl subsided.

Then the tree fey whispered around Fenella again.

Walker's family has long, long roots in the earth, said the oak trees. *Lineage is complicated,* added the willows. *He is human, but he is also ours,* said the tree fey, all together. *Just as you are.*

Fenella stood quietly then, as she remembered.

Her first drive with Walker in the truck. Walker talking about his family. *My family's been taking care of trees for generations. Trees are in our blood.*

She had known. For a few moments, she had guessed, but then she had forgotten.

"I see."

"You have completed the three tasks," said the queen.

"Yes," said Fenella absently.

She was still absorbing the information about Walker. He had really loved her? Though scarcely knowing her? Apparently he had. Love needed to exist before it could be destroyed.

She felt the trees sway against her. "I'm sorry," she murmured to them. To her family. "When one live limb is chopped off, it hurts the entire tree. In hurting Walker, I hurt all of you too."

And yourself, they said.

"And myself," she acknowledged. Maybe that was what love was after all. A rootedness beneath the earth.

All along she had thought she was seeking personal peace. But in reality, she had sought to cut herself away from the roots that connected her to not only one, but two families. She understood that now.

But nonetheless, she had destroyed, and destroyed, and destroyed.

She kept on rocking the little girl gently in her arms.

"Fenella?" Queen Kethalia spoke. "Did you hear me? The tasks are complete. The life-curse is broken."

"I am fully human again?"

"You always were human. But now you are . . ." The queen hesitated. "Reborn."

"I feel no different." It wasn't really true. Fenella had a terrible ache in her heart, a physical ache.

She had awoken, somehow, she thought.

She leaned her cheek against the soft head of the child. Was Fenella's flesh as vulnerable now as any human's? Truly?

With decision, Fenella straightened. There was no point in questions or in delay. Her path was the same. She had done all that was required. Padraig was destroyed, her family was safe, and it was time to act for herself.

"Ryland?"

"Yes?"

"Will you see Dawn returned safely and swiftly home to Lucy?"

"I promise."

"Then I am ready to die."

Fenella felt nothing much. Not relief, not peace. But perhaps that was the way of it, in the final moment of decision, in the final moment before death.

She placed the child in a cradle again offered by the tree fey.

She held the queen's opaque gaze and nodded questioningly at the queen's ceremonial knife, held as ever in its sheath on the queen's forearm. Then she bowed her head, waiting.

Behind and around her, the oaks and the willows whispered in their own intricate language. Their leaves brushed against Fenella's arms, the skin of her legs, and the drooping of her skirt, as Fenella stood with her hand outstretched for the knife, her feet firmly planted on the ground, and her red head bowed.

Impatience rustled in Fenella. Why was it taking the queen so long to pull the knife from its sheath? She was tempted to send a message to Ryland with her eyes. *Hurry her up!*

But she didn't. The moment elongated. Finally she felt the queen move near her. She heard the deep inhalation of the queen's breath. At last there came the weight of the knife as it was placed on Fenella's palm. The queen's cool touch helped Fenella to wrap her fingers around the hilt.

"Look at me." The queen was close, but it seemed to Fenella as if she were far away.

Fenella looked.

"I will not help you do this," said the queen.

Fenella looked to Ryland. He had said he was her friend.

He lifted his manticore paws. "I have no hands."

"Oh," said Fenella. "Of course."

It didn't matter, she told herself. She wanted this. It was all she had ever wanted. She had struck at herself with this very knife before.

The queen released Fenella's hand. She stepped away.

Fenella adjusted her grip on the knife.

The world shrank around her. The only thing that felt real

was the knife in her hand. She felt outside her own body, up high in the air, watching a small, slender redheaded girl. A redheaded girl with trees at her back, and a tall, extraordinary royal creature before her, and a second royal creature out of myth to one side.

All of them were waiting.

The redheaded girl held the knife out before her. She reversed it so that the point rested on her stomach. She put a second hand on the hilt.

With all her strength, she pulled the knife toward her, and felt the cleanness of its edge as it entered her body.

Chapter 47

The knife had only just parted her skin when a tremendous weight knocked against Fenella from the side, tumbling her to the ground and sending the knife flying through the air.

"Stupid girl." Ryland was on all four paws, crouched low, with his face bare inches from Fenella's and his breath heavy on her face. "You can't die. I won't let you. I've worked too hard." He paused, eyes narrow. His tone turned cool. "At least, not until you've thanked me for helping you."

"Thank you," said Fenella sourly.

The floating, disembodied feeling had left her the moment Ryland struck. She had landed in the dirt on one elbow. It hurt. She sat up slowly, painfully, and pulled her arm around to peer at her elbow. Blood welled there.

"You're bleeding from your stomach too," Ryland pointed out.

Fenella could feel that now also. She put a finger curiously to the second wound, poking it through the hole she'd created in her shirt with the knife.

The willows all crowded close. They murmured soothing things. Soft green leaves were used to wipe her wounds. The blood kept trickling out, though, and after a few minutes Fenella realized that, unconsciously, she had expected the pain to fade and the wounded area to knit together before her eyes, the way her wounds once had.

That was not happening.

She stared at her blood in wonder. "I really am mortal again."

"I told you." Queen Kethalia crouched down a few feet away. The lily crown that grew from her scalp had gone askew, and she was shivering even though it was warm. She drew her wings in close around her shoulders.

"You really did almost kill yourself," added Ryland crossly. "Why? You're eighteen. You'll be dead soon enough. You've only got another seventy, seventy-five years. What's the point of dying now?"

He slid a sideways glance at his sister. "What you were thinking, Kethalia, I have no idea. Nobody wanted Fenella dead. Am I correct? I've figured it out. You wanted the opposite. You and the tree fey. You were plotting for her to win. And live." He took a long, thoughtful breath and then added, throwing the words like weapons: "And become an ally for us, in the human realm."

"We were waiting to see if *you* would intervene to save her," said the queen coolly. "Rather than one of us doing it." She was pale, however.

Ryland froze.

"As indeed you did," finished the queen.

"You manipulated me! I never meant—I never wanted—" Ryland paused in his outburst. He glanced at Fenella, and then at the queen, and then at the ground beneath his front paws.

"You never wanted to care about her?" The queen's voice was neutral.

"I didn't say that."

It seemed to Fenella that the queen and Ryland momentarily forgot there was anybody present except themselves. The queen straightened, and stepped closer to her brother. His body was so tense that you could see the definition of his muscles over his shoulders and back.

"Why did you save her?" asked the queen.

Ryland did not respond for a full minute. "I do like her," he said, finally, grudgingly. He lifted a paw and then seemed to forget it, for it hung suspended in midair. "I liked being with her. I liked seeing her grow stronger and more alive, even if she didn't realize that was what was happening. It has been . . . gratifying—to help her." He sounded surprised.

He looked up at his sister, and his eyes narrowed. "Have you grown more insect capabilities while I've been gone, Kethalia? I don't remember you being able to shoot your eyes out on stalks."

The queen retracted her eyes. "I don't quite have them under control yet."

"I knew the tree fey were with you. Now I see the insects are too. You've used this time I've been gone, haven't you?"

"Yes," said the queen simply. "I have."

Noticing his extended left forepaw, Ryland put it back down on the ground. He said reluctantly, "Fenella has made me think about a few things."

From her spot on the ground, Fenella blinked.

The queen said, "Such as?"

"For one thing, she thinks we made a mistake. About the Mud Creature. She thought he should have been cared for, when he was a child."

The queen stretched her wings. "And your opinion?"

"I don't know. Maybe." For a long time Ryland stood, his entire body tight.

"It changes you," said Queen Kethalia. "When you care for someone."

Ryland raised his tail aggressively high. "Don't lecture me on ethics. You are no pattern of tender perfection. You've been playing political games." He gestured with one paw toward Fenella. "Playing with her life, which you supposedly think is so important to our future."

"I trusted *you* with Fenella," said the queen. "And you proved trustworthy."

Ryland was silent.

"Well, then, brother?" the queen pressed. "You have guessed my intentions. My hope, I should say. You know Fenella as well as the tree fey now, and in some ways, better. If she gets over her death wish, could she be the human ally we so desperately need? Can she be our agent of change?"

It took Ryland another few moments. Fenella watched him, fascinated. His tail flicked from side to side. His eyes were hooded, their gaze internal. But finally he spoke, thoughtfully, temperately.

"Fenella is uniquely rooted in both worlds. She is naturally curious and enthusiastic. And if her family accepts her again, they too might ally with us. They have a long history of involvement with Faerie." He paused, and cast Fenella a direct, assessing glance. Surprised, she returned his gaze squarely and fully.

Still looking directly at Fenella, Ryland resumed speaking. But now his voice had a passion and involvement that Fenella had never heard before.

"If Fenella lives, she will not waste a moment. She will be one of those who leave a blazing comet trail behind. When the humans inscribe their history—if they survive to do so—they will need space for her inventions. Her ideas."

Fenella was glad she was sitting on the ground. If she had not been, she would have fallen over.

The queen's gaze was only for her brother. "You are poetic."

"I like her," he said again. He regarded his front paws.

"The tree fey were right," said the queen. "Not only about Fenella. About you."

Ryland did not look up. "I wanted to rule."

"You never shall," said his sister. "Nonetheless, you are needed."

"I know," said Ryland sourly.

Queen Kethalia laughed. Though Ryland did not join her, he looked up at her, and then at Fenella, and then at the tree fey. Then he was suddenly standing straighter, as if—even if he did not fully realize it—he had set down a burden.

Abruptly, he turned to Fenella. "Enough of this. Fenella! You've gotten into a bad habit of leaping too quickly. You need to take time to process before you make decisions. Especially a decision like death." He scowled into her face.

Fenella shook her head. "Wait. I'm confused. I'm not sure—"

He interrupted. "Forget what my sister and I were discussing. For now, focus on one question. What's your hurry to die, human girl? Why would you spurn the precious years you have been given back?"

"Because I want peace," Fenella protested automatically. "I want death—I want . . ."

Her voice faltered. She looked at Ryland, and then past him at his sister. At this moment, they had an uncanny similarity of expression. Then she looked up at the tree fey, her newfound kin. "I want," she said, and heard her voice fade away into uncertainty.

"What do you want?" The queen slid a quick glance at her brother. "Take your time."

"I want," Fenella tried again. "I want—"

Then all the wanting burst in upon her at once.

She wanted to be the one to return Dawn to Lucy. She wanted to see Lucy's face as Fenella placed her daughter back in her arms.

She wanted to stand before Zach and Lucy and Miranda and Leo and Soledad and apologize, and fully explain, even if they could not hear it, even if they could never forgive her.

She wanted to tell Miranda that she had been right, and that she could trust her own instincts, always, forever.

She wanted to hold Dawn again. She wanted to feed her, and play with her. She wanted to watch her grow up, safe.

She wanted to sneak Pierre a treat under the table at dinner.

She wanted to paint walls and scrub floors and put up a chart of chores on the refrigerator, and help her family make a new home.

She wanted to raise her voice and harmonize with Leo and Lucy and Soledad and Miranda, as they sang in the living room at night.

She wanted to eat a Boston cream pie.

She wanted to open the atlas to a random page and go wherever her finger pointed, just to see what was there. She wanted to find the place where she had been born and grown up, and stand on that land, and there say a prayer for the lost Scarborough girls, and for Robert, and for Bronagh.

She wanted to make a new friend, a woman who was strong of mind and will, who would grow into her heart and help fill some of the place that had once belonged to Minnie.

She wanted to weave ribbons in her hair, and put on a dress with a skirt that swirled and a bodice that enhanced everything she had, and dance all night beneath the stars.

She wanted to pull car engines apart, and talk to people about them, and think about fuel, because she felt quite sure that there was another way to power engines of all kinds, a way that would produce waste products that were healthful and in harmony with the earth, and that she might be the one to discover it.

She wanted to find out exactly what the queen and Ryland had meant, when they talked about Fenella becoming their ally.

She wanted . . .

She wanted to drive beside Walker for long miles through the forest. She wanted to pull the truck over when she was tired, and have Walker offer her his hand.

She wanted to walk beside him under the canopy of the trees. She wanted to inhale the scent of the wood and the moss, and the scent of Walker. She wanted to tell him about the tree fey, and listen to him talk about his family and their history. She wanted to find the biggest tree, and tug Walker down beneath it. She wanted to feel his arms around her, and she wanted to put hers around him. She wanted the trees to whisper a blessing around them, while Walker looked at her again the way he once had, when he wanted her, when he loved her.

She wanted to pull him into Faerie for a visit, so that he could meet their tree family. She wanted to visit his human family.

She wanted to be on his lap again, this time without any

distrust between them. She wanted to press herself into him, and have him press into her. Then one day, with him, she wanted—oh, she wanted—

Fenella discovered she was curling her arms into a cradle. She let them drop. She swallowed back the lump in her throat. She could never have those things, the Walker-things, for she had destroyed Walker's love, destroyed it when it was only a small, hopeful shoot.

But she could still want them.

The wanting filled her. It felt good to want.

It felt—*she* felt—alive.

She was alive. She was alive and she was mortal, and that was her elbow that hurt, and her blood staining her clothing. There would be bruises and scabs and scars on her body as she lived her life. She would wear them proudly, for scars were evidence of how once you had been broken, but now were healed.

She was not broken. She had not been destroyed.

She was alive.

And though she could not be with Walker, there were many things on her list that she could work toward, and she would add other things too as she lived out her life. Her seventy, seventy-five years.

Her life belonged to her again. It was waiting to be seized. And what if Ryland was right about her? What if she could become the Fenella Scarborough he had described, the one who might leave a blazing comet trail behind her, full of her inventions and her ideas?

What if?

"I want to live." Fenella stared in shock at the queen and at Ryland and at the tree fey. "I want my life."

"At last," said Ryland. "Now, please. Do something. I really, really want this. Say thank you to me. Just once. Say thank you like you mean it."

Fenella looked around at a whole new world, full of color and light and possibility. She heard the low pleased whispering of the tree fey. She saw a smile growing on Queen Kethalia's strange, beautiful, and tired face. She saw how the queen stepped forward and stood next to her brother.

Her mind was full. Her heart was full. Ryland's words penetrated only vaguely.

She sent an abstracted nod in his direction. "You're welcome."

Chapter 48

It was after daybreak in the human realm when Fenella pulled open the unlocked front door to the three-family house. She hesitated in the vestibule, feeling the quiet all around her. There was no time to be lost in returning Dawn to her parents, even though Fenella was terrified to face them. She could feel her heart thudding with that fear as she looked at the staircase.

She thought of how she would ascend the steps and knock on the apartment door. She thought of how Lucy would grab Dawn from her. She wondered if her family would be able to hear her, when she explained that the stakes had been higher than they knew. When she explained that she had had to steal Dawn, in order to save Lucy's and Dawn's futures.

Maybe they would simply throw her out, even after hearing it all. Probably they would. How could they forgive her? After all, her motives had hardly been pure and loving at the beginning of the three tasks. She had pursued her own selfish way.

But she had been dead, at the beginning. Now she was alive. Now she would do whatever she had to do to earn her family's trust and forgiveness.

"Keekee," said Dawn conversationally. She laid her head on Fenella's shoulder. The child was clutching in her little hand another oak leaf, a gift from the tree fey. Fenella was grateful for it. The leaf kept the child calm, and would ensure she presented a smiling face to her parents. That would be infinitely valuable in the firestorm ahead.

I said to my soul, be still.

"Mommy," said Fenella. "You're going to Mommy and Daddy."

Dawn nodded happily. "Keekee."

Kitty was not a word that Lucy and Zach would want to hear from Dawn, Fenella knew, even though it seemed to mean many things besides Ryland. The word *keekee* was another reason Fenella could not yet instruct her feet to climb the stairs.

Also, it was early. What if they were all sleeping?

She glanced at the closed door of Walker's apartment. She had looked in vain for Walker's truck outside. Was he away?

Could he have spent the whole night somewhere else?

Then she heard the house's front door open behind her.

She stiffened.

She didn't have to see Walker with her eyes; for him, she had antennae. She didn't have to hear his voice; the nape of her neck recognized his footfall.

She turned.

Walker wore a hooded gray sweatshirt, faded jeans, and work boots. His thick hair was firmly banded back, the way it had been when she first met him.

His gaze went from Fenella's face, to the little girl in her arms, to the oak leaf clutched by the child, to Fenella's feet on the stairs, and then back, finally, to Fenella's face.

She could not read his.

She blurted, "Dawn is safe and she's well. I'm bringing her upstairs, to her parents. Everything is all right now. The curse—I don't remember if you know about the curse—but anyway, it's broken. I broke it at last."

Her throat choked up and it was impossible to say anything more.

"Miranda told me," Walker said. "About this Padraig. And about the family curse." He was still expressionless. "She says the faerie stuff is real. That you were in danger, even if we don't understand what exactly it was."

Fenella managed to nod. Miranda, she thought. Perhaps

Miranda would be able to understand, and would risk allowing Fenella back into her life. Perhaps.

"I did see your arms heal from the cat scratches. The first day I met you." He sounded neutral.

Fenella swallowed. "There is a lot to explain, and it's complex."

"Yes."

Fenella nodded toward the staircase. "So here I am. I am going to explain everything to my family, and ask for forgiveness, though I don't really expect to receive it." She lifted her chin. "I know I can't undo the damage I have done."

"No," Walker said. "You can't."

This was hard to hear. She knew it for truth, however. She had inflicted terror on Lucy and Zach and Soledad and Miranda. Leo's rehabilitation lay ahead. There was an old home to mourn; and a new home to make. There were family financial losses too, and those were not small.

Wait without hope, for hope would be hope for the wrong thing.

Still, if they let her, she would face it all with her family. She would shoulder as much as she could, for them, with them. Now, or later. She would be useful. She even had a legal birth record now, inserted into computer records as a gift from Queen Kethalia. The first thing she would do with it was get a driver's license. Ryland's voice came back to her: *Seventy,*

seventy-five years. She wanted every minute of every day. Not one moment would be thrown away. Not even the hard ones.

Like this one.

Fenella shifted the weight of the child in her arms. Dawn's foot dangled against her stomach, where, beneath her clothes, Fenella's skin had scabbed over.

She said to Walker, "Yes. I did the damage I did. I am here to take responsibility and make amends and help my family in every way I can." She paused. "To you too I owe explanations and apology."

Walker's eyes flickered. "It's hard to believe any of this. Even though your family says it's true about the faeries. I almost think you were all having a mass hallucination."

"It's real," Fenella said, as if the words could make him believe it. "You saw my arms heal from the cat scratches. You said it yourself."

"Unless I imagined that." Walker looked away.

Dawn brushed her leaf up against Fenella's cheek.

"Well," Walker said. "Don't let me keep you. Go on upstairs." He turned, and Fenella meant to let him go—it was right that he go. But—

There is yet faith.

She called after him.

"You told me once about your family. You said they were tree people."

He paused. He half turned back. "We have a tree farm."

"You said trees are in your blood."

He turned toward her again. "That's a family joke. I don't know why I mentioned it."

Following her instinct, Fenella pressed further. "Is it really a joke? Or are there some strange things about your family and trees? Things as unexplainable as what you've learned about me?"

Walker's gaze went to the leaf in Dawn's hand. "There was that business with the oak leaf. The other one, that took me to you when—when—" His face flushed. She knew he was remembering that night with her on the park bench, in the bower of trees.

Fenella wanted, as badly as she had ever wanted anything, to step close to him. To put her hands on his face, to make him understand.

The faith and the love and the hope are all in the waiting.

She stayed where she was. "Is that the only strange tree experience?"

"Well, it's like having a green thumb. We all love trees in my family. There's nothing strange about it."

"Did the trees ever talk to you?"

"No," he said quickly. Too quickly.

"It wouldn't be in language. It would be . . ." Fenella drew air into her lungs, released part of it, and then whistled softly, taking in new air through her nose and releasing it through pursed lips, a complex movement that resulted in a rustling sound. She repeated the words she knew. *You are kin. You are part of the whole. You are beloved.*

Walker shuddered.

"Have you ever heard the trees say something like that? Somehow, you *feel* what they mean. In your spine. On your skin."

Walker had an arrested look on his face.

"I am part tree too." Fenella felt shy, saying this. Shy, but proud. "Not by blood, like you. I am adopted. In Faerie, the tree fey are—well, they're different from trees here, but they are still all one people. They became my friends. They looked after me. They loved me and I loved them, and I think that I grew strong again only because of them. I never really knew how important they were to me, but they knew."

And I believe, she thought suddenly, that the tree fey sent Walker here originally, all the way across the country, to wait for me. Long before I knew that I would have the chance to return to the human realm. Time is different for them.

"Tree fey," said Walker.

"Yes. I wish you could meet them. I'd take you to Faerie if I could."

A long, long silence. Then Walker said, "The night I

turned thirteen. I woke up and went outside in the dark. I felt pulled."

Fenella waited.

"I went to the middle of the forest. Then—that noise you made, just now? That's what I heard from the trees. I understood it. Like you said. In my spine. On my skin."

"What did you understand?"

He said it simply. "That I am part of them. That they are me."

They looked at each other. Fenella felt all the things she wanted to say; all that she wanted to give. But she held back. It was enough that Walker was talking with her.

Perhaps, tomorrow, he would talk with her again.

She would water and nurture. She would give space and sun and air. And who knew what might grow? Destruction need not be the end. Creation could follow. What was broken might be remade, stronger than ever.

She was living proof.

Walker put a hand into his pocket. He pulled out the oak leaf. Fenella's jaw dropped down right against the top of Dawn's head.

"This came to me again," he said. "I don't know how it got into my pocket, but there it was."

Now Fenella did take that step forward. Cautiously, so as not to jostle Dawn, she reached out.

Walker made to put the leaf in her hand. But at the last second, he didn't let go. They both held the leaf, their hands near each other, not touching.

A minute passed.

Fenella said, "Would you—by any chance, would you come upstairs with me? Would you bear witness when I tell my family my full story?"

Walker's eyes were wary, but still he held on to his half of the leaf.

He said, "Yes."

Fenella closed her eyes, just for a second, not daring to believe. Then she opened them to see Walker's face.

"Yes," he said again. "I will."

Acknowledgments

Asking for other people's ideas can get you into serious trouble, but I always do it.

Scottie Bowditch at Penguin told me she'd love to read a prequel to *Impossible*, focused on the backstory of Lucy Scarborough's ancestress Fenella, the young woman with whom the Scarborough Fair song-curse began. I thought this was a bad idea and I told her so. "We already know Fenella's story ends sadly!" But then time passed and I wondered: What if Fenella were magically still alive? Could the prequel also be a sequel? Could I transform Fenella's sad ending into a new, hopeful beginning? I wrote excitedly to my editor, Lauri Hornik, that the new book would be "about healing, and 'becoming strong in the broken places,' and the re-embrace of life."

Scottie's bad idea had hooked me.

I knew Fenella's prequel/sequel story would be tricky to write. Among other problems, there would need to be a new puzzle in the present day, which would somehow be entwined with the curse from the past. I consulted my writer friend Mark Shulman. After five whole minutes of concentration, he suggested Fenella be forced to pursue three destructive tasks, to balance out the three tasks of creation in *Impossible*. "Brilliant," I said.

Halfway through writing the first draft, having fallen totally in love with Fenella—in other words, when I was too far gone to turn back—I understood that I actually had things backward. Scottie's was the good idea, whereas Mark's was insane.

Insane.

I take full responsibility for the badness or goodness of all the other ideas in this novel, which arose out of wrestling with those first two.

My thanks—along with a shake of my fist—go to those devil-angels, Scottie Bowditch and Mark Shulman.

Thanks are also due to the friends who read and/or discussed the novel with me in its various drafts and parts along the way. Some of them won't even realize how much they helped. Sarah Aronson, Franny Billingsley, Toni Buzzeo, Pat Lowery Collins, Carolyn Coman, Jacqueline Davies, Amy Butler Greenfield (who also vetted the historical sections), Alison James, A. M. Jenkins, Liza Ketchum, Jane Kurtz, Ellen Kushner, Jacqueline Briggs Martin, Jennifer Richard O'Grady, Lisa Papademetriou, Mary E. Pearson, Dian Curtis Regan, Leda Schubert, Delia Sherman, Joanne Stanbridge, Tanya Lee Stone, Deborah Wiles, Ellen Wittlinger, and Melissa Wyatt. My mom, Elaine Werlin. My steadfast agent, Ginger Knowlton. Linda McCoy and the extended

McCoy family, who over a holiday meal debated the best way to blow up a house. My workshop group at Vermont College for the Fine Arts, led by Betsy Partridge and Sharon Darrow, which discussed and dissected the first chapter. The novel workshop attendees at the New England SCBWI spring 2012 conference, who told me that I could indeed make it work. My audience at the Florida SCBWI summer 2012 conference, who said that they thought I could not.

Thanks also go to the folks at Penguin Books for Young Readers, who are such great partners and whose professional expertise means I can focus on writing.

My wonderful editor, Lauri Hornik, gave me honest critiques and encouragement, as well as time to work—the deadline came; the deadline went—until we were both satisfied with Fenella's story. Our editorial partnership goes back over nine books now, and I look forward to our getting into the double digits together.

Final thanks go to my own true love and husband. Jim McCoy is not only loving and supportive, he is wise. He never reads a book until it's done.

About the Author

Nancy Werlin is the author of seven previous novels: the *New York Times* Bestseller *Impossible* and Indie Next List pick *Extraordinary* (companion novels to *Unthinkable*); National Book Award finalist *The Rules of Survival*; Edgar Award winner *The Killer's Cousin* and Edgar Award finalist *Locked Inside*; ALA Best Books for YA picks *Black Mirror* and *Double Helix*; and the ALA Quick Pick *Are You Alone on Purpose?*

A graduate of Yale College, Nancy lives with her husband near Boston, Massachusetts.